MW01125990

Academy for Misfit Witches
Academy for Misfit Witches, Book One
A Reverse-Harem Fantasy Romance
Tara West

Edited by Theo Fenraven.
Artwork by Vanesa Garkova.

Seraphina Goldenwand, heiress to the largest fortune in all four magical realms, isn't really a bad girl. At least she tries not to be. A small indiscretion with her professor shouldn't have resulted in the major scandal that got Serah kicked out of her posh private school and sent to Dame Doublewart's Academy for Misfit Witches. Her new school is a dungeon—literally. Luckily, three sexy dragon shifters save her from a miserable and lonely detention, and they enjoy a night that will forever alter the course of their lives.

Draque, Teju, and Ladon Firesbreath, wayward dragon princes and masters of mischief, can't believe their good fortune when they rescue the beautiful witch from a night of fright, then discover she is just as turned on by them as they are by her. Little do they know that while they're locked away in their protective magical cocoon, someone will raze the school to the ground and frame them for the crime. Left with no choice but to flee, Serah and the dragon princes are forced to rely on one another. But when their trust in each other is shaken, they must learn to overcome their fears before their enemies find them.

Dedication

This book is dedicated to my beautiful and loving mom. Thank you for all of those book club subscriptions when I was a kid and for designated reading time every evening. Thank you for believing in me and for inspiring me to become a writer. I hope I'm making you proud. I still can't believe you're gone. I miss you every day. I love you.

Special Thanks To

To Theo, God of Grammar, blessed by the goddess, and tasked to save my ass with your red pen of shame. Thank you, thank you, thank you.

To Ginelle, thanks for always finding my oopsies.

To Sheri, thanks for being there when I need a beta.

Laura, I always appreciate your suggestions.

Pamela, your feedback was phenomenal. I'm so glad our paths crossed.

Chapter One

"How long will they make us wait?" Miss Pratt whined, checking the time on her wand while she hovered above the floor across the room, her wings angrily buzzing like she was a hummingbird on crack.

Serah fiddled with a gemstone on her gaudy emerald bracelet and ignored her annoying chaperone, AKA the five-foot clumsy hummingbird. She wasn't looking forward to starting a new school, but she couldn't wait to get rid of Miss Pratt. That pixie had been a thorn in her side since Grandfather ordered her out of his office, refusing to hear her version of the story and threatening to disinherit her if she brought any more shame to their family name.

Serah checked the backings on her earrings to make sure they were secure—a nervous habit—and recalled her grandfather's dark scowl. She felt like an utter failure for disappointing him, but did that mean she had to attend the worst school in the third realm? It had been one tiny transgression.

She looked at the cobwebs in the corners, the black mold exposed beneath the peeling wallpaper, and the dust-covered trophy case displaying awards from the Department of Magical Corrections for strict disciplinary action. Apparently this shithole was her last hope. None of the other magical schools would take a siren with a penchant for seducing professors. Actually, it had been only one professor, and he'd seduced her, but try as she might, she couldn't dispel the rumors that had spread faster than a dragon's inferno.

Slumping in her seat, she picked imaginary grime out of her fingernails and avoided eye contract with the female troll sitting behind the admissions desk. At least she was fairly certain the troll was a woman. The big pink bow covering that bald patch on her head might have been a good indicator. Or maybe the bright red lipstick leaching into her upper lip hairs. Steam poured out of the troll's wide nostrils as she glared at Serah from under a unibrow that looked like someone had glued a strip of shag carpet to her forehead. The admissions clerk at the Dame Doublewart's School for Misfit Witches had to be the ugliest troll in all four realms, and that was saying something, considering the last one she'd had the misfortune of encountering had had a thumb-sized brown wart hanging out of her nostril.

The plaque on her desk announced her name was Lady Hoofenmouth. She wore a huge rock on her bloated wedding finger. Serah didn't know if she was more shocked that Lady Hoofenmouth was a member of the gentry or that there was another Hoofenmouth.

When the ancient black phone on Lady H's desk rang obnoxiously, sounding like a bleating, sick cow, the troll picked up the receiver, nostrils flaring, and listened to a shrill voice on the other end.

Grunting, she hung up and gave Serah the once-over. "Seraphina Goldenwand, the headmistress will see you now."

Serah jumped to her feet, fingering the wand in her pocket and clutching her purse. "Thank you." Turning up her nose, she walked haughtily past the troll, ignoring the annoying buzzing of Miss Pratt's wings, who preceded her, as she banged into furniture, trying to keep up.

Once they reached a dark, musty hall, Serah covered her mouth, breathing into her palm while picking up the pace enough to zip past the pixie. This place smelled fouler than a rotting crypt.

"Wait up," Miss Pratt called, coughing and choking behind her. "Oh, my. This place smells like dragon farts."

Serah strode straight toward a tall slender woman with a long beak nose and hair pulled back in an austere bun, who glared at them from a doorway at the end of the hall.

"Hello." She smiled at the woman, not surprised when she didn't smile back. "It's a pleasure to meet you." Serah infused a bit of siren charm into her words, hoping her seductive voice would be hard to resist, then arched back when the woman's lips twisted into a scowl.

"I'm Dame Doublewart." Her face was a mask of stone. "Siren charms don't work on me." She held the office door open and motioned to a chair in front of a wide, gray desk. "Come in."

Serah's eyes widened as she walked past Dame Doublewart. In the magical world, sometimes one's name was an indication of one's appearance. Dame Doublewart had no visible warts on her face, but that didn't mean she didn't have them somewhere. Her imagination raced with possibilities, most of which made her stomach churn.

"Thank you so much for seeing us." Miss Pratt's rapidly buzzing wings ground to a halt when Dame Doublewart held out a staying hand. She dropped to the floor with a squeak and a curse and jutted tiny hands on her hips, glaring at the formidable headmistress.

Dame Doublewart arched a thin brow and scowled down at the purple-haired pixie. "And you are?"

"Penelope Pixiefeather Pratt." Miss Pratt pulled back narrow shoulders, flashing a triumphant grin. "I'm Lord Goldenwand's personal assistant."

Serah fought an eyeroll. She suspected her grandfather's name didn't carry much weight with Dame Doublewart.

"Miss Pratt, I don't believe your name was called." Dame Doublewart crossed her arms and impatiently tapped her foot.

Miss Pratt's jaw dropped. "But Serah's grandfather—"

"Has no influence here." Dame Doublewart shooed Miss Pratt away as if she was swatting a bug. "Now, if you'd excuse us."

"Fine," Miss Pratt huffed, eyes crossing.

Shoo, Serah mouthed, waving Miss Pratt into the musty hall, her grin widening when Dame Doublewart slammed the door in the pixie's face. She'd never liked Miss Pratt, and not just because she was a whiny, impatient little mouse. Miss Pratt had a habit of shadowing Serah at the most inopportune times and reporting everything back to Grandfather, including the rumors that Serah had slept with every professor at her former school. Miss Pratt was a short snitch with a dragon-sized grudge wedged up her twat.

Looking her over with an assessing glare, Dame Doublewart motioned for Serah to sit.

She sat in a slick, squeaky chair, cringing when it wobbled beneath her. She wasn't surprised this school couldn't afford decent furniture, given the condition of the place. The outside had been just as decrepit, a crumbling, gray building located in the heart of an old cemetery. This was a far cry from her last school, which was located at the edge of the beautiful city of Sawran, overlooking a tropical beach. That school had been beyond luxurious. If only her former headmistress hadn't believed those stupid rumors.

"Serah Goldenwand?" Dame Doublewart's lips twisted into a tighter scowl, as if she'd just finished sucking on a rotten lemon or the timer on her fifteen-minute enema had expired.

Refusing to be intimidated, she brushed a strand of her wavy auburn hair behind her ear and turned up her chin. "Yes."

If it was at all possible Dame Doublewart's disapproving expression deepened. "The correct response is 'Yes, *ma'am.*'"

She fought back a curse. Grinding her teeth, she spit out the words. "Yes, ma'am."

She had no choice but to kiss Doublewart's ass. This school was her only hope. One-hundred-and-fifty billion merlins were at stake, thanks to Grandfather's ridiculous rule. No diploma, no inheritance. She enjoyed designer purses and shoes too much to end up poor.

Dame Doublewart perused a file as thick as a tomb, shaking her head. "Let me get this straight. You seduced every one of your professors at your previous school, ruining no less than five marriages."

She tensed. "Only one professor, and he wasn't married as far as I know."

Her face contorted with distaste, her gaze practically boring holes in Serah's skull. "One professor is bad enough."

Unnerved by Dame Doublewart's penetrating, black eyes, she pretended to admire one of the many old cuckoo clocks in a small collection hanging behind Doublewart's desk. It was covered in cobwebs. "I realize that now."

"Your disciplinary report says you slept with all the male professors." The matron's voice rose in pitch with each word, making her sound like a squawking hen. "They were found guilty of giving you passing grades in exchange for sexual favors."

Though she shouldn't have been surprised the exaggerated tales of her exploits had preceded her, she resented the judgmental tone in Dame Doublewart's voice. She was a Goldenwand, the sole heiress to the largest fortune in the third realm—probably in all four realms. She didn't have to tolerate Doublewart's self-righteous attitude. "Believe the report if you want, but I only slept with one professor." The rest she bought off, thanks to Grandfather's generous allowance.

She repressed a sigh when she thought of Professor Prometheus Periwinkle's calm, deep voice, wavy blond hair, and blessedly large wand. He'd been so kind during their early tutoring sessions. So attentive. That first kiss had been the next natural progression after months of mutual flirting. By the time they ripped off each other's clothes and he draped her across the top of his desk, she'd been so horny, she couldn't see straight. After repressing her siren instincts for so long, she'd lost it. And she'd certainly paid for her transgression ten times over.

"Doesn't matter if you slept with one professor or a dozen." Dame Doublewart folded her hands and glared at Serah like a hawk zeroing in on a mouse. "It seems no other magical school in our realm will take you."

Tension stiffened her spine. "Correct."

"We are your last hope."

Dame Doublewart's lips twisted so tight, Serah thought they would snap. "Yes."

"Miss Goldenwand," Dame Doublewart said and sighed, "you are already eighteen, a year older than most other high school twelfth years. Why don't you just drop out?"

If only. She fought to maintain a neutral expression. "I would if I could." It's not like she needed an education. Potion and spell classes were now obsolete, thanks to the Goldenwand 2050. Why did she need to memorize spells when the Goldenwand did all the work for her?

Dame Doublewart eyed her expectantly. "What do you mean?"

She refused to answer. Why give Doublewart ammunition that she could use against her to get her to behave? She studied the woman's face, wondering exactly where those two warts were hiding.

The matron had an assessing look in her eyes. "Your silence confirms that other rumors are true. You will be disinherited without a diploma."

She found the nerve to make eye contact with Dame Doublewart for a moment. "Are you going to accept me or not?"

Dame Doublewart lifted a thin, graying brow. "Are you aware of our academy's rigorous course load?"

She thought of a half dozen different spells she'd like to use on Doublewart. "I've heard it."

"Each student is responsible for his or her own work." She pointed her beak nose at Serah, eyes narrowing to slits. "You can't suck your way into passing grades here."

Heat flamed Serah's cheeks. "I'll manage." She swallowed an angry retort and clutched her wand so hard, her knuckles ached.

"You're aware of our disciplinary policy?"

Serah shrugged. "I heard it was strict."

"Strict?" Dame Doublewart let out a grating laugh that sounded like two rabid cats mating. "Oh, Miss Goldenwand. I promise that when you find yourself on your knees at my school, you won't be begging for more." Shadows fell across her features and a wicked gleam shone in her eyes. "You'll be begging for mercy."

Well, fuck. She swallowed a lump of bile. "Noted."

"You're okay with this?" Laughter rang in Doublewart's words.

Serah bit back a curse. "I don't have a choice."

"No, you don't." The matron's eyes lit like fireworks. "Here at Dame Doublewart's, we like to get a jump on discipline." She picked up an old, gnarled wand that was as long as a yardstick and slapped it across her palm. "Our students spend their first night in the dungeon to get a taste of our disciplinary procedures. We generally find that after that first night, our students are much more receptive to our rules."

Dragon balls! This woman was mental. "So you're throwing me in detention, and I haven't even done anything yet?"

"That's right." Her smile widened, revealing sharp incisors. "If you accept these terms, I will grant you admission. If not...." Dame Doublewart slapped her palm in rhythm with the ticking cuckoo clocks behind her.

Serah released a shaky breath. "I accept."

"Excellent." Dame Doublewart set down the wand and stood. Turning, she thumbed through a stack of papers. "Let me just find the contract."

Sitting as stiff as a statue, she watched Doublewart locate the papers that would seal her doom. She only had one semester left until graduation—roughly four months with holidays. She didn't believe for a second that her grades couldn't be bought. This school was practically falling apart at the seams. If its condition was any indication, the teachers were likely underpaid, too.

If she and her potions professor had been more discreet, she'd still be at her posh school, dining at their custom sushi bar for supper and sucking the cream out of Periwinkle's éclair for dessert.

Dame Doublewart faced Serah, holding a faded scroll. Tapping it with her wand, she mumbled a reveal spell, and it came to life, the words jumping off the page and forming in the air in front of her like they were reflecting off a computer screen. She was impressed that Dame Doublewart's old wand could conjure such a modern spell.

"Sign here," the matron said, pointing at the signature line at the bottom of what must have been thousands of words of fine print.

Serah frowned. No way was she reading that contract. It would take her all day. It couldn't be too terrible. Grandfather wouldn't send her to a horrible school.

She pulled the wand out of her pocket.

"Not with that," Doublewart snapped, a wicked gleam in her eyes. "With your finger."

Serah pocketed her wand, biting back profanities, then leaned toward the signature line, jerking back when the contract crackled.

"I haven't got all day." Dame Doublewart turned her beak nose to the ceiling, rolling her eyes.

Serah reached toward the contract again, wincing when the screen pricked her finger, using her blood as the ink. Signing in blood? Grandfather had a lot to answer for.

By the time she finished, her finger throbbed and blood dripped down her wrist. She grasped her wand and silently asked it to heal her, sighing in relief when the pain stopped. There was a blood stain on her suede boot. Those boots had cost two thousand merlins. She zapped the stain with her wand, smiling when it disappeared.

The matron snickered at Serah's wand. "Follow me." She tapped dark chestnut panels on a wall, and it split open, revealing a secret tunnel.

Serah hesitated. "But my bags."

Dame Doublewart's eyes became cold, unreadable. "You won't need them. You'll be issued a uniform after detention."

A uniform? She made a face. At her old school, the only dress code was an unspoken one: dress like you had money. Needless to say, Serah had exemplified proper dress code. She couldn't imagine being forced to wear some starchy polyester or cotton-blend monstrosity.

"Of course I need them." She looked at Dame Doublewart as if she'd grown a second head. "My grandfather just bought me those bags from Elysian."

Ignoring her distress, the matron impatiently waggled her fingers. "Your wand."

Clutching her wand to her side, Serah took a big step back. "My wand?"

"We don't allow Goldenwands at Doublewart's. Every student is issued a standard PF Wand."

"A Pegasus Feather Wand?" Hysterical laughter bubbled from her throat. "Those are so last century."

"I know, which is how I like it." Doublewart flashed a smile so tight, her face looked ready to crack. "Forces our students to think for themselves instead of relying on their wands to do all the work for them."

Serah cocked a hand on her hip. This woman had definitely lost her mind. "Seriously?"

"Seriously." Doublewart lunged forward and snatched Serah's wand before she had time to react. "You'll get it back after graduation."

She threw up her hands. "What a load of crap." She had no right to take away her wand, considering the resolution Parliament was about to pass, requiring all schools to use the current Goldenwands.

"*Tsk, tsk.* You should've read our wand policy before signing the contract." Doublewart wagged a finger in Serah's face, and that's when she noticed what appeared to be two black bugs stuck to her fingernail. Gross. Why hadn't she noticed before? What a horrible place to have warts.

"I've changed my mind." Holding up both hands, she backed up another step. No way in Hades was she attending a school that refused to use her grandfather's wands. He'd understand why she had to drop out.

"Too late," Doublewart shrugged. "You signed."

"Well, unsign it." She held out her hand. "And give me back my wand."

Doublewart waved her big ugly wand at Serah's hands and feet, binding her in place. She tried to scream, but the woman sealed her mouth with another spell.

She flashed an evil grin. "Enjoy your stay in detention, Miss Goldenwand."

With one flick of the wrist, Serah was swept off her feet and traveling along the corridor at breakneck speed. Suddenly the bindings snapped off her limbs and mouth, and she screamed as she went over a chasm into pitch black.

She hit soft ground with a thud and groaned as she spit out a mouthful of dirt. Sitting up, she wished she had her wand for illumination. Wherever she was, she could distinctly hear water. After checking her earlobes to make sure she hadn't lost an earring, she stood and brushed dirt off her clothes, then picked debris out of her palms. That's when she noticed the emerald bracelet Prometheus had given her had fallen off. She fell back on her knees, frantically searching for it to no avail. It was all she had left of him. Releasing a shaky breath, she told herself it was for the best. He was never going to be part of her life again, so why keep mementos to pine over? Besides, the gems were fake. No way could he afford real emeralds on his salary. She didn't need that ugly bracelet and was glad it was gone. That's what she kept telling herself anyway.

She got to her feet, squinting at a pinprick of light above her. The light grew brighter, illuminating the uneven cavern walls.

"Hello! Can anyone help me?" she called, disappointed when the only answer was her own voice echoing back.

Stumbling forward, she came to the edge of inky black water that splashed the rocks under her feet. She rubbed warmth into her arms as goose bumps pricked her flesh. She'd landed on a small island rising up from the cavern floor no more than twenty feet in diameter, and she could make out the shapes of triangular dorsal fins moving in circles around her. Though she was an expert swimmer, thanks to her siren blood, no way was she getting in that water.

What kind of fucked up detention was this, and how in Hades was she going to escape this school?

SERAH HUGGED HER KNEES to her chest, trying not to wince every time a shark splashed her. They were magical illusions. They had to be. Sharks the size of elephants didn't swim in shallow water. Not to mention their teeth were disproportionately long, making them look like sabertooth fish. She had no idea how long she was supposed to serve detention, but as soon as she got out of there, she would call her grandfather and demand he come get her. There had to be another school that would take her, with enough financial incentive. No way could she survive a semester in this hellhole.

"Hello, there. You called for help?"

She blinked at the oddest thing she'd ever seen—three drop-dead gorgeous guys, smiling at her from inside a giant, translucent bubble that hovered about three feet off the ground. She rubbed her eyes, then blinked again. They were still there, still gorgeous, with their rippling tanned muscles, thick, black hair, and broad smiles. They looked like ancient Greek gods who had descended from Mount Olympus.

She slowly came to her knees. "Hello?"

The tallest of the three, wearing jeans tight enough to reveal a beefy bulge that proved he definitely didn't need to drive a fast broom or monster truck, smiled while palming a longneck beer. "You don't look like you're enjoying your detention."

She scratched the back of her head, squinting at him. "Ya think?"

He crossed muscular arms, slanting a knowing grin. "Need a lift?"

"In that thing?" She jumped to her feet and backed away from the bubble. "What if it pops?"

"It won't pop." The stud standing next to him, wearing nothing but boxer shorts and an unbuttoned dress shirt, jumped up and down, his bare feet making deep indentations in the bubble. "See?" He pushed his wire spectacles up the bridge of his nose, a gesture that reminded her too much of Professor Periwinkle.

"Where are you going?" she asked.

The tallest stud nodded at the cave wall. "To the next dungeon over. We've got detention, too."

They had detention? They didn't look like high school boys. They looked to be in their early twenties. Tall stud even had a full beard.

It didn't matter how old they were. Floating in a bubble with three good-looking guys was a far cry better than her current situation. Unless, of course, Grandfather found out. "What if we get caught?"

"We won't," the one wearing navy sweats said, his cheeks flushing, making him look adorably sexy. "They're not coming for us until morning."

That Doublewart bitch was more sadistic than Serah had realized. "I have to spend all night here?"

"Not if you come with us." Bearded Guy held up his beer. "We've got music and drinks."

Please say yes! the siren inside her begged.

"Come on," Boxer Shorts said. "You don't want to spend all night there, do you?"

Serah grimaced. She feared these guys could be a trick of the imagination, a tempting illusion sent by Dame Doublewart to make her hellish stay in detention even more miserable. When Boxer Shorts poked through the bubble, holding out a hand, she drew back, apprehension twisting a knot in her gut.

"We won't bite," he said with a wink.

"Unless you want us to," Bearded Guy added.

Fuck yeah, she wanted them to, and that was the problem. She'd repressed her siren until Periwinkle had revealed her inner goddess, introducing her to the carnal pleasures she'd denied herself too long. Now that her siren was awakened, Serah didn't know how to put her back or even if she wanted to. Grandfather would be so disappointed.

Go to them, Serah, her siren hissed, releasing a wave of pheromones that nearly swept her under lust's tide. Gritting her teeth, she reached for her savior's hand, praying to the goddess these men weren't an illusion. If she did end up sleeping with them, she hoped Grandfather never found out.

DORIS DOUBLEWART DIDN'T know if she was more worried or relieved. Apprehensive, definitely. Why had she admitted this girl into her school?

Half a million merlins, that's why.

She pressed the intercom button on her ancient landline. "Lady Hoofenmouth, will you please come to my office?" She waited anxiously, listening for the heavy footsteps of the one woman whose opinion mattered most. Clenching her teeth, she grabbed her coffee cup when thunderous stomping rattled her desk.

The door swung open, slamming into the wall with a thud. Athena Hoofenmouth looked like a bull ready to charge as she stared her down. "What took you so long?"

Doris slowly stood, smoothing invisible wrinkles out of her gray, polyester slacks. "I was showing our new student to the dungeon."

Steam poured from Athena's flared nostrils, and her pupils turned red. "I thought you weren't going to admit her."

Trolls were notorious for their short tempers, and though Doris loved Athena, she also feared her ever-changing moods. She instead pulled out the deposit slip she'd been keeping in her desk since this morning and waved it in Athena's face.

Doris's breath hitched when Athena snatched it from her hands, glowering at the slip of paper attached to a carbon copy of the check with Nathaniel Goldenwand's signature scrawled across the bottom.

Athena frowned. "What's this?"

Doris cleared her throat, summoning the courage to face her lover. "Half a million merlins from Lord Goldenwand."

"Great goblin gonads!" Athena shrieked, dropping the paper on the floor.

Doris snatched her wand and used it to retrieve the receipt, zapping it back into the safe under her desk. She'd be a nervous wreck until the money cleared the bank.

"No wonder you admitted her." Athena rubbed her hands together and licked her lips. "We could retire to Elysian."

Doris sighed. "Or build a bigger and better school."

Athena's eyes glazed over as if she was lost in a dream. "Or travel all four realms."

Doris cleared her throat. "Or remodel the gymnasium."

"Doris," Athena said with a groan, stomping her foot so hard, the cuckoo clocks rattled against the wall. "I'm tired of school life."

A heavy weight settled on Doris's chest. Athena knew how much the school meant to her. How could she expect her to just walk away? She fought to keep the edge of panic from her voice. "But this has been my dream."

A look of pity flashed in Athena's eyes, making Doris's heart sink to the pit of her second stomach.

Athena shook her head, snickering. "Even after Resolution 424 passes?"

Doris gritted her teeth. "It won't pass." A nagging voice in the back of her head told her it would, though, and then what? Would she shut down her school rather than violate her one golden rule? Mandatory Goldenwands for all students assured her they'd never learn another thing.

Athena's black eyes hardened. "Goldenwand owns everyone. Now he owns you."

Doris stiffened. "Nobody owns me. He told me his granddaughter was not to spend her first night in detention, but did I listen?" Even Goldenwand's goon who'd delivered the check had insisted that the heiress wasn't to serve detention. Doris simply scowled at him but refused to give him an answer.

Athena tilted her head, that ridiculous pink bow flopping sideways like an extra set of ears. "Really?"

"It's just a semester." Doris's voice sounded small even to her ears.

Athena cocked a brow. "She must pass."

"She will." She had to. Doris was not prepared to give back that check.

Athena's heavy brow lowered over her eyes. "A girl that pretty doesn't care about education."

A surge of jealousy flooded Doris's chest. "You think she's pretty?" she snapped, unable to keep the hurt form her voice.

Athena rolled her eyes. "I'm not blind."

Doris had known when she'd fallen for Athena that the troll had a wandering eye. How could she not, after her relationship with the beautiful Miss Bubblebosom, whose curves and wavy hair reminded Doris so much of Seraphina Goldenwand?

A slow smile spread across Doris's face when an idea occurred to her. With a flick of the wrist, she moved her wand over her body, reciting the transformation spell. She gasped when she shrunk a good foot and had to look up at her lover. When the pearl buttons popped off her shirt, she smiled at her generous cleavage and smoothed her hands over curvaceous siren hips. No wonder the little tramp couldn't keep her legs closed. She had a body made for loving.

Athena arched a bushy brow. "What are you doing?"

Doris zapped the lock on the door. She shrugged out of her jacket and threw it across the desk. Athena's eyes widened when she slipped off her shoes and unzipped her pants. When Athena broke into a lusty grin, steam pouring out of her nostrils, Doris hoped she'd won. If not, there was nothing to be done. The school came first. Athena had known this when they started dating.

Chapter Two

Serah was pulled through the thin, slightly sticky film that made the bubble. It looked nothing like what she'd seen from the outside. It was ten times bigger and a total bachelor pad, with a tiki bar at one end, a flat-screen television on the other, and a round, crimson velvet sofa in the sunken center of the room.

"I'm Teju." Boxer Shorts adjusted his wire glasses and slapped his chest. "And this is my brother, Draque." He gestured to Bearded Guy, who was casually leaning against the translucent wall, sipping a beer.

When Draque tilted his bottle toward Serah with a wink, she thought her knees would buckle. He was sinfully sexy. Something about the way he mentally undressed her with his eyes told her he'd be an amazing fuck.

Teju pointed to the crimson-faced guy in sweats, who was going around the room, shoving empty beer bottles into a bag. "And our other brother, Ladon."

Ladon's cheeks flushed even brighter. "Sorry about the mess," he said. "We weren't expecting company."

"I don't mind." She shrugged. "Beats that hellish island." She rubbed her arms when chills raced across her skin.

Ladon dropped his bag, snatched a blanket off the sofa, and wrapped it around her. "Come sit down," he said and led her down shallow steps to the sunken area.

She hugged the blanket tightly and smiled at him as she sat. When his fingers brushed her skin, her chilled flesh burst into fire. "Thanks." She looked into golden eyes that sparkled like gems, then was drawn to his full, sensual lips.

He flashed a dimpled grin. He had the longest, thickest black lashes she'd ever seen. "My pleasure. We didn't catch your name."

"Serah," she answered.

"A pleasure to meet you, Serah."

He licked his lips as if the sound of her name made him hungry, and there was no mistaking the fork in his tongue. Witches didn't have forked tongues.

Was he a shifter? She wracked her brain, trying to remember which ones had forked tongues and wishing she'd paid more attention in her Anatomy of Magical Creatures classes. Her mind wandered to all the naughty things he could do with that tongue.

"Would you like a hot cup of tea?" he asked.

His irises contracted into long, narrow slits before changing back again, and she had no doubt he was a shifter, which meant his brothers were, too.

She eagerly nodded. "Yes, please."

"Okay. Be right back."

Licking her lips, she sighed when Ladon disappeared behind the tiki bar. She could've gotten lost in those golden eyes of his. When his brothers sat beside her, she scooted back against the plush cushions, casting a cursory glance at the pile of pillows on the floor. Had they brought other girls to their bubble or was she the first?

The thought of being in a shifters' den sent a jolt up her spine. Shifters were considered the black sheep of the magical world, and the more dangerous the beast, the more taboo the immortal. Teju and Draque also had golden irises. She closed her eyes as the image of a golden-eyed dragon with a forked tongue flashed across her mind. Her grandfather loathed all shifters, but he especially hated the dragon race, which made her want them more.

Moisture flooded her underwear at the thought of all the fabulous things three forked-tongued shifters could do to her. Merlin's balls!

You can't take them home to dear old Granddad, but you can have some fun, her siren hissed.

Though Serah's siren was considered part of her, she had conversations with that part of herself. Thelix, as her siren preferred to be called, was short for Thelxinoe, an ancient ancestral name, since inner-sirens were basically recycled ancestors.

Shut up, she whispered to Thelix, unnerved when she was answered with a laugh.

She peered over Teju's shoulder; their bubble hovered in the air as if it was suspended on a string. She made the mistake of looking down. The earth moved beneath them as they floated to the top of the cavern, over a wall, and into another cavern. "You guys sure this is safe?"

"Relax." Draque chuckled. "We do this every detention."

"How many detentions have you had?"

"Meh." He shrugged. "Usually one a month."

"And you use that time to party in a bubble?"

Teju popped the top on a beer. "Pretty much."

"How many girls have you brought in here with you?" Serah couldn't deny the jealously that twisted a blade in her heart at the thought of other girls sharing the dragons' den.

They froze like deer in a broomstick's high beams. When they shared dark looks, she knew they were telepathically speaking to one another, as was the way with most shifters if they were in the same family. She and her siren mother and grandmother had been able to telepathically speak, too.

"Only one other," Teju answered, averting his eyes and pushing up his glasses.

Liar. Oh, well. She shouldn't have cared anyway. It's not like she was interested in anything more than a good time from these three studs.

No, Serah, she chided herself. *You can't sleep with them.*

Yes, you can, Thelix argued.

Draque brushed his denim-clad leg against hers. "But she wasn't nearly as pretty as you."

"Oh." She bit her lip, batting her lashes and feigning innocence. Carefully cultivated expression drove men wild.

What was wrong with her? Why was she capitulating to her siren so easily? *Because you need to get fucked,* Thelix chuckled.

"What brings you to the Academy for Misfit Witches?" Draque asked, as he not-so-slyly draped an arm behind her.

She turned into him, "accidentally" brushing her knee across his thigh, though she knew she was playing with fire. "I got expelled from my other school."

Draque's full lips pulled back in a feral smile. "Us, too."

"What did you do?" Laden asked as he returned and handed her a steaming cup of tea.

She was pleasantly surprised that he'd also included two sugar packets on the chipped, porcelain saucer. He wasn't such a brute, especially for a dragon. Her grandfather had told her they were all fire and no finesse.

"Got caught in a compromising position." She blew steam across her tea, looking up at him with an innocent air. "You?"

His nostrils flared and his gaze flickered to her breasts. "Burned down the boy's bathroom."

"Not on purpose," Teju said. "Draque was trying to smite a rat."

Ladon nodded. "The school was infested."

"Why are you allowed to bring your wands to detention?" She glanced at the long stick poking out of Draque's jeans.

"We're not." Draque slipped a wand from his pocket with a grin. "Teju knows every concealment and enchantment spell there is."

"He's the smart brother." Ladon tapped his forehead. "His mind is like a Goldenwand."

"Nice." She shifted uncomfortably at the reference to her grandfather's invention. People were always talking about the revolutionary wand that had the features of a cellphone (an electronic communication device used in the human realm) and the memory of a seasoned witch. It was the perfect blend of technology and magic. It was also seldom used by shifters, and she didn't know if that was due to their animosity toward the Goldenwand or the wand's hatred of them. Either way, she had a sinking feeling these shifters wouldn't be impressed if they found out she was the Goldenwand heiress.

"What kind of compromising position?" Draque asked with a hint of mirth.

She watched the steam rising from her cup, feeling as if he could see into her soul with his penetrating eyes. Smiling softly at the memory, she said, "Me bent over my professor's desk and him bent over behind me."

Panting heavily, Thelix perked up to see their reactions.

"You screwed your professor?" All three brothers said simultaneously, their jaws dropping.

"Just one, but if you listen to the rumors, I've fucked between ten and ten thousand." Though she was a siren, and naturally sexual, she did have standards. Even though he'd offered, she wasn't about to sleep with Professor Slugstack for a passing grade. Periwinkle had been too tempting to resist, though. It was almost as if he'd cast a spell on her libido.

"Why did you sleep with him?" Teju asked.

Though she wasn't always attracted to men in glasses, she couldn't deny Teju looked adorably sophisticated. The round lenses kept sliding down his nose. She studied his eyes and saw no judgment there, just a sense of wonder.

"It was a lot more fun than studying." She bit her thumbnail. "Professor Periwinkle wasn't just my teacher; he was my tutor, and we spent a lot of time together after school."

"Periwinkle, huh?" Draque chuckled.

She supposed his name was odd. There was once an infamous witch named Pressy Periwinkle, who'd been accused of shrinking her former lovers' testicles.

She eyed Draque coolly and then caught the thick scent of their desire. Thelix clawed at her, demanding to be sated. Serah refused to surrender to her siren, no matter how badly she wanted to bang the shifters.

Teju cleared his throat, shifting his legs and not-so-inconspicuously adjusting the bulge in his jeans. "The teachers are all women here."

She instinctively licked her lower lip, instantly regretting her action. Before Grandfather had taken her from Siren's Cove, she'd enjoyed the sexual company of two girls her age. They'd helped Serah unlock the secrets of her body. But she wasn't about to sleep with a professor again, even though the girls she'd been with had pleasured her far better than Professor Periwinkle.

"Most of them are trolls," Teju added.

She blinked at him, thinking of Lady Hoofenmouth with the unibrow, wide nose, and a face that had been struck a few times by a really big ugly stick. No offense to trolls, but they were the most unattractive race in the magical world. "Really? Most of them?"

"Everyone except for Miss Bubblebosom." Ladon chuckled. "And they're all loyal to Doublewart."

Holy dragon dong! She didn't think she could stomach sleeping with a troll. No wonder Grandfather had insisted she attend this school.

"If you need tutoring," Teju said, "I'm happy to help."

"Thanks, Teju." Heat flamed her cheeks when she looked into his piercing eyes. She had a feeling his idea of tutoring would be much like Periwinkle's. "But as soon as my detention's over, I'm calling my grandfather to come get me." He wouldn't want her to stay here after he learned Goldenwands were forbidden. Sure, he was often hard on her and not very affectionate, but he cared enough to see that she got a decent education, didn't he?

"You signed the contract, right?" Teju asked.

"Yeah." She shrugged, but Grandfather could get her out of it.

Draque gave her a forlorn look as if he'd accidentally eaten her puppy. "It can't be revoked."

She sat up straighter. "Excuse me?"

"Dame Doublewart owns your ass until graduation," he said.

She tossed long, wavy hair behind her shoulder. "I'm sure I can get out of it."

"I'm sure you can't." Draque snickered. "Doublewart's never lost a student. She prides herself on her record."

She slumped in her seat. "Fuck."

Ladon gave her a sympathetic look. "What year are you?"

"Twelfth." She should've finished school last year, but she'd gotten a late start.

"You only have a semester to go." Teju's enthusiasm sounded forced. "You'll get through it."

"How long have you been here?" she asked them.

"Three years," they answered simultaneously.

"We're twelfth years, too," Ladon said.

Merlin's dirty buttplug! "How have you survived that long?"

The brothers shared sly looks.

"We've managed," Teju said.

And by "managed" she suspected they'd seduced every wayward witch in the school.

"We had no choice," Ladon said. "We should've graduated two years ago, but no other schools would take us."

"How old are you?" she asked.

"Just turned twenty."

Hmmm. Triplets. She thought she'd read once dragon eggs hatched in threes. They looked older. Then again, she'd heard dragons were usually mature beyond their years. These guys didn't act too mature, though.

"You?" Ladon asked.

Thelix purred when he flashed those sexy dimples. Hot damn, he was cute. She wondered if he'd meant to turn her on or if he was genuinely sweet and sexy.

"Almost nineteen," she said. "I'm a year behind." Not that she was a dummy. Grandfather hadn't taken her from Siren's Cove until she was sixteen.

Teju puffed up his chest, looking far too sophisticated and sexy as he pushed his glasses up the bridge of his Roman nose. "We'll help you get all caught up."

Yesss, please, Thelix begged. *More tutoring sessions.*

"Thanks." She didn't have the heart to tell him she wasn't staying. Contracts could always be broken with enough payoff.

"Our pleasure," Ladon answered, his cheeks flushing so red, she feared he'd catch fire.

"What is it, Ladon?" she asked.

He looked at her with big doe eyes, and her heart melted. "You're the prettiest girl I've ever seen."

She swore she heard Thelix faint. "Uh, thanks." She forced herself to look away.

"Sorry." He leaned into her, getting so close she could smell him, a blend of heat, magic, and tempting pheromones all his own. "I hope I'm not making you uncomfortable."

She fought and the desire that coursed through her when she spied the bulge in his jeans.

Grab it! Thelix commanded.

"I'm quite comfortable, thanks," she answered him while ignoring Thelix. She knew she was attractive, with her wavy, auburn hair, luminous violet eyes, and generous curves. She was built like a siren, after all. But even she knew the power of the siren's call. Her mesmerizing voice was meant to lure sailors to their deaths, tricking them to fall so madly in love, they completely forgot their imminent danger. Kind of sucked for her at times, because she never knew if men were attracted to her or simply bewitched.

"I'm sure you get loads of compliments," Teju said, leaning closer, too.

Rip off their clothes! Thelix wailed. *Or let them rip off yours.*

She should've been alarmed that she was being squished into a stud sandwich, but she gloried in it.

"I do," she said, "and I'm sure you've met prettier girls."

"We haven't," they said in unison.

They want you. Spread your legs, already.

She would've been flattered if not for the fact that her pheromones were so strong. She wiped a bead of sweat off her brow, knowing her glands were reacting to the scent of three virile men.

"Listen," she said, clenching her hands into fists as she braced for their reaction. "I have to be honest with you. I'm part siren. You're reacting to my pheromones. All men do."

Don't tell them that! Thelix scolded.

They froze like gnomes caught in a trapper's net.

Draque shared wide-eyed looks with his brothers. "Seriously?"

"Yeah." She twisted the end of her belt in her fingers. "My grandmother is the siren queen."

Draque's jaw dropped. "No shit."

"D-do you eat guys after you have sex with them?" Ladon stammered.

She stiffened. Even though sirens had stopped eating men after the curse had been broken two thousand years ago, their reputation as man-eaters persisted. "No, I don't." She gave them each a direct look. "Sirens don't eat people anymore. Get with this millennium."

But we swallow, Thelix giggled.

All three brothers simultaneously sighed.

"Thank the stars." Ladon clasped his hands in a prayer pose, licking his lips like a kid in an ice cream parlor. "Not that we're afraid of you eating us. We're dragon shifters."

She glared at him. "Who said I was having sex with you?" So they'd already assumed she would spread her legs? Did they think her a whore? Was that why they'd rescued her from the dungeon? They'd already planned on getting laid? They made her horny, but they didn't have to be so crass.

"Sorry." Ladon dragged a hand down his face with a groan. "I don't know what's come over me."

"We're not usually like this," Draque said. "You must think we're cads."

She pretended to be offended, but the nagging siren in the back of her head urged her to jump them, telling her she wanted it as much as they did. She smoothed trembling hands down her jeans. She needed a way to shut the siren up. Either that, or give her what she wanted.

"That's okay." She frowned at her tea, cooling on the coffee table. "Do you have anything stronger than beer and tea?"

Ladon jumped to his feet. "What would you like?"

Teju arched a brow. "How about a siren sangria?"

Something was going on here. "Never had it," she answered.

They all froze again. "Really?" Teju asked, looking like a kid who'd gotten his hand caught in the cookie jar.

She shot him an accusatory glare. "I'm guessing it makes you horny."

Let's drink it, Thelix squealed.

As if she needed anything else to make he pussy throb and her nipples ache.

He scratched the back of his head, averting his gaze. "Uh... maybe."

"What the hell, Teju?" Draque snapped and turned to Ladon. "Make her a pixie punch."

"Okay," Ladon said, casting a wary glance at her.

You want the sangria, her inner siren purred. *Then you'll have a good excuse for capitulating to their many charms.*

"That's okay," she blurted. "I'll try a siren sangria." She should've regretted the words that slipped off her tongue, but she was well on her way past regrets.

"Okay," Ladon practically roared, "siren sangrias for everyone."

His brothers growled their approval, eyeing her like they were starving lions, and she was a choice cut of prime beef.

Ladon hurried to the tiki bar, but not before she saw the big bulge in his sweats. His brothers were also sporting erections. The heat radiating from their skin said they were ready for a night of primal passion.

She fought the urge to reach for them and free their flesh wands from their pants. That's when she knew there was a good chance she was getting laid that night. Not by one, but by three dragon shifters. She'd regret it come morning, especially if Grandfather found out, but there was nothing to be done. She was so damned horny, she couldn't conjure up a spell strong enough to suppress her libido, especially as her wand was currently locked away. Goddess save her.

LADON FIRESBREATH COULD hardly believe their good luck. He and his brothers hadn't expected to rescue a beautiful siren when they were assigned detention. Honestly, they'd deliberately gotten kicked out of class because they needed a break from boring lectures and atrocious cafeteria food.

He inhaled her intoxicating scent from across the room, sending his libido into a tailspin. She smelled like honeysuckle and something else, strange yet familiar. He accidentally poured too much punch in the glass and swore when it overflowed. He knew siren pheromones were tempting, but her scent was far too alluring. Could she be their destined mate? Goddess, he prayed she was.

With her luminous violet eyes, wavy auburn hair, mile-high legs, and alluring curves, she was the definition of temptation and he wanted a taste of her forbidden fruit.

He looked at his brothers, who were crowding her on the sofa. When they made eye contact, he sent them a telepathic message. *You smell what I smell?*

Teju gave a curt nod. *I've never wanted a girl so much in my damn life.*

We have to have her, Draque growled.

Teju shot Serah a sideways look. *Don't worry brothers. She wants us, too.*

SATED AND SPENT, DORIS lay in her lover's arms, cooing while Athena stroked her back and held her on the worn rug by the fireplace. Logs crackled in the hearth, the light from the fire flickering across the walls, creating for the lovers the perfect ambiance for a magical evening. If only it could be like this always. Perhaps Athena was right. Perhaps Doris should retire with the money and close the school. The thought was tempting but her teachers and students needed Doublewart's Academy, and so did she. It had been her passion these past twenty-five years, transforming misfit witches into productive members of society. How could she walk away?

With a resigned sigh, she sat up and kissed Athena's forehead before slipping on her clothes.

Athena reached for her with a languid smile. "Don't go yet."

Doris took Athena's large hand in hers and kissed her calloused knuckles. "I have to, my love." It was almost time for light's out. Doris always wished her students a goodnight.

Doris shook wavy brown hair over her shoulder and buttoned her blouse. How much she'd enjoyed this siren's body she'd temporarily adopted. She was young and flexible, not to mention orgasms were so intense, she saw stars. No wonder sirens were promiscuous. Doris admired her perky breasts once more before fastening the last button, regretting she'd have to transform back into her old body before she was discovered.

Kneeling over her lover, she kissed Athena once more, then reached for her wand. When a loud crash filled her ears, she screamed, hitting the floor so hard, her head spun.

She gagged on acrid smoke and shielded her face with her hands. Dragon's breath! Those mischievous Firesbreath brothers must have escaped detention. She would make them pay!

"Athena!" she rasped, sitting up and rubbing her dizzy head. "Are you okay?"

Her lover answered with a groan.

Doris's heart seized. "Athena!" she cried, fanning her face. "I can't see you!"

Peering into the smoke, she saw that the wall with the fireplace had crumbled, exposing them to the elements and giving her a glimpse of the nearby graveyard, illuminated by thin shards of moonlight. She made out the shadowy figures of three winged dragons. "You miscreants!" She shook a fist at them. "Look what you've done! I'll have you in the dungeon for the rest of the year."

When the tallest of the dragons moved forward, snarling, her breath caught in her throat. He looked familiar, but he wasn't one of her students—not one of her current students anyway.

"Wh-who are you?" she demanded, wishing she had her wand.

The dragon's upper lip lifted, revealing rows of razor sharp teeth. "Never mind who we are." The serpent's head weaved, following her like a snake cornering a rabbit. "You're the Goldenwand heiress."

She opened her mouth to contradict him but thought better of it. This was a kidnapping, and she'd be damned if she let them take one of her students.

Stepping back, she nearly tripped over her wand. With a quick flick of the wrist, she brought it to her hand, then yelled in pain when it was zapped away with a shock so powerful, she was driven to her knees.

"Did you think you could best me?" he purred, nuzzling her hair.

She backed up until she was pressed against the door or what was left of it. Crying out, she shielded her eyes when a dragon lunged for her, her knees buckling as she slumped into his open jowls.

THE STUDENTS HAD JUST finished their supper when Bodicea Bubble-bosom noticed the change in the night sky. In a matter of seconds, the dark clouds had turned a brickish hue, as if illuminated by a fire within. Bodicea's veins solidified with fear. It was just as Doris had predicted. War had come to their school.

She blew her whistle three times, waving her wand above her head. "Students, this is not a drill. Wands at the ready!"

Her charges snapped their wands out of their robes and fell to their knees, ducking under the tables as they'd practiced in drills.

A dragon's roar was Bodicea's only warning before the walls went up in flames. Bodicea threw a protective shield around her students as the other professors aimed their wands at the five massive dragons hovering over the charred remains of what had once been their school. They fought fire with fire, until the scorched air was so stifling, it hurt to breathe.

They would not survive this battle much longer.

Dame Doublewart and Lady Hoofenmouth were nowhere in sight, so Bodicea chanted the illusion spell, creating what appeared to be a powerful explosion. Then she whispered the secret password to unlock the dungeon. Bodicea stifled a scream when the floor buckled and she and her students fell to the bottom of the pit.

After hitting the dirt, she blinked up at the gray bricks, which shifted back into place above them. Her charges were dead quiet, knowing the slightest sound could give away their hiding place. Goddess save them if they hadn't fooled the beasts.

Chapter Three

"What kind of wand is this? It looks like something from last century." Serah knew she was turning on Draque as she fondled his wand, but she just couldn't help herself. Maybe she was a bad girl after all.

"Probably." He worked a tick in his jaw, his eyes turning to stone as he scooted closer to her. "We get leftover supplies from other schools."

"I've never seen a wand so thick," she cooed, taking on a sultry, siren tone. Great Goddess! Thelix was taking over. So not good. The last time she surrendered to her siren, she'd been kicked out of school.

"The older ones are thicker," Teju rasped, his voice cracking as he wiped sweat off his brow.

"Do you like thick wands?" Draque asked, his voice low and dark.

Yes, we do, Thelix purred.

She inhaled the scent of his pheromones. "Are you being bad?" she teased, batting her lashes.

"Trying to be." He ran a hand through his beard. "Are you?"

She handed back his wand. "Maybe."

"I've got a thick wand, too, if you want to see it." Ladon bowed his head, looking at her intensely.

We want to see all the wands, Thelix cried, *making messes across our breasts.*

Her siren watched too many porns.

Ladon's boyish charm made her cream her panties. He was so damn cute. She knew she'd be dominant if they ever had sex, riding her dragon until they were both roaring with pleasure.

"Let me see." She waggled her fingers, and he placed his wand in her hand. It was thick, like his brother's. Judging by the bulges in their pants, their wands were a good indication of their anatomy.

Crossing one leg over the other, she fought to push wayward thoughts out of her mind and took another sip of her siren sangria. It tasted nothing like she'd expected. Fruity and sweet, with a salty/sour aftertaste, sort of like sex with a siren. Blissful and sweet until she finished with her lover and tossed him aside, which she supposed was better than when they used to eat them. Her mother and grandmother had expected her to be like them—love men and then send them on their way—but sadly, she had a witch's heart. How she wished she could be as indifferent as the rest of her kind. Maybe then she wouldn't still be nursing a broken heart.

She shoved thoughts of Periwinkle aside. He didn't deserve her attention, anyway.

Thelix told her to dip Ladon's wand in her drink and suck it dry, but she resisted, knowing her dragons would lose all control if she did that.

Admit it, you want them to lose control.

She silently admonished Thelix and handed Ladon back his wand. "It's very nice," she said, forcing herself to look away from his big, sweet eyes.

"Look what mine can do," Teju said with a wink, handing her his wand.

It vibrated in her hand, and the tip bulged, making it appear to be a sex toy.

Ask him to slide it into your pussy, Thelix demanded.

"One drink, and you're already trying to get in my pants."

He blushed. "Sorry."

Clucking her tongue, she handed it back to him, a buzz going through her when their fingers touched. Great Goddess, she was in so much trouble. How could she resist these three tempting brothers all night?

Maybe she shouldn't. Maybe a tryst with them was exactly what she needed to heal her shattered heart after Periwinkle's rejection.

Teju and his brothers looked nervously at each other, each with a hopeless look that told her they were all out of tricks. Maybe they weren't the practiced flirts she'd assumed them to be.

"Tell me more about this school," she said, changing the subject and hoping to put them at ease.

Draque's eyes turned from brown to gold and back again, which meant he was probably warring with his shifter's desires, too. "Dame Doublewart is a hardass."

She rolled her eyes. "I gathered that."

"But she cares about her students," Ladon said.

She was beginning to suspect Ladon didn't have an unkind bone in his body, which made her want to fuck him even more.

She took several deep swallows of her sangria, finishing it off and wiping her mouth with the back of her hand. "Could've fooled me." She accidentally slammed her glass on the table and was relieved when it didn't shatter.

Draque flashed a mocking pout. "You're still hurt over being sent to the dungeon?"

She crossed her arms, scowling. "Are you making fun of me?" Draque was the most mischievous of the brothers, judging by his attitude. Maybe even the reason they were always in trouble.

"Every student gets sent to the dungeon their first night," Teju said, leaning into her and giving her a sympathetic smile.

"Usually one night is all it takes to prevent us from acting up." Ladon blinked at her, clearly missing the irony in his statement.

She laughed. "Didn't seem to work on you."

Twin fires brewed in Draque's eyes. "We're a *special* kind of bad."

Oh, goddess! Thelix yelled. *Just fuck them already!*

She scooted away from him, the heat from his nearness setting her skin aflame. "I promised my grandfather I wouldn't go near bad boys again."

He'll never know, Thelix pleaded.

Draque's brows raised as he gave her a long look. "Did you love him?"

"Who?" She wrapped her arms around herself, feeling as if his gaze was boring holes through her soul.

"Your professor." He took a long drink of beer before setting the bottle on the table. He'd been the only brother to refuse a sangria, but something told her he didn't need a magical drink to stoke his libido.

She broke eye contact with him, unable to handle his penetrating gaze a moment longer. "I thought I did."

He didn't know how to lick pussy, Thelix spat. *We didn't love him.*

He leaned so close, she could smell the barley on his breath. "What made you change your mind?"

Serah released a shaky breath, hating that he was making her relive that awful day but also knowing she needed to acknowledge the ugly truth if she was to heal her broken heart. "He didn't fight for us."

There, she'd said it, though the truth stung like a thousand venomous cobra bites. Periwinkle's rejection had hurt far worse than when her grandmother and mother tried to kill her. Worse than when Grandfather called her a whore after she'd been caught with Prometheus.

Prometheus had told her he loved her, that he wanted to spend eternity with her, but he'd let her go too easily after the headmistress discovered their affair, refusing to even look at her when they were called before the school board.

"How old was he?"

She blinked at Teju, startled back to reality, angry with herself for pining for her professor when she had three virile young men at her disposal. "Age is just a number."

Draque tapped her knee with his wand, a determined look in his eyes. "How old?"

"Thirty-three." She hung her head, angry with herself for capitulating.

"You were just a fuck to him."

She jerked back, Draque's harsh words like a smack to the head. "Gee, thanks."

"He should've known better than to take advantage of a student," he added.

No way would she cry now. She'd shed enough tears over that jerk. "Who said I wasn't taking advantage of him?" she said haughtily, pretending her potions professor hadn't pulverized her heart.

"Your eyes say it." Teju tapped the rim of his glasses, giving her a knowing look.

Ladon splayed a hand across his chest. "You might have a siren's body, but you have a witch's heart."

Jumping to her feet, she held out a staying hand when they tried to follow suit. "Stop."

As if she needed to fall in love again. No, best to focus on her studies so she could graduate and get the hell out of this place.

Teju stood and grasped the tips of her fingers. When she didn't resist, he pressed her hand between both of his. "We won't do that to you, Serah."

"How do I know that?" Prometheus had used almost that exact same line on her.

"A dragon's word is his honor," they said in unison.

"Why would you give me your word?"

Ladon gave her a soft smile. "Because you have a pure soul."

Suspicion raised its ugly head. Releasing Teju, she sat back down. These guys were full of gnome dung. "How do you know anything about my soul?"

Draque sat dangerously close to her once more. "It speaks to us."

That caught her off guard. She'd thought Ladon was the sappy brother. Why was Draque being so kind?

After sitting opposite Draque, Teju tapped his forehead. "Our instincts are never wrong."

She imagined her eyes were twin wands, burning holes through their chests. "Obviously your instincts are bad, or you wouldn't keep landing in detention."

"Oh, that." Teju chuckled, waving at the tiki bar and flat screen. "Does this look like detention?"

Ladon grimaced as he sat on the ottoman across from her, his knees pressing into hers. "Once you taste dorm food, you'll understand why we need to get away."

There were platters of crumbs on the tiki bar and coffee table. This place was far better than what she'd seen so far of Dame Doublewart's. But they were full of shit, because if their instincts were so superior, they wouldn't have gotten kicked out of their other school. She decided to drop it for now. Their confidence was misplaced but charming. Grandfather had told her dragons were annoyingly smug. They certainly were smug, but she wasn't annoyed by them.

There was still one issue. All three brothers appeared to be vying for her affection. They were all so cute, how could she pick just one? She didn't sense any rivalry between them. Were they hoping to share her?

She scratched the back of her head. "You guys don't mind sharing a girl?"

"No." Teju gave her a no-bullshit stare. "We share a mate. It's the way of dragon prides."

A mate? She wasn't ready to be anything more than a fuck.

Ladon frowned. "What's wrong?"

"This is moving too fast," she blurted. So soon after her disgrace, how did she find herself in the lair of three tempting shifters? And what about Prometheus? Wasn't she supposed to be pining for him? Funny how she couldn't recall the details of his face while she was looking into Ladon's luminous eyes.

"Do you want us to slow down?" Teju asked, obviously disappointed.

"I-I don't know."

Wrong answer! Thelix screeched. *You want them. Stop fighting.*

"Look at me, Serah." Draque cupped her chin in his strong, calloused hand, forcing her to face him. "You want us. I see it in your eyes."

She shivered as a wave of desire coursed through her. Damn him, he was right. "But it's wrong."

His brow shot up. "Why?"

She thought of Grandfather, sitting in front of the headmistress's desk as she went into great detail about how she'd caught Serah in a compromising position with her teacher. Serah would never forget the look of disgust in Grandfather's eyes when he said he knew she'd turn out to be a siren slut.

"I don't want to be a whore," she said, blinking back tears.

Your grandfather is a cruel, selfish man. You are a beautiful pearl. Do not let him make you ashamed of who you are.

Serah sucked in a sharp breath at her siren's words. Never before had the siren spoken of Grandfather, and never had she offered comfort. Was she right? Was Grandfather cruel and selfish?

Ladon sat at Serah's feet and took her hands in his. "We'd never think that of you."

No, she thought, *but Grandfather would.*

"You're far from a whore," Teju added.

"If you want," Draque said, "we can just get to know each other tonight. Don't feel obligated to have sex with us, Serah."

The sincerity in his eyes was enough to break her heart all over again. She was relieved they didn't expect sex from her, but her siren certainly did, and Goddess save her, so did she. Her core throbbed so hard, it felt like a heart was beating between her legs. The moisture that pooled in her panties was bound to soak through the cotton, leaving a siren's stain of shame on her jeans.

Not if you take off your jeans, Thelix cooed.

She searched their eyes for signs of deceit. "I don't want anyone finding out."

They perked up like they'd just downed cups of magic espresso.

"We don't kiss and tell," Draque said with a devastatingly sexy sideways smile.

"What happens in the bubble, stays in the bubble." Ladon's goofy grin warmed her heart.

She wasn't quite ready to let her guard down. She gave them all sharp looks. "Promise?"

They drew pentagrams over their hearts. "On our honor."

She stood when another wave of moisture gushed in her undies. Unzipping her jeans, she shrugged them off, then made quick work of her shirt, throwing both behind her. She gave them bold stares. "Then make love to me."

They broke into deep growls that shook the marrow of her bones, but she wasn't afraid. She knew they wouldn't hurt her.

Draque stood in front of her, his skin branding her flesh as he gripped her shoulders. Her legs went boneless as she wrapped her arms around his neck.

"Thank the Goddess," he breathed against her lips before claiming her mouth in a passionate kiss.

He tasted like smoke and barley and a warm spice that was all his own. Deepening the kiss, she clung to him like a lifeline when he lifted her into his arms and gently laid her across the sofa.

Thelix moaned, expelling a rush of air. *Spread your legs for them,* she demanded.

She shut her eyes when Draque kissed her again, trailing hot kisses across her jaw and neck. When the other brothers knelt beside her, kissing and nipping the bend behind her knee and her abdomen, she thought she'd melt in a puddle of lust. Strong hands caressed her breasts while another released the clasp on her bra. She arched when Draque slipped off her bra, shoving her chest in his face and crying out when he bit on the swell of her breast.

Running his hands down her back, he sucked one nipple and then the other, feasting on her breasts as if they were manna from heaven, his talented, swirling tongue sending a zing straight to her lady parts. Great Goddess! Where in all four realms did he learn that?

When someone pulled off her panties and slid his forked tongue across her slick ribbon, she about flew off the sofa. She looked down into Teju's eyes. He flashed a wicked smile as he licked her again, his tongue working with the dexterity of an appendage as it dipped inside her well of desire, spreading moisture across her swollen labia.

She shuddered, sinking back into the cushions and spreading her legs wider. *That's right,* Thelix cooed. *Surrender to your desire.*

Teju purred while he licked her, a low deep vibration that rattled her insides and buzzed against her sweet spot. Flinging a hand across her forehead, she wept with joy, swept up in euphoria's clutches.

Sliding her hands down her hips, she then ran her fingers through Ladon's thick hair while he trailed kisses from her navel to her swollen center, his long, forked tongue circling her button while Teju's tongue speared deep inside her. All the while Draque worshipped her breasts.

The orgasm that came over her was sudden and powerful, slamming into her like a wall of water. She tensed, crying out, then gushed into Teju's mouth, too caught up in pleasure to care about the mess she made on the sofa as aftershocks pulsed all the way to her toes.

Teju chuckled, licking her juices. She was about to come undone again when Draque pulled her up and spun her around until she gripped the sofa's armrest, her ass jutting in the air.

She heard Draque unzipping his jeans behind her and gasped when his cockhead circled her dripping juncture. She pressed into him, sucking in a hiss when his massive erection filled her halfway. He latched onto her ass, digging into her flesh with fingers that felt like talons, anchoring himself to her with one thrust.

Ahh, Thelix moaned.

When she jerked forward, he gripped her hair, as she slowly slid back onto his full length with a satisfied groan. He tunneled into her, his cock stimulating every nerve ending with such intense pleasure, she was well on her way to another orgasm.

"Oh, Draque!" she cried, throwing back her head and surrendering to his intense fucking. Someone fondled her breasts, pinching and twisting her nipples until pain blended with pleasure. She didn't even know which brother was touching her, and she didn't care. She was getting the best fucking of her life.

With a roar, Draque stilled, grasping her hips so tight, she she reveled in the torture of his nails breaking skin. The pleasure of her throbbing orgasm was more intense than any pain. She could tell by the erratic twitching of his hips that he was spilling his seed into her. She didn't mind. She'd just have to remember to chew Maiden's Wart come morning to prevent any unwanted pregnancies.

After their breathing had slowed, Draque slid out of her. He took her in his arms and pulled her into his lap, kissing her forehead, nose, and lips.

"Thank you," he breathed against her mouth, still panting heavily.

"You're very welcome," she slurred like a drunk, high on orgasms. "And thank you, too."

He traced her jaw with the tips of his fingers. She giggled when he nuzzled her neck, his beard tickling her sensitive skin.

You don't need to guide these dragons, Thelix said. *They have powerful instincts, unlike the undeserving one.*

Her siren had picked a hell of a time to bring up the professor, but she was right. She'd had to tell the professor over and over what she liked and what she hated, but not with these studs. They knew exactly what buttons to press.

When Teju pulled her off Draque's lap with a low growl, she fell into his embrace, feeling as boneless as a gutted fish. She was so sated and spent, she feared she wouldn't be able to have another orgasm.

Cupping her face in his hands, Teju kissed her long and deep, his tongue swirling with hers and making her pussy throb anew. He laid her across the sofa, then removed his boxers, revealing an impressively long, thick erection. Gripping his wand, he knelt beside her with a wicked gleam in his eyes.

She tensed. "What are you doing?"

"Relax," he soothed, stroking her slick folds with the tip of the wand.

When it buzzed, her legs opened farther, like melting butter. She threw back her head with a groan when he slid the thick wand inside of her, fucking her with deep, hard thrusts before pulling out and swirling across her labia, the intense pleasure from the buzzing making her button spring back to life. She panted while he alternated between fucking her with the vibrating wand and circling her clit.

Just as she was about to fall to pieces, he removed the wand, the wood slick and wet from her juices, and slid his cock inside her, keeping the wand pressed against her swollen button. He fucked her while vibrating her tender spot. She only lasted a few strokes before she unraveled again, calling his name while her pussy walls clenched his cock like a vice, squeezing and pulsing until he stilled with a roar, his cockhead swelling and filling her with his seed. Turning off his wand, he set it down beside her, then leaned over her and planted a tender kiss on her lips.

"That was amazing, my love," he said.

My love? The endearment would've alarmed her if she hadn't been so sated and bone tired.

He kissed her several more times before pulling out and wiping up their juices with a towel Ladon handed him.

Ladon traced lazy circles across her nipple. "How do you feel?" he asked.

She was unable to stop from smiling. "Sated."

"Good," he answered, stroking her side.

Her skin broke into gooseflesh at his touch. She made soft sounds while he caressed her. By the time he found that magic spot between her thighs, she was primed and ready for more.

He stroked her until she begged for release. She hissed when he pulled back, then sighed with relief after he climbed between her legs and sank into her heat. So much for her taking charge. Oh, well. She was too tired to dominate him.

They made love slowly, tenderly, working up their desire until they were both calling out each other's names as bliss consumed them. When he throbbed and spurted inside her, she fell apart in his arms, surrendering to the climax that rolled through her like a gentle, cresting wave.

After he pulled out and tenderly cleaned her up, she climbed into his lap.

"Can I get you anything to eat or drink?" he asked.

"No," she answered, feeling like putty in his arms. "Just love me."

His cock lengthened and hardened, pressing into her thigh. With a giggle, she fell back against the sofa, opening her arms to him and joining with him once more. His brothers also made love to her again, much more tenderly than the first time, making her feel more loved and cherished than she'd ever felt in her life, casting aside all thoughts she had of that other guy. How could anyone else compare to her three amazing shifters? Goddess help her, she could easily fall in love with them.

SERAH SAT IN LADON'S lap, licking her fingers after helping her lovers devour three platters of barbeque chicken wings and Cajun fries.

"That was amazing." Ladon said against her neck. "*You* were amazing."

She giggled when he nibbled her ear. "Thanks."

"Serah," he whispered.

She nuzzled his soft cheek. She loved how affectionate he was. He was the ultimate cuddler. "Yes?"

"I'm not sorry you got kicked out of your other school," he said with a mischievous lilt. He wrapped a strong arm around her waist.

"Me, neither. Meeting you was worth it."

After he finished nibbling on her neck, her hands flew to her earlobes. She was always checking to make sure the earrings her grandfather had given her were in place, a habit she couldn't seem to break.

Teju flanked her other side, resting his chin on her shoulder. "So does that mean you'll be our girl?"

She froze. Their girl? Wow, these dragons moved fast. Then again, they'd just had an amazing marathon lovemaking session. So amazing that Thelix had gone completely silent, other than the occasional satisfied sigh. "Your girl? Like a girlfriend?"

Draque handed her a cup of hot tea. "Like a mate."

"Thank you." She peered at him from over the rim of her mug. A mate to three sexy dragon shifters? She'd never have to worry about unfulfilled sexual needs. There were just a few problems, the main one being that her grandfather would probably disown and disinherit her when he found out.

"I thought dragons had to mate with other dragons," she said and sipped the tea. It was the perfect temperature and tasted like spiced apples and cinnamon.

"Not always," Teju said as he massaged her shoulders. "Our fathers are dragons. Our mother is a djinn."

She groaned while he rubbed the kinks out of her sore muscles. "You have more than one father?"

"Yes," Ladon said, "they're triplets, like us. They are mated to our mom."

Lucky woman, Thelix opined. *She has a fuck ready whenever she wants one.*

I liked you better when you were quiet, Serah silently berated. "And you're okay with sharing one girl?"

"We share everything." As if to emphasize the point, Ladon snatched Draque's beer from him, took a long swig, and handed it back. "It's the dragon way." He flashed a crooked smile while Draque gave him a side-eye look.

Pulling Teju's hands off her, she scooted back, facing all three guys while rubbing warmth into her arms. She couldn't get Grandfather's disappointed look out of her head or the venom in his voice when he'd called her a slut. If she accepted their proposal, she wondered how long she could keep it from him. Probably until graduation, but then what?

"So what do you say?" Teju nudged her knee. "You want to be our girl?"

Chewing her bottom lip, she warily eyed them. She badly wanted to say yes. "I don't have to share you with another girl, do I?" Because unlike them she didn't like sharing.

"Nope. Just you," Draque said with a straight face. "And we don't share you with other men."

"Don't worry." She laughed. "Three mates is enough."

Again, her grandfather's angry scowl popped into her head. Why was she entertaining the idea of mating with three shifters? Were they really used to sharing everything? And what about school policy? She had a feeling Dame Doublewart wouldn't allow it. Damn, she should've read that contract. "What about school rules?"

"No romantic relationships allowed," Teju said. "Which means we'll probably get thrown in detention if we're caught kissing."

"Oh." She hid a smile behind her hand.

"So?" they asked simultaneously, looking at her with such a hopeful gleam in their eyes, she couldn't bear to tell them no.

"Sure," she said, biting down on her lip. "I'll be your girl."

She inwardly cringed when her siren howled with joy. The last time Thelix had been this excited was when Serah had agreed to be Professor Periwinkle's lover. Actually, her siren hadn't howled that loud for Periwinkle, but she was practically blasting a hole through Serah's ears.

Great Goddess, what had she done?

Ladon took her in his arms, kissing her so passionately, he robbed her of breath. By the time they both came up for air, she was panting heavily and Thelix was swooning.

"You don't know how happy you've made us," he said, his eyes alight.

When Teju rubbed her shoulders again, trailing hot kisses down her neck, she was sure he was going to ask for another round. "Let's get some sleep," he whispered. "You have a long day tomorrow."

She turned to him. "I do?"

He grimaced. "Placement tests."

Her heart sank. "I'm not good with tests." That was why she'd gone to Professor Periwinkle for tutoring sessions.

Draque sat beside her, taking her hand in his. "Good thing your mates stole the keys to the placement tests."

"Really?"

"Don't worry." Ladon smiled. "We'll hook you up."

"You're awesome." She threw her arms around his neck and gave him a big kiss, then kissed his brothers, too. "You sure we need to go to sleep?" she asked, trailing a finger down Draque's chest and resting her hand just below his navel.

The brothers shared happy grins. "Maybe we could stay awake a while longer."

SERAH ROLLED OUT OF Ladon's arms and made the mistake of looking at him. He was smiling in his sleep. Whatever he was dreaming about, it was certainly making him happy. She wondered if it was about her. She kissed his forehead before stumbling to the bathroom behind the tiki bar. After relieving herself and freshening up, she poured a club soda and drank it. Sex with three hot dragon shifters sure worked up a thirst. Casting a wistful glance at her men, sleeping at various angles on the sectional sofa, she poured herself another drink, contemplating the giant pile of gargoyle shit she'd just stepped in.

"I wish Grandfather wasn't so prejudiced."

Why had she agreed to be their girl? Her grandfather would kill her if he found out. And then what? She liked them so much, maybe even more than Professor Periwinkle. How could she give them up?

You can't, her siren cooed. *I won't let you.*

She startled when a familiar cloud of pink smoke burst before her. Holy Baphomet balls! She had said *wish.*

Hestia Goldenwand, Serah's fairy godmother, droopy-eyed and a few mystic martinis past a good buzz, stumbled into her arms and let out a deep belch.

Her pink updo wig tilted to one side, and her mascara was smeared in heavy circles below her eyes.

Ugh, Thelix groaned. *I'm out of here. Let me know when she's gone.*

As if. Serah refrained from answering. She enjoyed her peace of mind far too much to summon her siren.

"Oh, my darling child," Hestia slurred, throwing her arms around Serah's neck. "I'm so glad you're okay."

"Of course I am." Gagging on stale alcohol fumes, she pried Hestia's arms off her, fanning her face as she stepped back. "Why wouldn't I be?"

"Your new academy was attacked by dragons!" Her godmother's eyes nearly rolled into the back of her head as she fell onto a barstool. Flicking her wand at a bottle of whiskey on the shelf, she magically poured a tall glass and beckoned it to her, licking her lips.

"It was?" Serah snatched the whiskey out of the air before it reached Hestia. "Are you sure?"

"Fairly certain." She looked at Serah with glassy eyes and a scrunched brow. "Or maybe it was a dream."

"Fairy Godmother, you have *got* to quit drinking." Serah loved the eccentric, kind old woman. She'd been like a mother to Serah after Grandfather had taken her from Siren's Cove. According to Grandfather, she'd served their family nearly eight hundred years. Given her thirst for liquor, Serah was surprised Hestia hadn't accidentally fallen down a wishing well or flown into a ring of fire pixies by now.

"My evening cocktail had nothing to do with it." She scratched her head and her wig flopped to the other side. "I'm fairly certain your grandfather was ready to wage war against the dragon king to avenge your murder."

"Well, I'm not dead." She shook her head and clucked her tongue. "And we both know it was more than one cocktail."

Hestia tilted her head again, and her wig fell off, revealing a bald head as shiny as a crystal ball. She snatched up her hairpiece and planted it firmly back on her head. "Maybe it was a dream."

"I'm sure it was." She latched on to her godmother's arm, pulling her off the stool when she heard one of the guys stir. "Look," she whispered, "you need to go."

"But I just got here, and I've been worried sick about you." She jerked free of Serah's grip, nearly tripping over her own feet, and fell into another chair. "I can't believe your grandfather let you go to Dame Doublewart's. Do you know that students are sent to a dungeon with sharks their first night?"

"I know, but I'm fine." She looked over her shoulder again as Ladon changed position, clutching a nearby pillow and moaning her name.

Hestia's eyes widened as she looked that way. "Bippity boingity boing!" She flicked her wand, and it turned into a folding lace fan with a pearl handle. Fanning her face, she shot Serah a sly look. "Did you?" She pointed the fan at the men.

Heat crept into her cheeks. No use lying. Hestia had always been able to see through her ruses. "Hell yes." She rubbed her face. "But please don't tell Grandfather."

"Don't worry, my dear." She splayed the fan across her chest. "Your secret's safe with me." She gave each partially-clothed stud a long look. "All three?"

Serah released a slow breath, her shoulders slumping with the movement. "Yes." She braced herself, preparing for her godmother's judgment.

"Mercy!" Hestia nudged Serah's ribcage. "That's my girl."

Relief washed over her. "So you're not mad at me?"

"Heavens, no!" She swatted Serah with the fan as Draque rolled onto his back. "Oh my, those pecs! Looks like you don't need me to fulfill any wishes," she said with an exaggerated wink.

Holy dragon dong! She'd had no idea her godmother was such a horny old lady.

"Actually...." Serah twisted her fingers, thinking of the right words to say. "Can you make Grandfather like shifters?"

"Shifters?" Hestia dropped her fan, eyes bulging. "They're shifters?" The words sounded like Hydra venom, dripping off her tongue.

She repressed a grimace. "Dragons."

"Oh, dear." Her godmother clucked her tongue. "He loathes them the most. I can't fix prejudice. You know that."

"Damn." A boiling cauldron burned a hole through her heart. "What do I do?"

"Have fun with them while you can," she said with a disinterested air. "You'll tire of them in a few weeks anyway."

"Yeah, probably," she lied, but she wasn't about to get into it with Hestia. Serah might have had a siren's lust, but she had a witch's heart, and giving them up would crush her. When she heard them moving around again, she pulled Hestia to her feet. "You need to go before they wake."

"All right." She let out a loud hiccup. "Which way's the exit?"

"Godmother," Serah groaned, "use your magic."

"Oh, yes, of course." She slapped her forehead with the fan. "I knew that. One drink before I go."

"No more drinks," Serah hissed. "Please go."

Hestia pouted. "Well, you're no fun."

When Serah dug her fingers into Hestia's arm, giving her a stern look, she snapped her fan back into a wand and poofed away, leaving behind a coating of pink sparkle dust on Serah's fingers. Returning to the sofa, Serah slipped the pillow out of Ladon's arms, and slid into its place. She let out a satisfied sigh when he squeezed her tight and feathered a kiss across her temple. How the hell was she supposed to walk away from this?

DRAQUE FIRESBREATH blinked at the canopy of black and silver crystals he saw through the top of the translucent bubble, contemplating how tonight had gone from the best night of his life to the worst.

She'd said she'd be their girl, their mate. She hadn't named any conditions. She hadn't warned them she'd tire of them in a few weeks, which is what he'd overheard her tell her godmother. Was she prejudiced against dragons, like her grandfather, and just using them? Or was it part of her natural siren instincts to toy with her lovers and move on? Either way, it burned.

When her tantalizing perfume tickled his senses, he rolled onto his side away from her. It did little good. Her scent was everywhere: on his skin, his tongue, even ingrained in his mind. It was going to take one strong memory spell to forget her. Sadly, she'd probably forget him and his brothers much more easily.

Chapter Four

Serah woke up the next morning to the sound of a rooster crowing. She jerked upright, startled. When she saw the smiling stud next to her, memories came rushing back.

Merlin's balls! Did I seriously have sex with three dragon shifters?

Yes, you did, Thelix answered, *and you're going to do it again and again.*

Teju leaned over and kissed her cheek. "Good morning, beautiful."

Heat crept into her cheeks, and she pulled a blanket up over her bare chest. "Good morning." She winced. That stupid rooster kept crowing, the sound like a wand scraping a chalkboard making her insides rattle.

Ladon sat up, rubbing sleep from his eyes. "Turn that damn thing off."

Teju waved his wand, and the crowing stopped.

"What was that?" Serah asked.

"Our alarm clock," Teju said, pointing at a rooster-shaped clock hanging beside the flat-screen TV.

She kissed Ladon, then looked around the room for Draque. The sound of a toilet flushing, followed by running water, revealed his whereabouts. When he appeared, looking far too sexy in a navy dress jacket, tie, and tan slacks, she gave him a bright smile and patted the space beside her. "There you are." She'd had no idea a guy could look so hot in a school uniform.

He stopped as if he'd run into an invisible wall, giving her a look that was part confusion and definitely part disgust.

"Bro," Ladon asked. "What's wrong?"

Draque gave each of his brothers hard stares, and she knew they were telepathically speaking. Was it about her?

There was no mistaking the hurt in Ladon's eyes when he turned to her. "Did you tell your fairy godmother you'll tire of us in a few weeks?"

Fuckity fuck! Draque had been listening.

You and your big mouth, Thelix cried.

All three brothers stared accusingly at her, and feeling self-conscious, she wrapped the blanket tightly around herself. "I didn't mean it."

"Then why did you say it?" Ladon demanded, sounding as if an arrow was lodged in his heart.

"I had to."

Teju knelt beside her. "Why?"

She scooted back, uncomfortable under the weight of his stare. "Because my grandfather doesn't approve of me dating shifters." She felt ten shades of gargoyle dung when Teju winced.

"Why not?" Draque asked accusingly. "*You're* a shifter."

She technically wasn't, since she hadn't seen her fish scales in ages, and she doubted she ever would again. "Look, I don't want to argue."

"Why doesn't he like shifters?" Ladon asked.

Of all the brothers, she hated hurting him the most. He was the most sensitive and the most kind. "I don't know." Unable to gaze into his sad eyes a moment longer, she picked imaginary grime from under her nails. "He's got some old grudge against the late dragon kings."

"Our grandfathers?" they said in unison.

Her head shot up as if she'd been shocked by a bolt of lightning. "You're the Firesbreath princes?"

Draque's scowl deepened. "We are."

Well, shit. That changed everything. Her grandfather wouldn't just disapprove of their union, he'd probably disown her if he found out about their tryst. "Why didn't you tell me?" she snapped, jumping to her feet and snatching her clothes off the floor.

Teju stood, giving her a look hot enough to melt her wand. "It didn't come up when my face was planted between your legs."

Heat raced through her as that exact image of his tongue buried in her girl parts popped into her mind.

Her knees weakened. Thelix groaned. Why did they have to be such amazing lovers?

"How many dragons do you think there are?" Teju asked her mockingly.

"How am I supposed to know?" She definitely should've paid more attention in her magical creatures courses.

"Not many. Most dragons live with the fae," Draque said wryly. "Who is your grandfather?"

"It doesn't matter," she mumbled. Hugging her clothes to her chest, she eyed the bathroom door. "I need to freshen up." And by "freshen up" she meant hide in the bathroom until it was time for class.

Draque stepped between her and the bathroom door, blocking her escape. "It does."

She hated how all eyes were on her. They'd been so sweet and passionate last night. Surely, they wouldn't hurt her now. "You'll judge me."

Or burn you to a crisp, Thelix said.

She did her best to ignore her siren. She didn't need her neurosis making things worse.

"Tell us, Serah," Draque demanded, clutching his wand in a white-knuckled grip.

She didn't like his smirk or the way his hand twitched when he raised the wand. She knew damn well he was conjuring a compulsion spell, so even if she tried to hide the truth, he'd pull it out of her. Bastard.

"Nathaniel Goldenwand," she said through tight lips, refusing to give him the satisfaction of forcing the truth out of her.

"Holy fuck!" they exclaimed.

"You're the Goldenwand heiress?" Draque's wand was in danger of being snapped in two.

She refused to be intimidated. "I am."

"Are you aware that your grandfather is the most evil wizard who's ever lived?" Teju asked, eyes flashing bright gold as his voice dropped to an ominous rumble.

Hiding her sudden fear, she did her best not to let him see how much he'd offended her. "You don't know him."

"Oh, we know him." Draque chuckled. "We know he's brainwashed most of the magical world, and he's trying to control all five realms through his wand."

"Four realms," she corrected, mentally slapping herself when they all growled.

"Five." Draque pointed his wand at her chest. "And the fact that you won't acknowledge our race's ancestral home as a sovereign realm just goes to show that he's brainwashed you, too."

These dragons were so ignorant, and to think she'd wanted to be their girl. "The Grotto isn't a realm. It's a wasteland."

What are you doing, stupid girl? Thelix cried.

Draque let out a roar so loud, the breath whooshed from her lungs when she stumbled back against the sticky bubble wall.

He advanced on her, waving the wand over his head, which smoldered like a lit cigarette. "Only because your grandfather has cut off all trade in an attempt to starve our people!"

"Hey!" She swatted the wand when it came close to burning a hole through the top of the bubble. "He manufactures wands. He doesn't control trade."

Draque threw up his hands, his face contorting into a golden mass of scales while his nose flattened. "He controls everything!"

Fuck, he was shifting. If she wasn't careful, he'd fully turn into a dragon big enough to burst their bubble.

"Then why am I, his only heir, stuck in this shithole and not at a posh school?" When her voice cracked, she bit down on her knuckles to keep from losing her cool. She wasn't about to put up with his animosity toward her grandfather.

"Because he's a heartless bastard, Serah," Ladon said. "He only cares about himself."

She turned to Ladon, who was watching her from the sofa with his big, sad eyes. Ladon's comment cut deeper than Draque and Teju's insults. She expected Draque to be a major asshole, maybe even Teju, but not Ladon.

Blinking back tears, she forced herself to speak calmly. "I need to get dressed. If you'll excuse me."

Refusing to make eye contact with them, she brushed past, holding it together until she reached the bathroom. Only after she shut the door behind her did she give into her tears. Standing in the shower, she hung her head and cried, muffling her sobs. When she heard Thelix wailing, she wiped her eyes.

They got to you, too? she asked, shocked to see this level of emotion from her siren.

Of course, Thelix sobbed. *Teju won't lick our pussy now that he knows we're a Goldenwand.*

SERAH SAT ON THE CLOSED toilet, gazing blankly at the faded floral paper on the walls and waiting for detention to end. She worried about what would happen if Dame Doublewart discovered her with the Firesbreath brothers. Would she make her serve another detention with the sharks? It didn't matter, though. After she told her grandfather about the conditions in this school, and that the Firesbreath Kings' sons were students, he'd get her out of here.

She didn't want to take the chance of getting caught with the shifters, so it was best she left their bubble. Squaring her shoulders, she stood, getting up the nerve to face down the dragons.

A knock on the door startled her.

"Serah," Ladon called, "are you okay?"

Her heart did a little backflip. Why was he asking if she was okay? Did this mean he still cared about her?

She cleared her throat. "I'm fine." Wiping her eyes one last time, she opened the door and her heart skipped a beat.

Ladon's thick, black hair was pulled back into a queue, and he wore a suit and tie like his brothers, but instead of khaki pants, he'd donned a plaid kilt, revealing thick, muscular legs. Holy gargoyle shit on a shingle, he was one hot shifter.

How could you give all this up? Thelix demanded.

Shut up, she said, then stiffened her spine, determined to put her sexy shifters out of her mind. As soon as this detention was over, they'd all go their separate ways, and she could nurse her broken heart in private. How could they think her grandfather was evil? He'd brought many helpful advances to the magical world. He should've been praised, not reviled.

"Our detention should be ending soon," she said haughtily, hoping they didn't notice how much she was dying inside. "You need to drop me off in my dungeon."

"Our alarm will go off before they come for us," Draque said, refusing to look at her. He sat at the bar, looking at a steaming cup of tea.

"Would you like tea?" Ladon asked so cheerfully, it appeared forced.

"No, thanks." She refused to look at him, knowing his big, sad eyes would be her undoing. Great Goddess, she had to get away from these shifters. "What time is it?"

Ladon pulled a rusty bronze pocketwatch from his vest. "Half past eight."

Teju paced. "Advanced Sorcery and Spells is about to start. I have a test."

"Did they forget about us?" she asked. She couldn't imagine being stuck with them for another day.

Ladon frowned. "They haven't before."

"Check the monitor," Draque said to Teju.

Teju waved his wand at the flat screen, pulling up an image of charred walls and smoke rolling across the decrepit graveyard that adjoined the school.

Draque slid off his barstool with a slackened jaw. "Fuck."

Ladon went to stand beside his brothers. "What the hell happened to our school?"

Teju scratched the back of his head. "Is the whole thing burned?"

"Looks that way," Draque said, then swore again.

You and your lovers are fucked, Thelix said.

Which means you're fucked, too, she said, pleased when Thelix went silent. Serah hugged herself, rocking on her heels. Had her fairy godmother been right? "Is everyone okay?"

Ladon shook his head, but didn't turn around to look at her. "I don't see anyone."

Her legs felt encrusted in sludge as she walked over to them. "My godmother told me dragons burned down our school."

Draque spun on her, twin thunderstorms brewing in his golden, elongated eyes. "And you're just now telling us this?"

"She was drunk." Her veins turned to ice as she stepped back, trying not to show Draque how much he unnerved her. "I didn't believe her."

He growled and turned to his brothers. "We need to check for survivors." He pointed at her accusingly with his wand. "You're staying here."

She leveled him with a glare. "No way in seven hells am I staying alone in this dungeon."

"No way in seven hells are you coming with us," Draque said, though it sounded more like a snarl.

She didn't think twice before summoning her siren voice. "You're taking me with you, and that's final." She prayed it would work, since it wasn't always reliable. She didn't want to bewitch them, but no way in Hades was she being left behind.

All three brothers gave her blank stares, then shook their heads as if trying to clear sprites from their ears.

"Fine," Draque relented, shoulders slumping, "but we're taking the lead."

She was relieved her power of persuasion had worked. "Whatever."

As if she wanted to go first anyway. As soon as they got out of there, she was calling Grandfather and asking him to take her home.

AFTER HER FORMER LOVERS used their wands to transport them out of detention, she trailed them, cursing when she stumbled over a pile of rubble. Nobody offered to help her, not that she blamed them. They were too consumed in digging through the charred remains of their school. She prayed they wouldn't find any bodies in the wreckage.

Who could've destroyed their school and why?

Thelix had gone quiet, other than the occasional sniffle, refusing to offer Serah any comfort. Pissed that her wand had been taken by Doublewart, she searched the rubble for another one she could use to call her grandfather, but the place was a pile of ash and dust. She'd have to call Hestia, who'd probably cause a scene when she saw Serah in the center of the destruction.

Ladon veered off from his brothers, walking through the rusty iron gate until he reached the edge of the cemetery. Overgrown foliage covered the tombstones. "Hey, guys!" He waved his brothers over. "You might want to see this."

Serah followed, halting when Draque swore and thrust a fist into the sky.

She cautiously joined them, noticing the enormous four-toed footprint that was easily three feet in diameter. A dragon print. "Whose is it?" she asked Ladon.

He gave her a dark look. "Ours."

"What?" she asked. "You're not making sense."

He grimaced. "Only the Firesbreath dragons have four toes."

"Could it have been your fathers?" she asked.

"Are you fucking mad?" Draque roared. "They wouldn't do this."

She held out her hands defensively. "Okay, chill."

Draque turned to his brothers. "Is it a coincidence the Goldenwand heiress distracted us last night while we were being framed?"

Oh hell no. "You think I had something to do with this?"

He turned to her, venom in his eyes. "Did you?"

"No." She shook a fist at him. "So much for that troll shit about your great instincts and my pure soul. You guys picked *me* up in *your* bubble of love and seduced *me*, not the other way around." She was so angry, she was seeing red. What a major fucking asshole!

He flashed a condescending grin. "And your siren charms had nothing to do with why we seduced you? You said it yourself. We were reacting to your pheromones."

"Merlin's balls!" She threw up her hands, wishing she had a wand so she could turn that troll into a toad. "I knew sex with shifters was a bad idea."

His lip curled back in a snarl. "There's nothing more pathetic than a shifter who's prejudiced against shifters."

Ohhh, this guy was royally pissing her off. She was a vegetarian siren, but she'd make an exception to bite off his head. "How do I know you didn't raze the school before you found me and you weren't just using me as an alibi?"

Draque's face hardened to iron. "You think us capable of this?"

"No. After the intimacy we shared, I don't think you'd commit this atrocity." She crossed her arms, unable to keep the hurt from her voice. "Sucks to be accused though, doesn't it?" How had their relationship gone from sensual, loving, and safe to this pile of dragon dung?

"Look," Draque said and groaned, smoothing a hand over his face, "I'm sorry."

"Don't be." She turned up her nose. "I'm leaving." Looking at the clear morning sky, she cupped her hands around her mouth. "Fairy Godmother," she called, "I wish you'd get me out of here!"

A poof of pink sparkles exploded near a tombstone, and Hestia materialized, clutching her wand. Serah braced herself, expecting her to launch into a drunken tirade when she saw Serah's surroundings.

"Ah, there you are." Serah casually waved at the three slack-jawed brothers with a dismissive flick of the wrist and marched toward her godmother.

"Stay back!" Teju hollered, shoving Serah aside and aiming his wand at Hestia.

"What are you doing?" Serah screamed seconds before she hit the mossy ground.

"Stay down," he said over his shoulder. "Something's wrong with her."

She brushed dirt off her hands. "What in seven hells?"

Hestia pointed her wand at Serah. "Kill the heiress," she mumbled, eyes dazed as if she was in a trance.

Serah froze. "W-What?"

"Separatum!" Teju yelled and zapped her godmother with his wand.

Hestia shrieked when her wand flew from her hand and landed on a nearby tombstone. That's when Serah noticed the wand was glowing ghoulish green. What the ever-loving fuck?

Hestia fell back, landing on a dirt-encrusted concrete slab with a grunt. Hanging her head, she let out a low moan. "Oh, my head. What happened?"

Ignoring her, Teju zapped the glowing wand. "Infernus!"

The wand exploded, shattering into a million tiny shrieking shards.

Hestia gaped at the hole left by the blast and then looked at Teju. "My wand? You blew it up!"

Ladon helped Serah to her feet. "You were going to kill Serah," he spat.

"What?" She clutched her chest, eyes wide with fright. "I'd never hurt my godchild. Never!" She got up on her knees and reached out to Serah. "My dear."

"Stay away from me." She clung to Ladon, turning away from Hestia. She didn't understand what was happening. First the school was destroyed, and the students either missing or dead, and now the woman who'd been like a mother to her had tried to kill her?

"We need to go, Serah," Ladon whispered in her ear.

She looked up at him. "Where?"

His face hardened. "Away from here."

When Hestia called to her once more, Serah's heart shattered. "I-I don't understand."

"Someone wants you dead," Draque said, his voice like sandpaper.

"That can't be." She vehemently shook her head. "There must be a mistake." Hestia answered to Grandfather. He wouldn't order her to kill his only grand-child.

"Serah," Draque said grimly, holding out a hand, "take my hand."

She shrank from him. "Why would my godmother try to kill me?"

"She's in shock." Draque's voice echoed as if they were inside a tunnel. "Let's go before more trouble finds us."

Ladon frowned down at her, concern reflecting in his eyes. He squeezed her hand and then Teju grabbed her elbow. Before she could argue, Teju recited a spell, and they were swallowed by another bubble, this one just wide enough to hold the four of them.

In the next moment, their bubble was racing so fast through space that her head spun. Where were they taking her? Stars spun around her. A weightless feeling spread to her extremities until she was falling and then landing in a pair of strong arms. The world whirled faster.

Chapter Five

With a groan, Athena Hoofenmouth pushed the crushed remains of Doris's bookcase off her. Sitting up, she rubbed the smoke from her eyes, swearing as she looked around the charred wasteland that was once her school.

Had those dragons burned down the entire school? No. She'd recognized them as the eldest Firesbreath brothers. They'd been mischievous, but never heartless.

Then what happened?

She vaguely remembered the elder Firesbreath brothers knocking down the wall to Doris's office. Athena had thrown a protective barrier around her after the first dragon had poked his head through the smoke. She was about to zap him with her wand, but then the bookcase fell on top of her. By the time she'd freed herself, Doris had been taken. She'd rushed outside, only to stop dead in her tracks when she saw the crimson cloud descend on the school. She'd no time to warn the staff, but she prayed they'd known what to do. Doris had made them practice at least a dozen times this school year alone.

Athena had no choice but to throw up another protective shield right before the entire school had gone up in flames. Then another bookcase somehow fell on her, which was how she ended up inhaling charred dust the rest of the night.

Strange how there were no detectives on site yet, how she could hear not a creature stir in the forest. It was as if the evil that had descended on their school yesternight had snuffed out all signs of life. As she stumbled toward the dungeon, she prayed it wasn't so.

PENELOPE PIXIEFEATHER Pratt fluttered around her office, wings angrily buzzing. Those idiots had failed. They had two tasks: destroy the school and kill the heiress, and not in that order. They'd said they fulfilled their assignment, that no witch could've survived their inferno. They were wrong, because the little bitch's fairy godmother had just been summoned. Penelope had just sat down to breakfast with the hungover old hag when she poofed away, Seraphina's name on her lips. Penelope was ready to bust some balls by the time Goldenwand's goons strutted into her office.

Penelope hovered above them, waving her wand in their faces. "Sit down!"

They did as they were told, glaring at her. Insolent fools!

Prometheus Periwinkle, loyal follower of the Arcane and the reason for Seraphina's fall from grace, glowered at her the longest, making her feel so uncomfortable in her own skin, she was compelled to look away. He knew she was a sucker for a handsome face, and Prometheus had good looks in spades. He was tall, blond, and beautiful, with vibrant blue eyes, high cheekbones, and a symmetrical nose. A modern day Adonis. He lit a pipe without asking her permission, blowing smoke rings toward her. Satyr's hairy butt wart. Penelope had spread her legs for him a few times, and now he thought he could abuse her?

Fanning her face, she buzzed to the other side of the room, With a flick of her wand, she zapped the pipe out of Prometheus's mouth and flung it against the brick wall, smiling when it smashed into tiny pieces.

Shooting to his feet, he raised his wand, ready to fight. "What the hell was that for?"

She eyed him coolly. "Seraphina's godmother was just summoned."

The beautiful, peach glow of his skin turned ashen gray. "No. Serah was at the school when it was razed."

"How do you know this?"

He played with a silver band on his wrist. "Because she wore a tracking device."

"What kind of device?" she asked, annoyed this was the first she was hearing of it.

"None of your business," he said coolly, casually folding one leg across the other.

"It damn well is my business." Her voice rose to a feverish pitch, along with her ire. Ugh, she hated him even more for upsetting her. "I'm running this operation, and I need to know your methods."

He gave her a serpentine look. "You don't need to know shit."

Frustrated, she let out a huff of air, then smiled when she remembered that ugly fake emerald bracelet Serah had been wearing when she'd dropped the girl off at school. Serah wouldn't have been caught dead wearing knockoff jewelry, unless it had sentimental value. She didn't want to give Prometheus the satisfaction of knowing she thought his tracking device was brilliant. "Did this tracker tell you if she was at or below the school?"

He shrugged, feigning indifference. "I couldn't tell."

She eyed him through slits, smug satisfaction at his shortcomings warming her chest. "Not a very good tracking device."

Prometheus's sidekick, Saul Slugstack, who resembled a slug with the many folds on his bald head and neck, spit phlegm into his handkerchief, not even bothering to fold it when he shoved it back into a vest pocket. "She had to have been in the dungeon."

Prometheus's cheeks turned bright pink. "I delivered the check to Dame Doublewart myself, with the instruction that she was not to serve detention."

Penelope angrily buzzed back to him, wagging her wand in his face. "I told you the old witch couldn't be bought."

"We'll take care of it." Jumping to his feet, Prometheus swatted Penelope as if she was a fly.

Squealing, she flew into a wall, then angrily bounced back. "No! One failure is enough." She refused to show Prometheus how much his rough treatment offended her. Had their trysts meant nothing to him?

"If we don't kill her," Slugstack whimpered, "our master won't have reason to wage war against the dragon kings."

Penelope flashed a triumphant smile. "She's dead by now. I've activated her godmother's wand."

Prometheus gave her a look that made her want to crawl into a cocoon and never come out. "Her godmother will tell."

Penelope squared her shoulders, forcing herself to be brave. Prometheus was her subordinate, after all. "No she won't, because *you* are going to dispose of her."

The men shared wary glances, then Prometheus cleared his throat. "When?"

"Now," she shrieked, "or there will be hell to pay."

She was pleased when Slugstack jumped to his feet and rushed to the door. Anger welled, threatening to split her skull in two when Prometheus shook his head at her before slowly sauntering toward the door. She wanted to curse him when his back was turned, make his nose grow three times in size, and shrivel up his balls.

He paused at the door, his back ramrod straight, as if he had read her thoughts. He was trying to usurp her. She'd fought too long and too hard to rise to the rank of semis-wizard in the Arcane Army. She'd smite him to dust before she let that happen.

HESTIA GOLDENWAND FELL back against a tombstone, rubbing her aching temples, her wings drooping. One minute she was lying in her feather bed, sleeping off a hangover, and the next she was in a smoky cemetery, trying to kill her beloved godchild. Then she remembered her wand had been enchanted and she'd been possessed. Great Goddess, she'd no idea her wand had such a function. Having served the Goldenwand family for the past eight hundred years, she was always gifted with the latest in wand technology. The Goldenwand 2050 had just come on the market. It was too expensive for the average witch, but Nathaniel Goldenwand had gifted all the members of Parliament with the wand.

Could they be programmed to possess their witches, too? How could Nathaniel create such an evil device? She straightened and looked 'round, her wings erratically flapping, when she heard a twig snap behind her. The next thing she saw was a massive fist coming at her face. She had no time to duck; her nose was split open and starbursts went off in her head. Falling over like a pile of dominoes, she stared up at the shadowy figure hovering over her, unable to make out her assailant's features before she succumbed to darkness.

IT TOOK ALL OF SERAH'S willpower not to throw up after they landed with a jarring thud, their magical bubble popping and coating her skin in a fine, sticky film.

Wherever they were, it was as black as pitch. Teju's wand illuminated first, making his face orange and frightening in its hazy glow.

Teju waved his wand over the group. "Purifico."

She was relieved when the sticky film dissipated. Ladon and Draque lit their wands, making everyone glow like demons. Their shifter eyes were bright gold, revealing the dragons beneath.

Trying to adjust to the strange light, she blinked at Ladon, thankful he'd been holding her. The air was thicker here; a sulfuric smell filled her lungs like soup and she had trouble breathing.

Dragon breath. Bleh.

Draque and Teju jumped down from wherever they'd been standing and went down a long tunnel, leaving her and Ladon behind.

She pulled out of Ladon's arms after she found her footing, then grabbed his elbow when she slid on a slick surface.

"This way," he said, clambering down the rocks and holding out his hand. "It will be easier once we leave the tunnel."

She took his hand, grateful for his support.

They walked through a winding tunnel for what felt like an eternity, their path lit by Ladon's wand. She could no longer hear his brothers, who were far ahead, their wand lights flickering before they disappeared.

She was perturbed that Teju and Draque had abandoned them. Why? Were they ashamed to be seen with the Goldenwand Heiress or were they that much in a hurry? It wasn't her fault she wasn't used to walking on mossy rocks. She was thankful for Ladon, the only kind brother, for dropping his grudge and keeping her safe.

I think they're right, Thelix said.

What?

Who else could've bewitched Fairy Godmother's wand but Grandfather?

I'm going to say this once, and only once, Serah mentally hissed. *Shut the fuck up.*

Thelix huffed and then went silent. Good. Hopefully, she'd stay gone a long time.

By the time the tunnel spit them out, she was dripping with sweat, and her muscles ached from tension. What a shitty portal entrance. She didn't have to ask Ladon where they were because obviously this large cavern was the smelly, dirty butthole of the magical world, the fringe of the four realms beneath the surface of the earth, and the one place she never wanted to visit: The Grotto.

She turned to Ladon when a pack of monkey men hopped up to them, screeching and pounding their chests, then sniffing her back. When Ladon covered her ears and roared, they scurried away, whimpering and bouncing off the walls.

She clung to him as they went deeper into the cavern that had a ceiling so high, it disappeared into darkness. Long rock formations as sharp as daggers hung from the ceiling—massive columns of white with sparkling crystals. They looked so precarious, she feared one would fall and impale them. After they'd navigated through a maze of lavender pools and more jagged crystal rock formations jutting up from the ground, they went even deeper into the bowels of the earth and came upon a massive gathering. They wound through what appeared to be a center for trade, with all kinds of makeshift stands and shops, where shifters bartered their wares.

Draque and Teju were talking to a tall man who appeared to be part tree. Draque impatiently waved them over.

As they approached, she realized the shifter was indeed a walking, talking tree, with flowery leaves growing out of his head.

Tree Man glared at them. "You boys are in a world of hurt."

Draque threw up his hands. "We didn't do it."

Tree Man snickered, his branches shaking with mirth. "Why is that always the first thing out of your mouths?"

"This time it's true," Teju said.

Serah pressed closer to Ladon when Tree Man looked over their heads and directly at her.

"Who do you have there?" Tree Man asked, his voice dark and rough.

Ladon wrapped a protective arm around her. "A friend."

She was grateful beyond words for his protection. Too bad she couldn't mate with just one brother.

The lines framing Tree Man's eyes deepened. "Smells like a mermaid."

Teju flashed a crooked smile and adjusted his glasses. "Close enough."

He nodded at rows of makeshift tents. "Go see your fathers."

Ladon puffed up his chest. "That's where we're headed."

Two more trees stomped up behind Tree Man, one of them so tall, she could barely make out the whites of his eyes and long, drawn mouth.

"Leave the mermaid with us," the tallest said as he leaned over and studied Serah with big, bulging eyes.

Ladon squeezed her tighter. "Over my dead body."

Her insides churned. Thank the Goddess for Ladon. She wanted to show her appreciation for his loyalty with makeup sex. If only she could leave out his brothers.

The tallest tree's leaves drooped. "We won't hurt her."

"You heard my brother," Draque growled. "She's coming with us."

She was dumbstruck. Why was Draque protecting her? Did he trust her now? Did he care about her? Her heart did a little backflip until she caught him scowling at her.

He waved them forward and pushed his way through the gathering crowd of shifters.

Holding tightly to Ladon, she struggled to keep up with Draque's long strides, falling farther behind him and Teju while they barged through the throng of sweaty, smelly onlookers. So much for Draque caring about her. Obviously whatever grudge bug had crawled up his ass still hadn't died.

BY THE TIME THEY ESCAPED the noisy throng of people, they had reached a pair of massive golden gates guarded by a three-headed dog as big as an elephant.

"Cerberus," she breathed.

"Not exactly," Ladon whispered. "That's Garm, a distant descendent of Cerberus."

The dog let out three barks, followed by three growls, the hair on the back of his necks standing on end.

Draque's shift happened so fast, she was taken by surprise. A massive golden dragon ripped through his mortal skin. Roaring, he hovered over the dog until it whimpered three times and backed away from the gate.

Teju shifted, too, snapping at the dog until he tucked his tail between his legs and ran inside a shallow cave, looking at the two dragons from behind paws that shielded one pair of his eyes. Holy heck! She'd had no idea dragon shifters got so big. They were easily twice the size of the three-headed dog.

She was grateful Ladon didn't shift. Holding her hand, he urged her to follow the two massive beasts who'd been her lovers. She gaped at the dome of sparkling stones overhead. Was the ceiling dusted with diamonds? It would make sense, since dragons were known to have an affection for sparkly things. They walked across the polished stone floor of a wide hall to another set of tall double doors made of dark wood. Though the doors were open, she could barely see into the darkened cavern. Why did it feel like they were taking her to be sacrificed? She cleared her throat, readying her siren voice should she need it. Her power of persuasion was all the magic she had left, since Doublewart had taken her wand.

"Ladon," she whispered, "what's happening?"

He squeezed her hand. "You must be quiet and let us do the talking."

"But why?" She'd done nothing wrong.

Draque spun on her so fast, she barely had time to jump back. He hovered over her, his long, serpentine neck glowing like he'd swallowed hot coals.

"You say nothing," he growled, his voice low and deep and sounding like a steam train rolling through her ears. She'd no idea they could talk in dragon form. The only other dragons she'd encountered had been dumb beasts, not shifters. This monster hovering over her was no dumb beast, and he had teeth as long and sharp as daggers.

"Whatever, asshole," she muttered. Fanning her face, she gagged on his hot breath. If she had her wand, she'd shrink his head. Or maybe his balls.

Careful, you may need those balls later, Thelix warned.

Not likely, Serah grumbled.

"He's only looking out for your safety," Ladon whispered.

She rolled her eyes but said nothing, and not because Draque intimidated her. She was still trying not to choke on sulfur fumes. How could he be so concerned about her safety when he was obviously the most dangerous creature here?

A thunderous roar shook the ground. She lurched forward, nearly falling face-first onto Draque's spiky tail. Ladon clutched her elbow, steadying her.

Another roar shook her to her core.

"Where are those cursed boys?" The deep bellow resounded in her skull.

Draque quickened his pace, then leaped upward, beating hot air down on her with his heavy wings. "We're here, Fathers."

Teju jumped into the air, too, soaring through the cavern after his brother.

She and Ladon sprinted to keep up with them. It would've been easier for Ladon to shift and fly as well, and she was even more grateful to him for staying with her.

By the time she ran through the double doors, her chest was heaving and she was out of breath. Three massive dragons sat atop a dais carved from shimmering stone. Few wall sconces lit the dark cavern, and their long necks cast eerie shadows across the uneven walls.

The dragon in the center of the dais had dark bronze scales and long, white whiskers that hung down over his jowls like an old man's moustache. He let out a rumble so deep, she felt it in her gut.

Turning his long neck to a ceiling so distant she saw only darkness, he released a stream of fire and then looked at his two dragon sons. "The school burned to the ground, and there are no signs of survivors!"

Serah wondered why the kings were in dragon form when they could easily meet their guests as humans, but she quickly realized this was a means of intimidation. It certainly worked, because she was one cough away from crapping her pants.

Draque sat stoically before his fathers, wings pulled back and tail tucked under his legs. "It wasn't us. We were down below in detention. We had no idea until this morning."

"Don't lie to us." The dragon beside him had scales the color of warm honey and one empty socket where his golden eye should have been. "Our spies saw you three flying over the Werewood Forest last night with the Goldenwand heiress in your talons."

Teju puffed up his chest. "Your spy is lying. We spent all night in detention. We swear it on the Scrolls of Makarios."

The third dragon father, with golden scales so pale they appeared to have been bleached by the sun, snarled, revealing rows of criss-crossed, jagged teeth. "Who is that girl with you?"

Draque's massive body went rigid. "She is the Goldenwand heiress."

When all three fathers broke into low murmurs and growls, glaring at her through slitted lids, she thought she'd die from fright. "She spent last night in detention with us," Ladon said, then averted his eyes when his dragon fathers looked at him like a hawk spotting a mouse.

"We would speak with her," the whiskered dragon said.

She wished these dragons would all shift, so they could speak as humans and not terrifying beasts.

Awww, fuck! Thelix groaned. *I'm outta here.*

Thanks for your support, Serah grumbled.

"Child," the pale dragon said, "tell us what happened."

She summoned the courage to speak. "Exactly what your sons said. We spent the night in the dungeon, and when nobody came for us, we surfaced and saw the destruction."

The one-eyed dragon arched a brow. "How did you escape the dungeon?"

She gestured to the brothers. "They had their wands."

The one-eyed dragon shared skeptical looks with his brothers. "I thought wands weren't allowed in the dungeon."

Teju guiltily cleared his throat. "They're not."

The whiskered dragon said, "Nathaniel Goldenwand will use the attack on your school to press Parliament into declaring an act of war on the shifter race."

"Your sons had nothing to do with it," she blurted. She'd no idea why she felt so compelled to defend them, but she couldn't let the night she spent in their arms turn into an act of war.

The whiskered dragon gave her a pointed look. "Will you tell your grandfather this?"

She nodded eagerly. "Yes." Though she feared her grandfather's wrath after he discovered his granddaughter had slept with shifters, it was worth it if her confession prevented war.

The whiskered dragon shook his wings like a bird ruffling its feathers. "Then we must return you to the witches immediately."

"No!" all three brothers bellowed in unison.

She clutched her throat. Why wouldn't they want her to go back after their argument?

"You dare defy us?" the whiskered dragon roared.

"Fathers, her fairy godmother just tried to kill her," Draque said. "There was an enchantment on her wand."

"Any idea who would do that?" the pale dragon asked Serah.

She shook her head, her shoulders falling. "No, I don't."

She did her best to ignore Draque and his brothers when they grumbled her grandfather's name.

"How many families does your godmother serve?" the one-eyed dragon asked.

She swallowed back a lump of emotion. She knew where he was going with this. "Just ours."

"Who does she answer to?" the one-eyed dragon continued.

Her heart sank. "My grandfather."

The dragon kings' large luminous eyes shone with pity. They looked at her as if she was a ghost.

"Goddess save us," they whispered in unison.

I told you, Thelix said wanly.

"Take the heiress to your chamber and await our instructions," Kron said to his sons.

Forget hiding in the chamber. Serah wished the earth would open up and swallow her whole.

Chapter Six

Strapped to an uncomfortable chair, Doris Doublewart tensed when a massive golden dragon sidled up to her, steam blowing out his wide nostrils.

"Are you comfortable?" he asked.

She turned her head. "Go away, sulfur breath."

Roaring, he spun around, nearly knocking her over with his barbed tail as he stomped out of the cavern.

She knew how to escape her bonds—she was a djinn, after all, and could easily transform into a small child and slip away—though she pretended to be trapped by her captors. She'd been terrified when they'd first grabbed her, but now she was more annoyed than anything.

She knew these men—correction, boys. They were her former students, and though they'd been tricky, mischievous dragon shifters, they had good hearts like their fathers and younger brothers.

They'd captured her for leverage over Nathaniel Goldenwand. She didn't blame them. The evil wizard was plotting an attack against the shifter race. She felt it in the marrow of her bones.

Even if the dragons managed to capture Seraphina Goldenwand, it wouldn't have done any good. She knew Nathaniel's type. He cared for no one but himself. All Doris had to do was convince the dragons of that before it was too late.

SERAH WAS RELIEVED to see Draque and Teju turn back into humans. Her relief was short-lived, as she still had to run to keep up with them. She had no idea where they were going, but she hoped they stopped soon. She had many questions. First, when would they find out about their school? There had to be survivors. She couldn't imagine every student and teacher perishing. Second, when would she get to leave The Grotto?

They entered a smaller cavern after traversing another maze of stalls, and she passed a furry woman with ears as big as platters, trying to sell her moldy cheese. She didn't like it here and couldn't wait to be elsewhere.

Her dragon princes appeared to be unfazed, waving off the woman with laughter. As she admired Draque's confident stride and round ass, she wondered what magic he and Teju had used to shift from giant, hulking dragons and back to humans, and still have their school uniforms be intact. She hadn't shifted in almost three years, but she'd always destroyed her clothes, especially pants. Her long, scaly tail tore through them. Whatever spell they'd used, surely her Goldenwand had a similar one stored on its memory card.

"My grandfather would never try to kill me," she whined at Draque's back as he pushed through a throng of shifters. "He loves me." At least she thought he did. He never gave her any indication he didn't love her. "Where are we going?"

"To our chamber," Teju said over his shoulder when Draque ignored her. "Just like our fathers ordered."

"Are they going to tell the authorities I'm here?"

"Yes," he answered tersely.

Good. Maybe they'd demand her safe return. Her grandfather couldn't be behind her attempted murder. He had no reason to want her dead. He'd saved her after the sirens had tried to murder her. No way was he the monster they made him out to be. Someone else had enchanted her godmother's wand. Maybe Miss Pixiefeather Pratt. She wouldn't put it past the annoying little bitch. "I know you think he's horrible, but—"

"Oh my Goddess!" a woman said shrilly in the distance. "There are my sexy dwagon-wagons!"

A tall girl with flowing pale hair, clad in a skimpy dress that barely covered her crotch, came barreling toward them. Her tits, which were even bigger than Serah's, bounced like boulders strapped to her chest.

She threw herself into Draque's arms, wrapping her long, tanned legs around his waist and making him stumble.

Fucking bitch is trying to steal our man, Thelix complained. *Claw her eyes out!*

Serah latched onto Ladon's arm. "Who in Hades is she?" she hissed, wincing when she sounded like a spitting cobra.

"Fuck," Ladon said through clenched teeth. "Katherine." He looked at her with alarm in his eyes. "She's nobody."

Huh. Could've fooled her.

Draque untangled himself from Katherine like he was trying to take off a jacket that was two sizes too small.

She landed on her feet with a pout, thrusting her chest in his face and gazing at him with large, emerald-green eyes. "What's wrong?" she cried, dragging a long fingernail down his chest.

"Katherine, we don't have time to talk." When he pushed her aside, Katherine looked ready to spontaneously combust.

"Well, too bad." Jutting hands on her hips, she glared at him and then his brothers. "You will make time for your mate."

"Your mate?" Serah gasped. Those lying, two-timing lizards!

"No," Draque said firmly, giving Katherine a look that would melt steel. "She's delusional."

"Katherine." Teju groaned. "You're not our mate."

She raised her chin. "I'm as good as your mate." She cast a glanced at Serah. "Who's she?"

Ladon wrapped a possessive arm around her. "This is Seraphina."

She didn't try to shove him away when he squeezed her tight. Truthfully, the thought of pissing off Katherine gave her great pleasure.

"The Goldenwand bitch?" Katherine spat the words like they were made of venom.

Serah jerked back like she'd been slapped and wished she had her wand.

"Mind your choice of words," Draque said with a low growl.

Clenching her hands, Katherine's face hardened as she locked eyes with Draque. "Who is she to you?"

"None of your business," Teju answered.

She shot him a glare. "It damn well is my business. Don't tell me you're fucking her?"

Claw the bitch's eyes out! Thelix demanded.

"Again," Draque said coolly, "none of your business."

He could've just told her Serah was their mate, but he didn't, and she didn't know where she stood with them after Draque overheard her damming conversation with her godmother.

"Listen, bitch." Katherine advanced on her and poked a long, curved finger that looked more like a talon at her chest. "I don't know what spell you've cast over them, but their parents chose me to be their mate."

Ignoring the low growls coming from her dragon shifters, she straightened her shoulders, refusing to be intimidated. "Maybe they should let their sons pick their mate."

Katherine's lip pulled back in a feral snarl. "Maybe you should just fuck off."

Thelix let out a screech that sounded like an enraged hellcat. *Kill the bitch!*

"Enough, Katherine," Teju said.

When Draque stepped between them, Katherine peered over his shoulder. "She's bewitched you!" she shrieked.

"Not hardly." Serah rolled her eyes. "You're lucky I don't have my wand."

"Ohhh!" Katherine threw up her hands, which were definitely curved into sharp bird-like claws. "Your special Goldenwand that does all the work for you? You're lucky I don't slice open your neck with my talons."

A low rumble erupted from Draque's chest as his skin transformed into glistening, golden scales. "You touch her, and you'll regret it," he said in a deep, dragon baritone.

"Draque, dearest," Katherine cooed, stroking his cheek. "You wouldn't hurt me, would you?"

He smacked her hand away. "Back off, Katherine. I mean it." He turned to Serah, eyes glowing yellow and narrowed to slits. "Come on." He led her through the throng.

She would've been touched by the way he'd defended her if he wasn't dragging her so hard, it made her arm throb.

"Draque," she complained, fighting his grasp. "You're hurting me."

His golden eyes became more feral, lengthening to oblong slits. "You keep away from her, do you understand me?" He clutched her shoulders.

She winced when his nails dug into her skin. "I'm a big girl, and I can defend myself," she said more harshly than she meant but she was overwhelmed and confused by his sudden attention.

"Not against a Griffin." Shadows fell across his features. "She will cut you open before you can defend yourself. I've seen her do it."

Well, shit. She'd heard of psycho ex-girlfriends, but this shifter-bitch brought "cat fight" to a whole new level.

Thelix gulped. *Forget what I said about killing the bitch.*

DRAQUE KEPT HOLD OF Serah's hand as they trekked through a maze of dark tunnels lit by ancient wall sconces, heading toward the living quarters he shared with his brothers. She hoped his protectiveness meant he'd forgiven her for their earlier misunderstanding. She was pleasantly surprised as they passed several normal-looking, smiling shifters who didn't smell like old cheese or have hair as thick as twine growing out of their ears. Other than the fact that The Grotto was in a deep, dark cave somewhere in the bowels of the earth, it wasn't as bad as the horror stories she'd heard from her grandfather. He'd told her the place reeked of raw sewage and was as hot as satan's sweaty armpit. But the scents of mint and fresh-cut grass overpowered the sulfuric smell, and the air that blew through the tunnels was refreshing.

They made their way down a narrow tunnel with doors and windows carved into the walls on either side and cheery fires reflecting from within. She recognized the mouthwatering odors of roasting meats and was painfully reminded that she hadn't eaten breakfast.

Draque opened a door and led her inside, and she noted the cleanliness and elegant decor. The walls were lined with plush tapestries of golden dragons, and the floor was covered in bright orange and gold furs.

She sat on a sofa of pillows and furs, watching nervously while Draque and his brothers paced. When two servants brought them platters of bread, cheeses, meat, fruit, and drinks, the brothers stopped, their nostrils flaring.

"What's this?" Draque asked one of the servants, who looked part were-gerbil, with a wide, flat nose and pink ears that twitched.

"A gift from the kings," he said, his gaze flitting to Serah before he bowed out of the room, the other servant following him.

Teju popped a piece of cheese in his mouth. "Our fathers usually make us fend for ourselves."

"But we usually don't have a beautiful guest with us," Ladon said with a wink.

Heat flushed her cheeks, but her growling stomach refused to let anything prevent her from eating.

He wants you, Thelix observed. *Maybe you haven't totally blown it.*

They ate in silence for the most part, other than when Teju threw back his head and let out a fiery burp, coating the ceiling with red and gold embers. She knew her grandfather would disapprove of his manners, but for some reason, she wasn't bothered. He was a dragon. She couldn't expect him to go against his nature.

That made her think. She'd been going against her nature the past three years to please Grandfather. Though she sometimes missed the water, she hadn't shifted since going to live with him. Swallowing a lump of food, she washed it down with several gulps of juice. No longer in the mood to eat, she set her goblet down.

Draque pushed back his chair, frowning down at his brothers. "Something's not adding up."

Teju leaned back, folding his hands behind his head. "A lot of things don't add up."

"Don't you think it's odd investigators weren't on the scene?" Draque asked.

Serah was stunned. No one was looking for survivors?

Ladon set down his drink. "Maybe they hadn't found out yet."

Draque turned to her. "Your godmother knew about it last night, right?"

She fidgeted, scared where this was going. "She did."

"What did she say?" he asked.

Clutching her hands in her lap, she said, "That my grandfather was ready to wage war against the dragon kings for my murder."

Teju and Ladon jumped up, standing beside their brother.

"So he knew about the attack last night, and he didn't alert the authorities?" Draque asked accusingly.

She crossed her arms. "Your fathers knew about the attack, too."

He leaned against the fireplace mantel, every muscle tensed. "They have spies."

She shrugged. "Maybe my grandfather has spies, too."

"Then why didn't he say something?" Draque demanded.

"Why didn't *your* fathers say something?" She hid her uneasiness. Something was very wrong.

Teju flashed a smug smile. "Because they'd suspect shifters were involved."

"The authorities could've been there." She twisted the cloth napkin in her lap. "They might have been hiding behind invisibility spells."

Draque shook his head. "Then why didn't they arrest us?"

"We were only there a few seconds," she argued, but she was lying to herself. They'd been there long enough to be approached by investigators.

"You need to connect the dots, Serah," Draque grumbled, staring her down. "Do you know why your grandfather hates our fathers so much?"

She balled the napkin in her hand. "No."

"He courted our grandmother, but she left him for our grandfathers," Ladon said.

Their grandmother? That had to have been ages ago. "I doubt he's still holding a grudge over that. He's never mentioned her."

Draque straightened. "Serah, Nathaniel Goldenwand doesn't know how to let go of a grudge. He's not the person you think he is."

Why was Draque doing this to her now after all she'd been through? Her godmother had just tried to kill her, for goddess's sake. Had he no compassion? "Stop saying that!" Her hand flew to her throbbing temple, a soft groan escaping her lips when her world tilted. She had a stress headache. She always got them when she had conflicting feelings about her grandfather.

Ladon knelt beside her and put his strong hand on her knee. "Are you okay?"

She fought back tears. "Is there somewhere I can be alone for a while? I have to lie down." And she didn't want Draque to see the waterworks that were about to spring from her eyes. Ladon gestured to a doorway carved into the far wall. "You can use my den."

"Thanks." She touched his wrist. "*You're* so kind."

"You think me unkind for wanting you to know the truth?" Draque said harshly.

She deliberately avoided eye contact with the brute. "I think you unkind for many reasons."

"It's not my intention to hurt you." His gruff voice rose an octave.

She shrugged, focusing her gaze on the door, still refusing to look him in the eyes. "Could've fooled me."

Without so much as looking in Draque and Teju's direction, she followed Ladon to the den.

Whispering soothing words, he held her, rubbing her back. He was so sweet. She wished his brothers were more like him. She sighed when he wrapped strong arms around her. Though she tried to hold them back, a few tears fell.

She told herself she was crying because Draque was such a jerk, but the real reason was a truth she still couldn't acknowledge. She absently fondled the earrings her grandfather had given her when he'd saved her from the sirens. He was the only family she had left and he wanted her dead?

Chapter Seven

Lady Athena Hoofenmouth grimaced at her surroundings. The school's underground emergency shelter was a sparse cell illuminated by old wall sconces. There were a few benches and old school desks, a rusty toilet against a stone wall, and a dilapidated water fountain not equipped to last them more than a few days.

She knelt in front of Serah Goldenwand's bound godmother, choking on the fairy's stale boozy breath. "I'm going to ask you once more: why did you try to kill Seraphina?"

"I told you, my wand was bewitched." The fairy sniffled, gobs of mascara running down her saggy, wrinkled face, her lopsided pink hair sticking to one side of her head like a matted ball of fur. "I'd never intentionally try to hurt my goddaughter."

Athena narrowed her eyes at the fairy. "Who bewitched it?"

"I-I don't know." She hiccupped.

She studied her face, unable to detect any sign of deceit. Still, she didn't trust her. She hadn't seen the woman's eyes when she'd tried to kill Seraphina, which would have helped determine if she'd truly been bewitched. She'd been hiding behind a tombstone, watching in awe as the Firesbreath brothers and the heiress suddenly materialized from detention. They'd been shocked to find their school in ruins. Good. Doris would've been crushed if those boys had been behind the destruction.

"Do you live with Nathaniel Goldenwand?" she asked the godmother.

"Yes." The fairy hiccupped again, then let out a rancid belch. "I've lived with the Goldenwand family for eight hundred years."

Cursing, Athena arched back, waving away the stink. Great Goddess, eight hundred years serving the Goldenwands would be enough torture to drive anyone to drink.

"Has Nathaniel been in contact with your wand?" she asked.

The fairy flinched, looking affronted. "Nathaniel Goldenwand personally inspects every Goldenwand before they go on the market," she said haughtily, "but he wouldn't harm his only heir."

"Are you sure?" Maybe that's what the fairy thought, but Athena certainly didn't believe it. During the few minutes she'd spoken to him in the waiting room, she could tell he was heartless, and not just because of his snake-like stare. He'd referred to his granddaughter as a whore no less than five times before being shown into Doris's office.

"It just doesn't make any sense," the fairy cried, seemingly oblivious to a long trail of snot dripping down her nose and into her mouth.

"Neither do you," Athena grumbled. Rising, she turned to the group of wide-eyed teens, looking at her as if she was their last hope. Doris had the connection to the kids, not her. Why were they looking to her as their leader? She waved to the potions teacher. "Bodicea, do you have any herbals to sober her up?"

The teacher stood, her wavy red hair floating around her shoulders in wild, untamed abandon, her porcelain cheeks stained with soot. When she smoothed her dress over generous curves, Athena was reminded they'd once been lovers, and she'd spent many nights with her face buried between Bodicea's creamy thighs. That was, until Doris Doublewart caught Athena's eye. Not that Doris was anywhere near as beautiful as Bodicea, but she was fierce and strong, two qualities Athena admired most in a woman. Bodicea was beautiful but lacked the grit Athena needed in a partner.

Bodicea nodded. "I believe I can brew something."

"Good. See that it's done," she said tersely. "I need a walk. I should be back in about an hour."

"You're leaving us?" Bodicea's eyes widened. "Where are you going?"

Athena fought the urge to roll her eyes. Doris wouldn't have been frightened, or if she had, she wouldn't have shown it. She would've taken charge and rallied the students until Athena returned.

"To see how the Firebreaths and the heiress escaped their dungeons," she said, then marched out of the cell.

"I'm coming with you," Bodicea cried.

"No." Athena stopped and glared at the pretty teacher. "Stay here with the children."

"Too bad. I'm coming." She raised her chin in a beautiful act of defiance. "The moss I need for the godmother's brew only grows in the dungeon." She nodded at a cluster of teachers behind her. "Hortensia, you're in charge."

Marching past Athena, she left the tantalizing scent of honeysuckle in her wake. Athena followed, remembering how she missed that scent.

TEJU'S HEART SANK AS Serah went into Ladon's room with him. He and his two brothers rarely competed with each other, because they'd been sharing everything since they were hatchlings. Though they'd hatched within a few hours of each other, Teju considered Draque the older brother and leader, and Ladon, as the youngest, the follower. Teju had been stuck somewhere in the middle, the most academic of the three, the one who helped bring Draque's outlandish plans to fruition by conjuring spells or designing potions.

But it seemed their order had changed. The baby brother had taken charge of their girl—correction, not their girl. She'd been theirs for only a short time before their world imploded. What Teju wouldn't give to return to their bubble, to feel the quickening of Serah's tight sheath while she moaned beneath him.

He was struck with envy as he thought of her in Ladon's bed. Would he make love to her without them? The thought gnawed a hole in his gut.

Draque paced by the hearth, swearing under his breath about a stubborn siren.

"Do you think we're being too hard on her?" Teju asked.

Draque's gaze snapped to his. "By telling her the truth?"

He felt like a cornered mouse under the weight of Draque's stare. "She's obviously not ready to hear it."

"Too fucking bad." Draque let out a primal roar. "She needs to face reality and show a little appreciation." His eyes shifted from brown to brilliant gold. "If it wasn't for us, she'd be dead."

Teju sure hoped Serah couldn't hear Draque from Ladon's den. She'd call him a few choice names and then their chances of getting her back would be even slimmer. "She's in shock."

His eyes shone brighter, and his skin rippled before transforming into golden scales. His deep, dragon voice took over. "She needs to wake the fuck up before the wizard army shows up at our door."

A loud knock at the door was followed by an obnoxious squawk and ruffling of feathers. Teju and Draque shared dark looks; they recognized the sound of their fathers' lackey, Lord Crowfoot, who preferred to remain in a half-shifter, half mortal state, as many other shifters did in The Grotto.

Draque unlatched the heavy wooden door. It squeaked and groaned when he pulled it open. Crowfoot ducked under the doorway, his feathered head almost scraping the top of their cavern as he filled the room with his imposing presence. Though his shifter line was supposedly derived from crows, Teju suspected he had some prehistoric blood as well.

Crowfoot looked at them from behind a long, sharp beak with eyes that looked human. He ruffled his feathers once more and cleared his throat. "Draque, Teju, and Ladon Firesbreath, you have been summoned by the kings."

"Again?" Draque grumbled. "We were just there."

Crowfoot let out a shrill laugh that sounded like a train whistle. "They said you'd say that, and I'm to answer that if you don't get your scaly hides to their chamber immediately, they will smoke you out of your den themselves."

Draque widened his stance and gave the bird a challenging look. "Teju and I will go."

"The youngest prince has been summoned, too."

"He's with the Goldenwand heiress." Teju glanced at the door to Ladon's den.

"And we're not leaving her alone," Draque added.

Teju smiled. Though he pretended to be vexed by Serah, Draque was still ruled by his protective instincts.

Crowfoot let out a noisy squawk. "Your fathers will be—"

Draque shot a stream of fire across Crowfoot's shoulder, smoking the tips of his feathers. "Shut your bird beak and let us worry about our fathers."

Crowfoot's long, spindly legs shook, then he flapped his wings and part walked, part flew from the room.

Teju and Draque shared nervous looks. Why did their fathers want them again so soon? Teju suspected they bore bad tidings.

"WAIT UP, BODICEA," Athena called, climbing through the narrow tunnel. A rat scurried past her feet. Who knew the pretty teacher could traverse slippery rocks so fast? Athena had forgotten what a treacherous climb it had been, getting from their emergency shelter to the detention dungeons. If it hadn't been for the glow from her wand, she wouldn't have been able to see where she was going, though perhaps that would've been better. The tunnel was littered with rat skeletons and spider webs.

Upon reaching the end of the tunnel, Bodicea leaned against moss-covered bars overlooking a treacherous drop into the cavern below. "Do you know which cell they were in?"

Athena shoved a hand through the bars, shining her wand into the darkness below and revealing inky black water surrounding a narrow, makeshift island. She barely made out the dorsal fins of the giant sharks that patrolled the water. They had been crafted from an illusion spell, based on Doris's poorly drawn sharks, but they were threatening nonetheless, even if the size of their teeth were so exaggerated, they were almost comical.

After she recited the password, the metal grate opened and stairs appeared, lengthening until they touched ground.

Athena waved her wand at Bodicea. "After you?"

"Thank you." Bodicea flashed a coy smile. "How polite."

Athena inwardly smiled. She'd never been polite when she'd dated Bodicea. In fact, she'd been gruff, even demanding. She suspected Bodicea had grown tired of her. Their relationship had started fizzling even before Doris had shown an interest in Athena. The thought of Bodicea thinking her a brute didn't sit well with her, and she made an extra effort to help her down the stairs.

"We will need to surface soon," Bodicea said when they reached the bottom. "We don't have enough supplies to stay for more than a few days."

One of the comical sharks splashed Athena's shoes. "We'll have to ration."

"The children are terrified." Bodicea nervously twisted the hem of her apron. "We've been here since yesternight."

Athena walked the perimeter of the island, searching for clues. "We will continue to wait until we receive a sign from Doris," she said. She had a feeling Bodicea had only wanted to tag along so she could nag her.

Following close at her heels, Bodicea refused to drop the subject. "But you said Doris was kidnapped by dragons."

"She was." Turning on her heel, she gave Bodicea a withering look. "Dragons who think she's Seraphina Goldenwand. As long as they keep thinking that, she'll be able to escape."

"What if she can't?" Bodicea clutched her throat. "What if they kill her?"

"They won't." She forced herself to look away from the rise and fall of Bodicea's ample bosom. "These are the elder Firesbreath brothers. They are misfits, but they aren't murderers." At least Athena hoped so. Hopefully Doris hadn't put too much faith in her former students.

"So why should we hide from them if they're not killers?" Bodicea pressed, advancing on Athena, her cloying smell enveloping her like a fog. "Why not surface and alert the authorities, so they can be arrested?"

Backing up a step, Athena struggled not to be distracted by Bodicea's honeysuckle perfume. "Because they didn't burn down our school."

Wagging a finger in her face, Bodicea said, "How can you be sure?"

What had they been talking about? That honeysuckle and those beautiful breasts were too distracting. "You said you saw dragons emerge from storm clouds."

"Yes."

"Those weren't dragons. What you saw was a conjuring."

Bodicea's draw dropped. "But conjuring requires dark magic."

"It does." Athena bit back a sardonic laugh. "And who else but a dark mage would burn down a school full of children?"

"But who would do such a thing?" she asked with a breathy whisper.

"Do you have to ask?" Athena rolled her eyes, and that's when she saw it: a giant bubble suspended in the air, tucked into the space between Seraphina's cell and the next. She squinted. "What in Goddess's name is that?"

"It looks like a giant bubble." Bodicea scratched the back of her head.

Athena aimed her wand at the bubble and pulled it toward her as if an invisible string connected the two. No bigger than a small car, the bubble landed at her feet. Remembering her father's modest boat, that was as big as a yacht inside, Doris suspected this was a trick of the mind. Tentatively, she pressed her palm against it and the structure gave way. Pushing her way through, she gaped at what could only be described as a pleasure pad. It offered a large sunken room with a round sectional sofa, a flat-screen TV, tiki bar, and even a ping-pong table. She scented the slightest residue of sulfur and knew this was a creation of the Firesbreath brothers. Sneaky fuckwads.

Bodicea fell through the sticky wall, somehow landing in Athena's arms.

"Sorry," Bodicea said while finding her footing.

"No problem." Coughing into her fist, Athena tried to appear unfazed. This woman was far too tempting. Besides, Athena was in love with Doris, though she didn't love Athena the same way. Doris was much too enamored of her school, which would always take priority over Athena's needs. Always.

"Great Goddess!" Bodicea turned in a slow circle. "This has Teju Firesbreath written all over it."

Athena inhaled the distinct smell of sex. Those horny fucks. "This kind of spell is far more advanced than what we teach at Doublewart's."

"I know. The boy's a genius." Bodicea clasped her hands to her heart. "Do you think we could fit all the students in here?"

Athena bit back a curse. "Possibly." Not that she wanted to hide in a bubble with fifty hormonal witches.

Bodicea squealed and ran through the place like a kid wired on sugar. "It has everything we need, including a bathroom and a pantry full of food."

"No wonder they didn't mind detention," Athena said wryly.

Bodicea raced up to her, eyes bright. "And neither will we."

"It's a shame to bring the kids here, though." Athena bridged the distance between them and twirled a lock of Bodicea's thick strawberry hair around her finger. "They'll probably trash the place."

Bodicea pouted, making her look adorably sexy. "We can't leave them in that shelter."

"I know, but maybe we could enjoy it for a while before letting them in." What the hell had gotten into her? Doris was a hostage somewhere, and she was flirting with another woman! She should have felt ashamed of herself, yet she couldn't stop.

"Athena," Bodicea whispered, leaning into her, her breath tickling her skin like a butterfly. "What about Doris?"

"She's tough. She can handle herself." She was probably finding a way to free herself at that very moment, eager to get back to her school. She hadn't even considered Athena's suggestion to use Goldenwand's bribe money to retire to Elysian. She'd use that money to rebuild the school, where she'd live out her life, probably dying there. How depressing. Was this really the life Athena wanted? She removed the ring she wore on her wedding finger and slipped it into her pocket. Doris had told her it wasn't an engagement ring, though Athena had pretended it was. It was just a promise ring, though what that promise was, Athena had no idea.

"That's not what I meant." The color that touched Bodicea's cheeks made her look even more beautiful.

"I'm sorry." Athena rubbed her face. This was so bad, so why couldn't she stop? "It's your perfume."

"It was your favorite." She batted her lashes. "That's why I still wear it."

How thoughtful. Doris refused to wear perfume for Athena, even though she'd begged her to on numerous occasions.

Bodicea looked at Athena as if she held the moon and stars. "This is wrong," she said, closing her eyes.

"I know," Athena said and kissed her.

Chapter Eight

"Make yourself comfortable," Ladon said and waved at his big bed, which looked like an animal den carved into the stone wall. "I'm just going to clean up."

After he disappeared behind a heavy drape, she heard the distinct sound of a stream of urine hitting the inside of a bowl.

She crawled into the alcove, smiling when her hands and knees sank into soft furs. The low cave wall acted as a cocoon, making her feel safe and secure. She fell into the bed, heaving a sigh and digging her fingers into a pillow. Ladon's bed was beyond comfortable, with just the right amount of bounce. Piled high with animal furs, it felt as luxurious as the magically enhanced Sparklefeather bed her grandfather had purchased for her.

Grandfather had spared no expense when it came to Serah's needs, buying her expensive clothes and jewels, and paying for the best school in the third realm—until she'd gotten kicked out. He'd never been overly affectionate, but he had always been there for her, which was why she was having trouble thinking he'd bewitched Hestia's wand.

Ladon joined her and sat at the edge of the bed. When she heard loud voices outside, Ladon shot to his feet. Her breath caught in her throat as she strained to hear what they were saying.

"We're not leaving her alone."

Her heart warmed when she recognized Draque's voice. Yeah, he was a jerk at times, but at least he was protective of her. She wondered if it was because he cared about her or if he was afraid of her grandfather's wrath. A loud roar startled her, then Draque's angry words punctured the air. "Shut your bird beak and let us worry about our fathers!"

Her libido sprang to life. Of all the times to get turned on!

"I'll be right back." Ladon shot her a sympathetic look and slipped out the heavy, wooden door, latching it behind him.

The sound of the lock turning unnerved her. Was he locking her in for her safety, or was she actually a prisoner?

She bit down on her knuckles to repress her nerves. Whoever Birdbeak was, she hoped it wouldn't come to blows with Draque. The door opened again.

"It's just me," Ladon said and crawled across the bed. "Everything's okay."

Well, that wasn't true. She stiffened when he grasped her shoulder.

"Can I get you anything?" he asked.

Curling into herself, she shook her head.

"Are you sure?" When he stroked her back, she fought reacting to his touch. The connection felt wonderful, and being cared for by him was a small shimmering beacon in the darkness, but his compassion almost made her to burst into tears.

"Serah," he said in low, soothing tones, spooning against her and wrapping an arm around her. "It's okay."

She turned into him, feeling bad that he was being so kind to her after what she'd said to her godmother the night before.

Placing a hand on his chest, she looked at him. "I didn't mean to agree with my godmother when she told me I'd tire of you. I just didn't want her telling my grandfather. I knew he'd try to break us apart."

Ladon cupped her jaw. "I understand."

"Do you believe me?"

"Yes."

She heaved a sigh of relief, hardly aware that she'd been holding her breath. "Thank you, Ladon."

"We told you our instincts were good." He gently caressed her face, his infectious smile making her feel less quilty. "I can see into your heart."

Being held by Ladon, embraced by his scent and electrified by his touch, made her pulse with desire. She wanted to show him she adored him. She needed to hold him and feel him deep inside her. Feathering her fingers across the bulge between his legs, she was glad to know he felt the same way.

Hissing, his eyes fluttered shut when she dragged her thigh across his erection.

"What is my heart telling you now?"

His eyes shot open. "I don't want you to feel obligated." He grabbed her wrist when she reached for him again.

She pushed against him. "What if I want to?"

He released her wrist and laid back, pulling her on top of him. "Then I'd be a fool to stop you."

LADON HAPPILY GAVE his lovely siren control and was not disappointed when she removed his clothes and wasted no time taking him in her mouth.

He surrendered to the mind-blowing pleasure of his cock buried in her throat while her tongue swirled around the sensitive foreskin. It was the single most exquisite feeling of his life.

He fell back with a shudder, fireworks exploding behind his eyelids. He tried to hold back, but the way her magical tongue made love to every inch of his shaft was more than he could bear. He barely managed a warning he was about to come. He was surprised when she continued to suck him. He shot off like a rocket, and she slurped his seed as if his cock was coated in chocolate. Hot damn, she was so fucking erotic.

He hissed when she pulled off. She threw off her clothes and straddled his thighs, sliding his glistening cock into her dripping mound, and he anchored her by grabbing her fleshy, round tits and rolling her nipples in his fingers.

She ground against him, gasping each time his cockhead slammed into her swollen center. When her tempo increased, he gladly met each thrust, their joined bodies slapping against each other harder and harder until she threw back her head with a gasp. Her sheath contracted, then shook with tremors that electrified him, milking him once more.

She captured his lips in a heat-searing kiss, and he moaned into her mouth. He didn't know if she was having multiple orgasms or one big long one. She kept pulsing around him. They panted into each other's mouths for several long heartbeats before she finally collapsed, her heavy breasts smashed against his hard chest. She didn't seem to mind. She practically melted all over him, like warm syrup dripping over hotcakes.

Stroking her back and hair, he enjoyed her sweet mewling sounds, his cock still buried inside her.

"How are you feeling?" he asked

"Like I'll never be able to walk again." She chuckled. "You?"

He feathered a kiss across her forehead, tightening his hold on her. "Like I never want to let you go."

"I don't want you to either." She rose enough to look into his eyes. "You have been so kind to me." Her voice cracked, and she looked away.

His heart lurched. What had upset her?

"Serah, my love." He rolled her over and reluctantly slid out of her, slipping his crumpled shirt between her legs.

She staring blankly at the ceiling. "You must think I'm an emotional mess."

"You've been through a lot." He nuzzled her cheek. "It's okay to let it out, Serah."

She heaved a shuddering breath. "I don't want to."

"You're going to have to eventually."

Latching onto his hip, she buried her face against him. "Why would he want to kill me?" Her voice was muffled.

"It's not anything you did." He cupped her shoulders. "He's evil."

Her lower lip quivered. "But he gives to charities, and he's always been generous with me."

"Gifts don't make someone a good person," he said, hating himself for having to make her see the truth.

"Ladon, he saved my life once. Why would he save me only to kill me?"

"He saved your life?" As much as he believed in Serah's goodness, he also knew a wizard as powerful as Nathaniel Goldenwand could have deceived her with an illusion spell.

She drew back and blinked at him. "When my mother and grandmother were going to sacrifice me."

Ladon's heart slammed against his chest. "Sacrifice you?" That couldn't be right. The sirens had a bad reputation, but never had he heard of them sacrificing their own. "Why?"

"In homage to our goddess, Maiadra."

Why would the sirens risk being called before the Mage Council and possibly sentenced to death? "But sacrifices were banished in all realms years ago."

"Sirens follow their own code."

"They're not worried about the law?" Ladon touched his neck, a shudder coursing through him when he thought about Parliament's brutal beheading of a renegade mage he'd witnessed when he was a boy. "Witches don't go to Siren's Cove. You know how they feel about shifters."

He knew witch prejudice all too well, which made it even more puzzling that her grandfather had sired a child from a siren. Perhaps her pheromones had been too tempting to resist. "But sirens are still obligated to follow magical code."

She let out a bitter laugh. "Who's going to enforce it?"

Clasping her hand in his, he brushed his lips across her knuckles. "I'm sorry." He wished he could conjure up something that would soothe the pain in her heart, but he wasn't as gifted with spells as Teju. He reminded himself to ask him for his help.

"Anyway," she continued in a disinterested drawl that sounded forced, "my grandfather saved me and took me home. It can't be him, Ladon. It has to be one of his assistants or a distant relative who wants my inheritance."

He arched a brow. "Who are these distant relatives?"

She averted her eyes. "Cousins."

He could tell she didn't suspect them, and she was still trying to convince herself her grandfather was innocent. He decided to play her game. She'd wouldn't accept that her grandfather was evil until she was ready. "We'd need to see the will to see who would benefit from your death," he added cautiously, "but he's been looking for an excuse to start a war with the shifter race for a while."

Sitting up, she wrapped her arms around herself. "I know he doesn't like shifters." Her smooth brow furrowed as she became lost in thought.

Maybe it was finally sinking in.

"That's an understatement," he mumbled. Nathaniel Goldenwand despised shifters and wanted to see their race destroyed. He'd said as much to his grandfathers once, and Ladon doubted such a wizard would set aside a grudge so easily. More likely it had festered over the years, a giant, oozing boil of hatred and vengeance, and poor Serah was caught in the middle.

"COME HERE, MY LITTLE mite."

Katherine hid in the shadows of an alcove, impatiently tapping her foot as her slag slithered down the uneven wall. Not much bigger than a worm, it left a thin trail of slime behind it wherever it went.

She held out a hand, and it dropped into it with a hiss. Capturing her pet, she kissed the top of its brown, bumpy head, letting its feathery antennae tickle her lips. Then she held him beneath the lobe of her ear. He latched on, squeezing hard enough to break skin and draw blood. After feeding for a few minutes, her pet crawled into her ear and slithered its way to her brain.

There he relayed everything he'd seen while spying on the Firesbreath brothers in their den.

Biting her lip to keep from screaming, Katherine's talons shot out, and she fell against the wall, grinding spiky nails into the mossy rock while she relived the memory of Ladon fucking the siren bitch.

She agonized over each moan and slippery thrust, biting back tears of frustration as she slid down the wall to the floor, falling on her rear with a painful *thud.* Time stood still as they pleasured each other, and then he held her in the cradle of his arms. When the sweet murmurs began, she wanted to rip out her hair by the roots until she heard the bitch's dark secret. The sirens had wanted to sacrifice her? Interesting. A dark seed of vengeance took root in her mind. That bitch would pay for stealing her mates.

Chapter Nine

Draque was pleased to see their beautiful mother, Rhea, when they walked into their fathers' chamber. The quickening of his heart reminded him how much he'd missed her. As the oldest of the three brothers, he had to put up a tough front, but he loved her gentle touch and warm hugs.

"My dear boys," she cried, her long silvery hair flowing behind her like wisps of smoke as she ran to them. "I'm so relieved you're safe." She hugged Teju first, kissing his cheek while Draque awaited his turn in anticipation.

Draque stiffened when she hugged him next, relishing her affection, but refusing to show his fathers any sign of weakness. When she kissed his cheek, he quickly hugged her back before pushing her away.

She frowned. "Where's Ladon?"

"We left him with Serah," Draque explained. "Katherine has threatened her."

Her frown deepened, the lines marring her otherwise smooth forehead. "We will speak to her father."

Teju laughed. "I doubt it will do any good."

She searched their faces, and Draque felt the discomfort of her scrutinizing gaze. As a djinn, she could practically see into his soul. "Do you care for this girl?"

"She's not like her grandfather," he answered, purposely avoiding her question. "She has a pure heart."

Her obsidian eyes narrowed. "But do you care for her?"

"How can we not?" Teju answered.

She clasped her hands to her heart and smiled. "Then I will pray to the goddess to guide your hearts until your stars align."

"Thank you, Mother," Draque said.

She fluttered back to his dragon fathers with the grace of a butterfly. His fathers preferred to be in full dragon form when they kept court. They were more intimidating that way.

Kron was the oldest of his three fathers. Long whiskers hung over his snout, a sign of his ancient dragon ancestry. He nuzzled the top of his mother's head, purring like a cat before taking her in the crook of his wing. As fierce as their three fathers tried to present themselves, Mother could reduce them to simpering kittens with one look. Funny, how certain women had a way of charming beasts.

Draque had felt the same way with Serah yesternight.

"So it truly wasn't you who burned down the school?" Dagon asked, glaring at them with his one eye.

Draque stiffened, clenching his hands until nails broke skin. They'd been unruly children and deserved to be sent to Dame Doublewart's, but it was past time their fathers viewed them as men. If only they could learn to trust them.

"No, Fathers," he said, "and I'm insulted you still don't believe us."

Teju's lip pulled back in a snarl. "Why don't you ask our brothers, or are we still pretending they're not fighting with the resistance?"

Draque gave Teju a sympathetic nod. Though he was close to his two hatchling siblings, he was not fond of his eldest brothers, who were first in line to the throne. They had been even worse than Draque and his brothers when they'd gone to Doublewarts, which was one reason the Firesbreaths had such a bad reputation. Though they were well past high school age, they'd yet to grow up or show any interest in inheriting the thrones and the responsibilities that came with it, which put more pressure on Draque and his brothers to conduct themselves as kings, should something happen to their fathers.

Goddess save them all should that day come.

Vepar pulled back pale lips, revealing either a jagged smile or a frown. "We believe you, sons, and we will be summoning your brothers."

Draque felt the threat behind Vepar's words and hoped his older brothers would be thoroughly punished for their misdeeds, for it had to be them. They'd joined the resistance against their fathers' orders and had been wreaking havoc ever since. Though the rebel army had initially banded together for the noble cause of preventing powerful witches from destroying the shifter race, somewhere along the way their mission had become warped. Draque wouldn't be surprised if they'd been the ones to destroy his school, murdering innocents in order to propel witches and shifters into war.

"Did you fornicate with the Goldenwand girl?"

Draque blinked hard at Kron, who twirled the tips of his whiskers in his talons while giving them a knowing glare.

Draque swallowed. His fathers expected them to save themselves for their true mate, which was unfair considering a dragon's insatiable libido. "Her name is Serah, and yes, we had sex."

His mother's gasp filled him with dread and then annoyance. She still treated them like babes, one reason why she insisted they finish school after they'd tried to drop out.

Vepar's pale scales colored a rosy pink. "You care so little for your people's safety that you'd sleep with our enemy's spawn?"

Teju cleared his throat. "We didn't know she was the heiress until afterward. Besides, she's not the enemy here."

Their mother advanced on them, her face shifting several times and revealing too many faces to count. "So you just randomly take strange girls to your den?"

"No, Mother," Draque said and sighed.

Dagon gave them his knowing look, as if his one eye was a crystal ball that could see into their souls. "Rumor is that she's a siren."

"She is," Teju said. "She told us before we slept with her. She has a pure heart."

"Did she seduce you?" Mother demanded.

Draque shook his head. "If anything, we seduced her."

And he'd do it again if given the chance, so long as he knew her heart was theirs, and she wasn't planning to discard them later. If only he hadn't heard her conversation with her godmother. He'd gone from trusting her to suspecting she'd bewitched them.

Vepar crossed one clawed foreleg over the other, looking like a complacent feline overlord. "Her grandfather will not be pleased."

Kron winked. "He will be even less pleased when we send him word that his granddaughter is betrothed to our sons."

"We're not betrothed," Draque protested. "All we did was sleep together."

"You will be betrothed," Vepar said in a tone so dark and threatening, Draque knew it would be impossible to sway him.

"I-I beg your pardon," Teju stammered.

"You will marry the Goldenwand heiress," Kron said, enunciating each word as if speaking to children.

"Why?" he demanded, currents of molten lava flowing through his veins. He decided he liked his parents better when they were treating them like babes; he was too young to marry.

"To prevent war," Dagon answered. "Nathaniel Goldenwand will be hesitant to attack us if his granddaughter is here."

"No, he won't!" Draque threw up his hands, frustration pounding a hammer in his ears. "He clearly doesn't care for her."

"But he cares about his standing in the magical world," Dagon said. "He will not be able to wage war over the death of his grandchild if she's safe with us."

Draque cursed. "I don't think she'll agree to it." In fact he knew she wouldn't. She only liked Ladon.

"You must make her agree," Vepar said with a disinterested slur, like a cat who'd tired of his pet mouse.

"Fathers, we're still at the academy." Teju steepled his fingers. "Don't you think we're too young?"

Kron shrugged. "Our fathers married when they were your age."

Draque's heartbeat quickened. They weren't backing down. "Times have changed."

"If we marry now," Teju said, his voice surprisingly calm considering what their parents were trying to make them do, "Goldenwand will know it was forced."

Kron released a stream of smoke from his nostrils. "No marriage yet then, but we must have a betrothal."

A betrothal? Draque clenched his hair by the roots. That was almost as bad. It meant they were destined for the inevitable bonding ceremony.

"This is insane!" Teju groaned.

"Would you rather send her back to the man who tried to kill her?" Kron asked, smirking.

Draque's dragon rose, clawing at his skin. The thought of her in that wicked mage's clutches made him want to destroy the entire third realm.

Dagon said, "Sons, it's the only way to keep her safe."

"Your Highnesses, I beg your pardon, but I don't think marriage between the Goldenwand heiress and your sons is a good idea."

Master Eagleheart, his fathers' mage and Katherine's father, was behind him, leaning against his ruby-tipped staff. Like Katherine, he was tall and lanky, though his nose was much bigger. His feral black eyes were framed by so many wrinkles, Draque wondered exactly how old the master was. He'd served Draque's grandparents and great-grandparents, and from what he'd been told, the griffin had been old even then. He'd never had a mate that Draque was aware of; his daughter had simply appeared one day sixteen years ago, a wide-eyed tot who some said had been born of dark magic.

"Master Eagleheart," Kron grumbled, pulling back his shoulders, "this is a private conversation."

Eagleheart waved his staff. "As your council, I assumed I was to be included, especially as your decision directly affects the arrangement between your sons and my daughter."

"We never agreed to any arrangement," Draque faced Master Eagleheart, speaking from between clenched teeth.

The mage fixed him with a hawkish glare. "It was an unwritten agreement. It's what's best for all shifter-kind."

A bitter laugh escaped Draque's throat. The only shifters who'd benefit from that arrangement would be the Eaglehearts.

"We have told our fathers and you that we do not love Katherine in that way." Teju's words were cool and controlled, which belied the thunderstorm in his eyes.

"She loves you." The mage turned a pout, so exaggerated it looked forced. "You're all she talks about. If you marry another it would crush her."

"Forgive me, Master Eagleheart. It is not our intention to cause Katherine pain, but we think of her too much like a sister," Draque said, "not a lover." He didn't want to lie to his fathers' mage, but he didn't want to hurt his feelings either. He thought of Katherine less as a sister and more like a giant, obnoxious, bitchy thorn in his paw.

"You loved her once." The mage shook his staff at Draque, his eyes glowing red like the hot coals of hell. "I know you did! That siren has you bewitched."

"Enough!" Kron's roar shook the stagnant air.

Draque and Teju ducked when dust and debris rained down on them. Draque cursed when a pebble sliced open his ear.

"Master Eagleheart," Kron continued, the steel in his voice leaving no room for argument. "There has never been an agreement between our houses that our sons would mate with your daughter."

"I'm sorry, friend, but they must bond with the Goldenwand heiress if we are to have any chance at preventing war," Dagon added.

"Perhaps a war is what we need." The mage's eyes lit with a strange gleam as he banged his staff on the stone floor, the sound echoing off the cave walls. "Between the dragons and the griffins, we can crush the wizard army."

Draque had thought Master Eagleheart and his daughter the only griffins living in The Grotto. He'd heard the rest of their kind were extinct. Did he really think two griffins and a handful of dragons could crush an entire witch army?

Mother stepped forward. "You have yet to feel the power of the Goldenwand 2050. The wizard army will obliterate us."

The mage threw back his head and released a grating laugh that sounded like a screeching hawk. "An enchanted wooden stick doesn't compare to the might of a griffin."

Vepar folded his paws in front of him, giving the mage a long, apathetic look through half-lidded eyes. "You are either too confident, too foolish, or both."

When the mage snorted, Kron let out a low rumble, straightening to full height, his long neck nearly scraping the ceiling. "I will not have your temerity lead our army to their doom. Our sons will bond with the Goldenwand heiress, and that is final."

The mage let out an enraged squawk. "If it's money you're after, don't bother. Her grandfather will disinherit her if she marries shifters."

Kron threw his head back and released his flame, lighting up the cavern in sparks of white, gold, and red. Vepar protected their mother under his wing, and Teju conjured a protective bubble around them both. Draque's fathers were protected by their thick scales, but Eagleheart had no such protection. He stood ramrod straight, his chin at a proud angle, and ignored the embers that burned holes through his robe.

"You insult us." Kron looked at the mage with blood-red eyes. "It's not about the money. It's about the continuation of our species."

The mage's hawkish eyes focused on the kings. "Your fathers wouldn't have cowered before witches."

When Kron roared and blew out an even more massive ball of flame, his brothers roared, too.

Dagon jumped to his feet, golden scales glistening, eyes shooting visual daggers at the imprudent mage. "Leave us, Master Eagleheart."

Eagleheart spun on his heel and marched back to the chamber's two massive doors, his staff sparking as he banged against the stones.

Draque and his brother shared dark looks. He'd never trusted Master Eagleheart, and he feared the duplicitous mage would seek vengeance for his perceived slight.

LADON WATCHED THE STEADY rise and fall of Serah's chest as she slept. Slowly he extricated himself from her arms when he heard his brothers return to their chambers. Tiptoeing to the door, he opened it, hoping the hinges didn't squeak too much. After closing it behind him, he locked it and pocketed the key. Though he knew it was for her safety, he felt like the lowest of scoundrels for locking his sweet siren away.

His heart dropped when he turned to his brothers. They were looking at him with accusatory glares.

"I smell her mating fluids on you," Draque hissed.

Ladon shrugged, regretting nothing. "She wanted me to."

"She's using you."

His blood ran cold as his inner-dragon raged, clawing at his skin. "No, she's not." His dragon spoke for him in a a low, warning rumble. "You know she's got a pure heart."

Draque gave him a cool look. "I know what she said to her godmother."

Ladon sucked in a breath.

"She had to," Teju answered before Ladon could speak. "Her grandfather would never agree to our match."

Ladon folded his arms with a stern expression. "Exactly."

"Ha!" Draque threw back his head. "I wonder if you'd feel the same way if she wasn't yanking your wand."

Ladon's talons involuntarily shot out, his inner dragon demanding to fight. He did his best to ignore the call of the beast. No good would come from fighting with his brother. He decided to appeal to Draque's reasoning.

"Of course I'd feel the same way," he answered plainly. "I love her."

Draque and Teju gaped at him, and Draque threw up his hands. "Great goddess!"

"You haven't even known her a day," Teju sputtered.

Ladon stiffened under his brothers' scrutiny. "I know her well enough. She's the one."

Brushing past them, he ignored their swearing and sputtering and sat at the table. After shoving several pieces of meat and cheese into his mouth, he poured juice into a tall goblet. Loving his beautiful siren sure worked up an appetite.

"Great." Draque snatched the goblet from his hands. "Maybe *you* can propose to her." He downed the juice in a few swallows.

Ladon should've been upset with Draque for stealing his drink, but he was too shocked by his mention of marriage. "Propose?"

Teju sat beside him, propping his booted feet up on the table. "Our fathers say we must marry her to prevent war." He snatched a piece of palma fruit from the basket and dug his fangs into it, not looking the least bit alarmed that they weren't yet twenty and being forced into marriage.

But Ladon was alarmed. Were they ready to be bonded? Was Serah? The thought of her reaction to the news made all moisture in his mouth evaporate in an instant.

Ladon snatched the goblet back from Draque, poured, and drank. After belching a ring of smoke, he waiting for the shock to wear off, praying they were joking. When their somber expressions didn't change, he cleared his throat. "Nathaniel Goldenwand won't allow it."

Draque snorted, a plume of smoke escaping his nostrils. "Nathaniel Goldenwand doesn't have a say in this realm."

Maybe not yet, Ladon thought wryly.

"So we're just going to mate with her against her will?" he asked. He suspected Serah's reaction would be almost as bad as Nathaniel's.

Dropping his legs to the floor, Teju frowned. "Not against her will."

Draque tossed a palma fruit above his head, caught it, and threw it again with casual ease, as if their entire world wasn't about to go up in flames. "She'll come around."

Draque was too confident. So far Serah had been a willing and amazing lover, but that didn't mean she would agree to marriage, especially not when she and Draque were constantly at odds.

"She won't want to go against her grandfather." Ladon grimaced. "He saved her life once."

Teju shot up, smoke pouring from his nose. "When?"

A knife twisted in Ladon's heart. "When her mother and grandmother tried to sacrifice her."

"They did what?" his brothers cried in unison.

"They were going to offer her to our goddess before he rescued her."

Teju scratched his head. "Are you sure he didn't put a memory enchantment on her?"

Ladon groaned. "I'm not sure of anything at the moment."

"Getting her to trust us isn't going to be easy," Teju said. "She's been hurt too many times, and we've hurt her even more with our treatment of her lately."

"We have to make her trust us." Draque leveled him with a dark look. "The fate of our people depends on us."

SERAH AWOKE TO DRAQUE'S familiar scent, a warm, tempting spice that was richer than his brothers and suited his brooding personality. His arm was draped over her waist, his solid chest pressed against her back, and his erection jutted against her buttocks.

She should've been angry with him for cuddling her without permission. When she turned in his arms, determined to tell him off, one look into alluring eyes that shone like tourmaline, and she lost her resolve.

He flashed a devastatingly sexy smile that revealed a deep dimple in his cheek. "Enjoy your nap?"

"Yes." She tucked her hands under her cheek.

"I'm sorry I upset you earlier." He reached for a lock of her hair and twirled it around his finger. "Are you still angry with me?"

"I probably overreacted. I'm a little stressed." She looked away, afraid she'd see censure in his eyes.

He stroked her cheek with calloused knuckles. "Of course you are, after what you've been through."

His sympathy hit a nerve, as if his compassion was attached to a poison arrow that lodged in her heart. She was almost angry with him for showing that he cared. Why couldn't he always be this sweet? "Have you heard anything from my grandfather?" She needed a diversion.

"No," he said, "but our fathers have sent him word that you are alive."

What if he demanded her return? Would they let her go? Would she want to go? He looked away almost guiltily, and she got the impression there was something he wasn't telling her. "Do we know yet if there are any survivors?"

"Investigators are on the scene. That's all we know."

If there had been survivors, surely they would've found them by now. She swallowed back a lump of fear at the implication. If she and her dragon studs were the only survivors, that left Serah with more questions than answers. Parliament might even accuse the dragons of murder.

"Do they think you did it?" she asked.

"Probably." His voice cracked.

She cupped his cheek, forcing him to look her in the eye. "I'll vouch for you."

His face colored. "We'd appreciate that."

Why was he being so polite? Maybe the reality of their situation had finally set in. "Now what?"

He sat up, stretching thick arms corded with muscle. "You've only seen a small part of The Grotto. How about a more extensive tour?"

Her stomach churned. So far her visit to The Grotto hadn't been awful, but what if he took her to the dregs her grandfather had warned her about?

"There's a special place we want to show you," he continued. "It's the underground lake."

"A lake?" Her veins solidified with fear. "With water?"

"Of course." He chuckled.

Heat crept into her cheeks. What else would a lake be filled with? She hadn't been swimming since she was freed from Siren's Cove. Three years, and she hadn't once shifted. Would she remember how to do it after so long? Would her tail work after years of neglect? "Do you expect me to swim?"

His expression softened. "Not if you don't want to. We won't pressure you, Serah."

Releasing a shaky breath, she slowly nodded. "Okay."

Great Goddess! What had she agreed to? She was about to go to a large body of water with three tempting dragons. Her libido sprang to life at the thought.

Chapter Ten

Serah held hands with Ladon while they followed Draque through the maze of damp underground tunnels that smelled like piss, no doubt from shifters marking their territory. It was no coincidence that Teju followed close behind them. She wondered if their sandwich was meant to protect her or trap her. Either way she was grateful that no strange shifters were able to accost her. When a band of rat-looking things, with long snouts and clawed hands, tried to approach her, Draque singed the hair off the top of their leader's head with a hot band of smoke. The rat scurried back with a squeal, his friends following him.

"What do you think they wanted?" she asked Ladon.

He squeezed her hand. "They're scavengers. They like shiny things. They probably want your jewelry."

She touched her earlobes, making sure her earrings were still there. There were only a handful of ambrosia diamonds in the world, making her rare treasure even more valuable. Grandfather had put them in her lobes after he'd saved her, one of the few times he'd shown her affection. "Rare jewels for a rare treasure," he'd said, then kissed her forehead.

She'd worn them ever since and she never planned on taking them off. She understood why the rats would try to steal them and was glad she had three dragons to protect her.

As they went down several steep steps, Ladon held tight to her, making sure she didn't slip. She thanked him several times with kisses, each one hotter and wetter than the one before. By the time they reached the bottom of a dark, humid cave, her calves and libido were screaming. Stealing a glance at his bulging groin, a zing of excitement shot through her. He was just as excited as she was. She wanted to pull him into an alcove and have her way with him. Heck, she'd love for his brothers to come, too. Damn these dragons! She'd always had a supercharged sexual desire, but these guys amped her horniness to new levels.

Thelix groaned. *When are we going to get laid?*

They wove through more narrow tunnels, some with ceilings so low that her dragon-shifters had to duck their heads.

"How much longer?" she asked Ladon.

"We're almost there," he whispered.

"Good." She straightened when she saw beams of vivid green light spilling into the tunnel. As they approached it, she was struck by warm, fragrant air that smelled like tropical flowers similar to the rich scents she remembered from Siren's Cove. They exited onto a ledge overlooking the most beautiful pools she'd ever seen. Hundreds of shimmering green, blue, and violet bodies of water were intersected by columns of crystalline rocks that thrust up from beneath the lake and also hung from the darkened ceiling. The sound of water trickling from the columns above filled the caverns with an oddly soothing melody and rippled the water in brightly colored circles.

"It's beautiful here," she said as Ladon helped her down the moss-covered steps.

"It's one of our favorite places," he answered. "I'm glad you like it."

They were alone, and she wondered if other shifters had an aversion to the lakes or if they were just lucky. She hadn't had sex in water in a long time, not since she and Acacia had experimented with each other back at Siren's Cove. She didn't know if it was because of her siren blood, but making love in water felt even better, her orgasms magnified as every inch of her skin hummed with sexual energy. She longed to feel the magic once again.

She arched back when Draque turned to her and thought she saw him flinch before he held out a hand.

"Do you want to go for a swim?" he asked.

She backed up as images of them gaping at her long tail and gills flashed through her mind. "You said you wouldn't pressure me."

"We're won't, but you want to swim." His voice dropped to a low, sensual rumble. "I can see it in your eyes."

"No thanks." She sat on a nearby ledge, gazing at the water that lapped at her feet.

Teju gave her a pitying smile. "You don't have to be afraid to shift around us."

"I'm not," she lied, drawing her knees to her chest.

"Do you mind if we go in?" he asked, his eyes too innocent.

She waved him off while her heart thudded. "Do what you want."

His brothers hooted and hollered and stripped down to their swim trunks, then ran into the nearest pool. When the water reached knee level, they partially shifted, sprouting long, spiked tails, fin-like hands, and horned heads.

She sat upright, admiring the way the torchlight reflecting from the pools bounced off their scales, creating prisms of color. "You look like swamp monsters."

"We are." Ladon chuckled, then dove head first into the pool.

Draque splashed her with his tail. "You don't get to be the only one with a tail."

She watched with envy while they played, their laughter echoing through the cavern as they worked their way deeper into the pool. Then all three of them disappeared in a maelstrom of bubbles. She waited several minutes for their return. Jumping to her feet, she scanned the water. The beautiful rainbow colors were only on the surface. Below was an inkiness that appeared to have no limits. What if something happened to them? They didn't have gills. How could they hold their breath so long? Pacing, she chewed her nails, sick with worry.

A solitary bubble popped on the surface, followed by another and another.

Draque sprang into sight, blowing out a stream of water and shaking droplets from his head. "You sure you don't want to come in?" he asked with a wink as his brothers popped up around him.

Hands on her hips, she scowled, unable to keep the tremors from her voice. "What took you so long? I thought something happened to you."

"We're fine. There's a whole new world down there. We were just exploring."

They were trying to tempt her but why? Was it that important they see her ugly tail?

"Come on, Serah." Ladon splashed her legs.

She frowned at her wet denim, feeling her skin tingle. *You want to release me, Serah,* Thelix said. *Why fight it?*

She wondered the same thing. Just because her grandfather had said siren tails were ugly didn't mean everyone thought so. She remembered her carefree days as a siren, how fast she could dart through the water, her hair fanned out behind her, tickling her bare back. She wanted to swim again.

ACADEMY FOR MISFIT WITCHES   103

Before she lost her nerve, she unzipped her jeans and tossed them on the rock shelf behind her, ignoring the appreciative whistles coming from the dragons. If they wanted her to become a siren, so be it. If they thought she looked unattractive, at least she'd know where she stood with them.

After stripping off all her clothes and checking to make sure her earrings were secure, she walked naked into the water, looking boldly into her lovers' eyes while they gaped at her breasts.

"Careful of the drop-off," Ladon said, holding out a hand to her.

She thanked him and slid off the ledge, her feet disappearing into the dark water. She treaded water, wrapping her arms around his neck.

When his scales chafed her skin, she knew she was being foolish. Releasing him, she swam backward and summoned the change. Her skin burned at first, and she cried out as her bones ground together before snapping and fusing. The shift was slow and agonizing, like learning all over again how to ride a broom, but by the time it was finished, her legs had transformed into a powerful aquamarine tail and her sides had sprouted gills. The rest of her upper half remained unchanged.

Giggling, she dove under the water, delighting in their protests when she hit them with a powerful wave. Her siren eyes saw three pairs of human-like legs and three dragon tails that acted as rudders. Their strokes were awkward and choppy. Clearly these dragons weren't meant for swimming, but they'd brought her here anyway. She dove deep until she saw a pinprick of light, her lovers following her, pulled toward the light by a current. She glimpsed a beautiful underwater world of colorful plants and creatures and heard someone call her name. Teju had fashioned another bubble, and he and his brothers were inside it. She swam toward them, and Ladon pulled her through the wall. She shifted to human form, and he draped a towel around her shoulders. Suddenly self-conscious, she noticed the brothers had transformed into humans and were wearing swim trunks, she wrapped the towel around her naked body.

This bubble was much smaller than the one she'd spent the night in for detention, set up like a day camp with a few folding chairs and an ice chest stocked with beer and sodas. Ladon handed her a grape soda, and she sat in a low folding chair meant for a sandy beach, praying the metal didn't pop the bubble when her weight dipped the chair.

Their transport carried them through a dark river of deep purple bubbles under the lake. Other than bubbles, there wasn't much of a view.

"Keep watching," Ladon whispered, sitting beside her. "It gets better."

A thrill coursed through her when he placed his damp hand on hers. She loved having him near. He was such a comforting presence.

The bubbles changed from a dark purple to violet and then lavender as light reflected off the current. She blinked hard when a tiny being no bigger than her palm attached itself to their bubble, two little eyes staring at her while its curved body pulsed violet and aqua and green. Another creature followed suit, and then more, until the entire bubble was lit up in blinking colors.

"What are those?" she asked Ladon.

"Sea sprites," he answered. "Didn't you have those in Siren's Cove?"

"No." She crawled off her chair and pressed her palms to the bubble wall, laughing when the creatures' buzzing bodies tickled her skin.

"We're about to land," Teju said, latching onto her arm. "Get ready."

"For what?" she asked, then gulped when they hit something solid and she bounced into Teju's arms. She panicked when the bubble began filling with water. "What do I do?"

"Don't worry," he said with a wink. "I've got you."

The bottom fell out from under them, and she sucked in a mouthful of salty water. Salt water? Had they traveled to the ocean?

She shifted, this time much faster than the last, and propelled upward, holding Teju's hand. He'd shifted into a half-dragon creature. They swam until they breached the surface.

They landed in a cove with a beautiful beach nestled beneath a rocky overhang, its wide shelf casting a curved shadow over the white sand. Behind them was an endless sea of undulating turquoise water. The ocean. She breathed in deeply, filling her lungs with the familiar scents of seaweed and salt. She hadn't tasted the sea on her lips or felt the ocean breeze ruffle her hair in three years, and she was long overdue.

Balancing above the water with her powerful tail, she frowned when Ladon and Draque surfaced beside their brother, all having shifted back into their human skins.

"Don't you like your tails?" she asked them.

Draque climbed on a rock, standing waist deep in the water. "We don't need them."

"But you can keep yours," Ladon said, shaking droplets from his hair as he sat beside his brother. "It's far prettier than ours."

"Thanks." She feigned indifference, afraid to let him see how much his praise meant to her. "It's just a tail." She circled the rock, careful not to scrape her tail against the colorful coral.

"It's a magnificent tail," Draque said.

Her breath caught in her throat. The intensity in his eyes was enough to make her bones turn as soft as seaweed.

A wave of pheromones washed over her as she looked at him with heavy-lidded eyes. "Thank you."

Did they really think her tail pretty? Grandfather had said it was unsightly, that it was unnatural for witches to grow tails. These brothers didn't seem to mind that she was both witch and shifter. In fact they appeared fascinated by her.

"Where are we?" she asked.

"Some people call this place the end of the earth." Ladon smiled. "We call it heaven."

The blood in her veins turned to ice. They'd called Siren's Cove the end of the earth. How close were they to her family?

"The sea smells familiar. A-are we near Siren's Cove?"

Teju climbed onto the rock. "Siren's Cove is a few hundred miles that way." He pointed.

She scowled, narrowing her eyes on the line of water that disappeared beyond her line of sight. Could her family swim hundreds of miles? She'd been the only siren to leave the cove in centuries.

"They can't hurt you here, Serah," Draque said, twin storms brewing in his eyes, "and if they tried, we'd burn them to crisps."

She swallowed back the lump of emotion that had lodged in her throat. "Thank you. I hope it would never come to that." Despite how badly her family had hurt her, she never wanted to see them harmed.

Ladon slipped back into the water, cupping her chin in his strong hand. "We know."

Her heart melted when he kissed the tip of her nose. Her siren purred as she wrapped her arms around him, nuzzling his neck. She wanted to make love to him and to his brothers, too.

She swam beside them as they traversed several rocks that acted as a bridge across the lagoon. When they reached the shallow end of the cove, she shifted back into human form.

Teju smirked. "You don't have to shift yet if you don't want to."

She froze at that. Did she want to remain a mermaid?

Yes, yes, you do! Thelix cried.

She flopped back into the water and swam in the cove, exploring every coral structure and petting as many sea sprites as she could. She discovered right away they liked to nibble bright yellow leaves from an odd looking fern that grew in the ocean. The sprites had human eyes and long, flowing hair, but long snouts and mermaid tails. They were silly looking but so adorable, she wanted to take them all home. Even more amazing was how trusting they were, following her as if they were ducklings and she was their mother.

Every so often she stopped to watch her lovers sunning on the shore, but they just let her be her, Serah the Siren, who until that moment hadn't realized how much she'd missed her tail.

This is where you belong, Thelix said, her gentle tone a sharp contrast to her usual snark.

I can't stay in this cove forever, she answered, her libido awakening when she swam close enough to catch their strong, masculine scent.

Not in the cove, Thelix chided. *With your dragons.*

Her heart thumped. "My dragons?" she whispered to herself. If only.

BY THE TIME SHE SURFACED, the sun was hanging low in the sky, and her dragons had built a campfire. She watched them from afar, her stomach rumbling at the scent of roasting meat.

After swimming to shore and shifting back, she was greeted by Ladon, who draped her with a large towel, kissing her shoulder. The feel of his lips on her skin made her siren moan in delight. Mouthing her thanks, she wrapped the towel around herself, tucking it securely by her breasts, and squeezed salt water from her hair.

"What are you cooking?" she asked.

"Salamin." Ladon nodded at a net filled with flapping fish.

"Mmm." She licked her lips. "My favorite." She'd been so consumed in exploring the cove, she hadn't even noticed they'd been fishing.

Sitting in a low folding chair, she warmed her feet by the fire and drank another grape soda, thanking Teju when he handed her a large filet on a wicker mat. It was delicious, the pink meat seasoned with the perfect amount of sea salt and lime. As the sun dipped behind the horizon, Draque stoked the fire with his dragon's breath.

Ladon nudged her, pointing to the lagoon. "Look."

She gasped when she saw the water was awash in millions of multicolored lights.

"The sea sprites are saying good night." He grinned. "They must really like you."

She was unable to keep the awe from her voice. "This place is magical."

Taking her hand in his, he brushed his lips across her knuckles. "Because you're in it."

"More fish, Serah?" Teju asked.

She patted her stomach and smiled. "No thanks. I'm full. It was delicious."

"I'm glad you liked it." He brushed a wayward strand of hair behind her ear, his gaze lingering on her lips.

Her heart hammered out a staccato she felt all the way to her toes. She caught Draque's eye; he was staring at her so intensely, it was hard not to look away.

When he stood and circled the fire, coming toward her, she fidgeted with the frayed end of her mat.

"Serah." His voice was a hoarse whisper as he gently pried the mat from her hands.

She didn't want to look at him. It would be her undoing. Her heart was still raw from their fight earlier.

Do it! her siren cried.

"Yes?" Against her better judgment, she looked into his eyes, and then she was undone. The longing in his eyes nearly took her breath away.

"Did you enjoy your swim?"

Her tongue felt weighted as she fought to find words. "I-I did."

He flashed a devastatingly sexy smile. "You should do it more often."

She turned up her chin while clenching her fists tight, praying he couldn't hear her racing heart. "Maybe I will."

"We enjoyed watching you from shore." He bit his lip, leering at her from beneath thick lashes. "We wanted to go in with you, but we thought you needed some time to get reacquainted with your siren."

She swore her heart did a backflip. "I did. Thanks."

How awesome were these guys that they could sense what she wanted? For too long she'd repressed her desires.

His dazzling eyes darkened, then turned bright gold, human irises becoming dragon-shaped. "Everything about you is beautiful, and don't let anyone tell you otherwise."

She nodded and felt strong emotion. For three years she'd longed to hear those words. Not even Prometheus had admired her siren. He'd agreed with her grandfather, that she needed to be locked away. After swallowing back her emotion, she finally found her words. "Thank you for bringing me here."

Still holding her hand, he gently stroked the back of her wrist, the simple gesture enough to make her heart pound wildly. "We're happy to share it with you."

Teju knelt beside her, placing a hand on her knee. "We hope we can share it with you more often."

She smiled. "I'd like that."

Did this mean they still wanted her to be their girl? She wanted these three amazing shifters as her boyfriends, consequences be damned.

"We can't let you go back, Serah." Draque squeezed her wrist.

Ladon said, "We want you to stay with us, where we know you'll be safe."

"I haven't graduated yet. I need to find another school."

"We can homeschool." Draque glanced at Teju. "Our brother knows as much as most professors."

He's an expert at licking pussy, too, Thelix growled.

Serah wished circumstances had been different, that her grandfather didn't despise shifters so much. "I'll be disinherited if I don't get a real diploma."

Draque flinched and released her. "Does the money mean that much to you?" he snapped, and she heard the dragon.

He acted as if it would be easy to walk away from her life. She absently fingered an earring. "It means security. I only need a few more months of school to graduate."

"The money means nothing to us," Ladon said, squeezing her hand. "Your safety is all that matters."

She thought about her grandfather's dire warning. She'd almost been disinherited after her affair with the professor. She'd given her heart to him and what had it gotten her? He easily turned his back on her when she'd needed him most. And what about how cold her dragon princes had been to her just that morning, after they'd discovered she was the Goldenwand Heiress?

Unable to stand the plea in their eyes, she shook off Ladon, and grabbed her grape soda from the cup holder, playing with the metal tab. "I'm afraid, especially after the way I've been burned."

"By the professor?" Ladon asked.

She nodded. It had only been a week since they'd been caught and her world had imploded. "He had me convinced he was in love with me. It was a lie. He didn't even fight for us."

Draque stood, towering over her while steam poured out of his nose. "He was a fool."

"He took advantage of you," Teju said, pity in his eyes.

Thelix swore. Serah wanted them to understand her hesitation, and she didn't want their pity.

"Look at me." Ladon pried the soda can out of her fingers and squeezed her hands. "We would never take advantage of you. We love you."

It was as if time stood still. It took her several stuttering heartbeats to finally find her voice. "You love me, Ladon? You've only known me twenty-four hours."

He placed a hand on his warm, bare chest. "My heart beats for you. It always has. I can feel it when we touch."

She was sorely tempted to melt into him and get lost in his golden eyes, but his love for her was based on a lie. "It's my siren pheromones."

"No, it's you, Serah." Eyes flashing with alarm, he pulled her closer. "It's your pure heart."

She wanted to believe him, but it had to be the pheromones, and there was her grandfather—.

Fuck him, Thelix growled. *He tried to kill you, for Goddess's sake.*

She wasn't about to argue with Thelix, too. Nobody knew who'd tried to kill her, and she refused to blame him without all the facts.

She touched Ladon's cheek, breath mingling. He smelled of barley and salted fish. She longed to kiss him, but she was painfully reminded they weren't alone. His brothers' eyes were boring holes into her. "You're sweet, Ladon, but your brothers are suspiciously silent." She shot them a look.

His mouth hitched in an impish grin. "They don't like to show their emotions."

"It's true we aren't good about showing feelings," Teju said, inching closer. "Draque more than me."

Casting a furtive glance at Draque, she bit back a sarcastic retort. Dragons afraid to show their feelings? What a load of troll dung. It was clear they wanted to get laid and were doing a bad job of talking her into it.

"We have tender feelings for you," Draque said, grazing her cheek with calloused knuckles. "But our fathers raised us to be fierce."

She couldn't deny his touch did something to her insides. "Then why do you kiss me so passionately?"

His cheeks flushed as red as molten lava. "Because we want you." Draque answered, tracing her lip with the pad of his thumb.

Take him, Serah! Thelix screamed. *Take him now!*

Her siren's lust took over all reason. She tried to fight it, to no avail. She scooted out of her chair, letting the towel fall to the sand and straddled him. She searched his expression for any sign of deceit. "So is desire all you feel for me?" she asked, her sultry siren voice taking over.

Damn that siren! That's not what she'd wanted to ask him. Why would she goad him into confessing his love when their relationship would never work?

His golden eyes shone with such intensity, she felt ravaged. "We feel more for you than just desire."

Cupping the back of his head, she pressed his mouth to her breast and murmured against his ear. "Tell me what you feel."

Chuckling, he swirled his tongue around her nipple. "You're determined to wrap us around your finger, aren't you?"

Her pussy clenched in response, leaving moisture across his skin as she rubbed against his thigh. "Perhaps your lust for me is clouding your hearts. Perhaps we should put some distance between us."

Roaring, she broke her siren's hold on her and slipped out of his arms. When he lunged for her, she retreated to the water.

"Don't go!" the brothers simultaneously hollered.

Water was lapping at her ankles when Draque grabbed her around the waist and turned her in his arms. The air was knocked from her lungs when she spun against Draque's chest. Bodies melded together, they tumbled into the soft sand, his lips on hers, his hands branding every inch of her.

"No." She broke the kiss, chest heaving. "You need to focus on what I mean to you."

"You mean the sun, the stars, and the heavens in all five realms." He showered her neck and breasts with kisses. "Is that enough of a declaration of love?"

Yes! It was enough! Great Goddess, what had she done?

She tried to push him away. "I can't tell if it's your heart speaking or that stiff protrusion between your legs."

"Both," he rumbled in her ear.

"Oh, Draque," she cried, Thelix spreading her legs for her. He buried his thick shaft inside her heat.

They fucked hard, desperation growing as she dug her nails into his back. Sea foam washed over them. When he planted a bruising kiss on her lips, Thelix wouldn't let her delay her pleasure; she fought for that pinnacle, that pulsing place of ecstacy that glowed brighter with each thrust.

She cried his name when her orgasm hit. It pounded through her, unraveling her last thread of sanity. She lifted her legs higher, and he poured himself into her, a look between pleasure and pain etched across his frozen features.

After several glorious aftershocks, he kissed her tenderly, stroking her hair. She giggled, the foamy waves tickling her sensitive skin.

When he pulled out, she reached for him, begging him not to go. But Teju took his place, sliding inside her and filling the void his brother had left. He made love to her with much more tenderness, reaching between them to stroke her swollen bud while plunging into her with choppy thrusts. It didn't take him long to build her next orgasm, awakening nerve endings she didn't even know she'd had. He rubbed her tight peak into a frenzy until all she could think about was falling off that glorious edge again. After they finished, he rolled off and took her in his arms, kissing her earlobe while the surf washed over them. "If you want to know how I feel about you," he murmured, nibbling her lobe, "I have more tenderness for you than a thousand orgasms and a million kisses."

When Ladon sat beside them, she gave Teju a last lingering kiss and turned to him. Wrapping her legs around Ladon's waist, she sat astride him.

He stroked her hips and her waist before settling his large hands on her breasts, massaging each globe. Groaning, she threw back her head when he pinched each nipple, then rolled them. She slid down his cock, sheathing him to the root, and ground against him while he dug his fingers into her ass. Their lovemaking was sweet at first, tender and gentle like the waves lapping at their feet. But soon they picked up the tempo, emitting joyous sounds as she road him hard. Orgasm washed over her like a rogue wave, holding her captive to its strength. After he came, she fell on top of him with a shuddering breath.

"Can't you tell when we make love how we feel about you?" he murmured.

She froze at that. Did they really love her? Oh, Goddess, what was she to do?

She rested her cheek against his heart, afraid to look him in the eyes. "Yes," she said curtly, then closed her eyes, hoping he didn't pick up on her tension.

This was all happening so fast, it made her head spin. She didn't have to do much soul-searching to know if she was falling for them, too. She was. Hard. And therein lay the problem. She was afraid the fall wouldn't just break her heart, it would shatter it to pieces.

Chapter Eleven

Penelope Pixiefeather Pratt glared at the detective who stood in the doorway, his bowler hat dripping, his thick, walrus moustache drooping over his lips like a limp squirrel.

He frowned at the storm clouds overhead. "I'm cold. May I please come in?"

"I'm sorry." Her smile was aloof and unwelcoming. "Mr. Goldenwand cannot be disturbed. He's mourning the loss of his only grandchild."

The detective removed his hat, revealing a bald head that shone like a marble, with the exception of a small tuft of black hair sprouting from the top of his head like a clump of crabgrass. He wrung the sopping hat over the doormat. "He's going to want to hear this."

"Again," she said haughtily, "he cannot be bothered." She started to close the door.

He threw his arm out, blocking it. "It's about his granddaughter."

She pushed on the door until he cried out. "Again, I will take a message."

"Miss Pratt, his granddaughter lives." He stuck his head in. "She was rescued by the Firesbreath princes."

"What?" Her jaw dropped. This couldn't be. She forced a smile, speaking through frozen features. "Oh, how wonderful. Tell me more."

"I've said enough." He slipped his head out of the doorway with a curse. "I'm speaking to Nathaniel Goldenwand from here on out."

"Very well then," she spat, slamming the door on him.

Ignoring his loud cursing and pounding on the door, she flew straight to Nathaniel's office. Pausing at the door, she released a shaky breath, fearing she'd be the object of his anger once she relayed the news. But he had to know. She tapped on the door, her insides churning while awaiting his response.

"Come in," he called.

Her wings buzzed so hard, her insides rattled. She tried to be gentle opening the door, but she ended up tumbling into the room. She sucked in a sharp breath at the throbbing in her shin when she struck the back of a brocade chair.

Nathaniel Goldenwand sat behind his morning paper, no doubt reading about his granddaughter's demise. The headline read, *Goldenwand Heiress Presumed Dead After Fiery School Massacre.*

"Forgive me, sir," she squeaked in fear, "but a detective was at the door."

He set down his paper, snarling like a were-bear waking up from slumber too soon, but it didn't detract from his handsome features. He had a pointed chin and turned up nose, making him look part fae, but his eyes were his most beautiful feature, wide and gray with flecks of violet. Though she suspected his hair had turned gray ages ago, he kept it black and slicked back, tied in a queue at his nape. He kept his thin black moustache well oiled and trimmed, and he was tall and lean, far more fit than men half his age. Penelope soaked in his beauty like he was manna for her eyes. If only he admired her the same way.

"Well? What did he want?"

Ever the polished gentleman, he was careful not to spill as he took a dainty sip from a porcelain teacup, his pale pinky turned up. If Penelope had such refined manners, perhaps Nathaniel would take her seriously as a lover.

All moisture evaporated from her mouth as she summoned the courage to speak. "Your granddaughter lives."

He jumped from his chair, spilling tea across his desk and soaking the morning paper. "Who saved her?"

She swallowed back a lump of fear, fluttering back. "The dragon princes."

He shook with rage. "If she slept with them, so help me goddess."

"I don't have the details yet," she said, the words tumbling out of her mouth like they'd tripped over her tongue.

His handsome features twisting, he threw the saucer at her. She ducked, yelping and wincing when it clipped her wing and shattered against the wall behind her.

"What did the detective say to you?" he demanded.

She willed her hands to stop trembling. "Not much."

"Did you give him time to speak?"

When he pulled a wand from his pocket, her wings skipped a beat, and she flew back into a bookcase, knocking several dusty tomes to the floor.

"No, but it doesn't matter." She forced a note of confidence into her voice. "My spies will be reporting within the hour."

She fluttered to the other side of the room when he waved the wand at her feet. The old books flew back to their spot on the shelf.

"I would've liked to know if Serah is injured and her whereabouts." His voice dropped to such a low, menacing whisper, she had to strain to hear him. That's when she knew she was in deep troll dung. He never whispered unless he was furious.

Her heart pounded so loudly in her ears, it drowned out the sound made by the rapid beating of her wings. "I don't know if she's injured," she rasped, "but I can guarantee they took her to The Grotto."

His eyes shifted from gray to inky black. "She's their prisoner!"

"I-I'm not sure," she cried, flattening against the wall, then falling on her ass when her wings drooped.

"She is!" He banged the chair beside her with his wand, sparks flying and setting the heavy emerald curtains framing the oak windowseat on fire.

The blackness in his eyes seeped into his skin, dripping down his cheeks like ink spilling from a well. "I will raze that rat-infested slum until every last dragon's fire has been extinguished."

SERAH CLUNG TIGHTLY to Ladon's neck, resting on top of him while the sea foam tickled their legs. Loathe though she was to leave the safety of his arms, they had to get back. Reluctantly she sat up, ignoring his erection poking her buttocks. "We should go. Your fathers might have news."

"Wait." He sat up and shared wide-eyed looks with his brothers, and she knew they were speaking telepathically.

"Hey!" She swatted him. "No secrets."

Teju knelt beside her, drawing a heart in the sand. "We want you to be ours for all eternity."

Her hand flew to her throat and her heart skipped a beat. "You mean that?"

Legs braced apart, Draque stood above her, blocking the setting sun. "Yes." His voice was as rough as sandpaper. He turned away, giving her a glimpse of a strong, determined jaw.

She squinted at him, wondering why it looked like he was hiding something. "I'll think about it."

"How long will you think?" He balled his hands into fists.

"I didn't know my heart was on a deadline," she snapped. The guy was on edge, but why? His brothers eyed her expectantly. Jeez. They'd just met!

"We want you, Serah. But more than that, we want to keep you safe. We can't lose you to that madman."

She groaned. "Why do you insist my grandfather is guilty before giving him a chance to explain?"

He has never been loving to you, Serah, and he loathes me, Thelix said.

Hating the truth that rang in her siren's words, she flinched and didn't respond.

"He will send for you when he finds out you're with us," Draque said. "He may have already done so."

"Which is why I need to get back." Jumping to her feet, she brushed sand off her legs, wriggling uncomfortably when she felt the tiny, abrasive grains chafing her crotch. Damn, she suddenly remembered why she didn't like beach sex. She stomped into the water to shift and swim back to The Grotto and hopefully wash out the sand.

Draque jerked her toward him. "Serah, don't pull away from us."

Breath *swooshed* from her lungs. His bare chest, solid and warmed by the sun, enticed her senses. His scent enveloped her, a mix of musk, sulfur, and sea salt that set her pheromones on high alert. Why did he have to be so virile and tempting? "I'm not pulling away."

Liar, Thelix jeered.

He traced a path down her cheek with calloused knuckles, his voice dropping to a sultry whisper. "You are."

Forcing herself to ignore her siren's lust, she turned up her chin. "I'm going to hear him out. It's the least I can do after all he's done for me. Then I will make my decision."

Draque's eyes shifted to brilliant gold, his voice dropping to a dragon's rumble. "He'll turn you against us."

There was no use arguing. "He'll try."

He caved inward, like a dam breaking under a deluge. "He'll make you choose."

Her heart fell, and she turned away. "I know."

PENELOPE FLEW INTO her office so angry, she saw stars. Prometheus had a lot of nerve, sitting in her chair with his boots propped on her desk as if he was the semis-wizard in charge.

"Where in Hades name have you been?" she shrieked, wings angrily flapping as she hovered over him.

He picked up a quill from her desk and twirled it between long, slender fingers. "Interrogating."

"Interrogating whom?"

He looked at her coolly, dismissively, as if they'd never been lovers. "None of your business."

She kicked a roll of tape into his lap and dropped to the desktop. "You do realize I'm the semis-wizard?"

"I don't give a damn what you are." He picked grime from under his fingernails.

That pigheaded prick!

She impatiently tapped her foot. "The bitch lives! Saved by the dragon princes."

"I know."

Falling to her knees, she shot him a glare, trying to intimidate him. "Tell me what else you know."

"I know that the elder dragon princes are working for the resistance," he drawled, not appearing fazed in the slightest when she leaned into him.

"Everyone knows that."

"I also know they've kidnapped Dame Doublewart, who's disguised herself as Serah."

She startled, accidentally tipping an ink well. "What?"

"I figured it was too complex for you to follow." He snickered. "We have the leader of the resistance in our custody. The elder princes have been cut off from communication."

Scowling at the growing blob of ink that seeped into her papers, she zapped it with her wand before it caused any more destruction. "And?"

He leaned back in her chair, casually folding his arms behind his head. "And when they panic, they'll reveal their location."

She wished she could zap that smug expression off his face, but he was quicker with a wand and she feared retaliation. "What does this have to do with the heiress?"

Thunderclouds darkened his eyes. "We don't need to kill the heiress to declare war. We can kill a dragon prince, and the kings will retaliate."

Her jaw dropped. "How are you going to kill a dragon?"

He patted her hand as if he was comforting a child. "You let me worry about that."

Her breath caught in her throat. "Don't tell me you'll use the unbreakable curse."

"Why not?" He chuckled. "You did."

"Not directly." She vehemently shook her head, her wings buzzing like rabid bees. "I activated Hestia's wand." Which meant that the drunk godmother would take the blame, not her.

He shrugged. "Same difference."

Gasping, she clutched her throat. "If you use the unbreakable curse, you'll be executed."

He shrugged. "Not for killing a dragon."

"You go too far," she breathed.

Shadows fell across his handsome features. "And you don't go far enough."

THE TRIP BACK TO THE underground cavern was awkward, to say the least. They traveled in silence, tension thick inside their bubble. When it popped to the surface of the water, she stood in the shallow pool up to her knees, taking in air as if she'd been suffocating.

Ugh. She'd been so used to the fresh sea air, she'd forgotten The Grotto smelled like sulfur. It had to be dragon breath. Serah wondered if she could ever get used to living with such a stink.

Ignoring her grumbling lovers, she trudged forward, staring at Draque's wet, black hair plastered against tanned muscular shoulders and wishing he wasn't so beautiful.

When Draque swore, kicking up water, Serah noticed Katherine was waiting for them on the shallow ledge surrounding the pool. She wore an odd smile that appeared to be mixed with a snarl. Either that or the act of smiling was too painful. Her clothes, or lack thereof, was what was most disturbing about her appearance. Her bottoms barely covered her skanky crotch and her top, if you could call it that, was like a giant rubber band wrapped around her tits, barely covering her nipples. This revealing attire was meant for seduction, and by the way Katherine's heated gaze centered on Serah's mates, it was clear they were the objects of her desire. No, wait. Not her mates. Not yet. She still hadn't decided.

They are your mates, Thelix said. *I've decided.*

Serah ignored her siren. She only had enough patience to handle one adversary at the moment. Clenching her fists until nails broke skin, she released an aggravated sigh. When Ladon tried to block her view, she went around him with a huff. She didn't need him treating her like a fragile flower. She could handle Katherine. At least she hoped she could.

"What are you doing here?" Draque snarled at the she-bitch.

Serah inwardly smiled at his tone. It was clear he didn't care for Katherine. *She is not as beautiful as you,* Thelix said, *and I'm not just talking about outward appearance. Her soul is rotten.*

For once Serah agreed with her siren.

Katherine appeared undaunted by Draque's rebuke. "I have come to apologize for my behavior earlier."

"Apology accepted," Teju said through clenched teeth. "Now please leave."

Katherine's eyes momentarily widened, then narrowed before she flashed a wicked grin. "You know...." She tossed a cursory glance at Serah. "Only shifters are allowed in The Grotto?"

Ladon said, "We know that."

She waved dismissively at Serah. "And yet you bring this witch here."

"You know damn well she's a shifter." Draque's voice dropped to a predatory rumble. "The portals are enchanted to prevent non-shifters from passing
through."

Katherine thoughtfully tapped her chin. "She might be a witch, but there
are rumors she is also part siren."

Teju waved a fist in her face. "So what's your point?"

She didn't even flinch. "My point is that she can use her voice to control
you, even make you fall in love with her."

"Go away, Katherine." Ladon shooed her off, then mouthed an apology to
Serah.

"Fine," Katherine said, tossing her shimmering, pale hair over her shoulders. "But don't say I didn't warn you. I'm only trying to stop you from getting
stuck in a doomed marriage."

Serah was affronted. "We're not getting married."

Uh oh, Thelix mumbled.

"That's not what the dragon kings say." Katherine let out a grating laugh.
"They say you *must* marry their sons."

Panic swept through her. "I'm not marrying anyone against my will." She
shot her lovers an accusatory look, not at all soothed when they averted their
gazes. Was that why they'd romanced her all day? Pressured her to be their girl?

"Against your will?" Katherine squawked like a predatory bird on the hunt.
"Do you not realize the honor the kings have bestowed on you?" She looked
Serah up and down, making a disgusted face. "You should be grateful they'd al-
low a Goldenwand to marry their sons."

That fucking bird bitch! Thelix shrieked.

"Oh, please." Serah cocked a hand on her hip, attitude locked and loaded.
"I'm the heiress to the largest fortune in all four realms."

"Five realms," Draque corrected automatically.

She eyed him with a snarl. "I'm not marrying you."

He turned to Katherine. "Why would you tell her she has to marry us? It
was not your place."

"I thought she knew." Katherine pouted.

Liar, Thelix said again.

Teju pointed at her. "You came to cause trouble."

In a bold move, Katherine grabbed his finger, gripping it in a curved hand that looked like a claw. "How can you marry someone who won't even acknowledge our realm?"

"Oh, trust me, I acknowledge it," Serah said, crossing her arms. "Just not as a realm. A real realm doesn't smell like Satan's sweaty armpit."

When Ladon turned to her with a wounded look in his eyes, her heart plummeted. She hadn't meant to hurt him, but she was angry and frustrated.

"This is our home you're slandering," Ladon whispered.

Katherine squawked again, flapping her arms as if they were wings. "I told you she's not a good match."

"Katherine, you've caused enough trouble for one day." Draque pointed to the darkened tunnel behind them, his voice a threatening rumble that rolled through Serah's head like a steam train. "Leave us with our mate."

Katherine huffed and spun around, sashaying away with an exaggerated swing of her hips.

What a skank, Thelix gleefully observed.

That's for sure, Serah said, realizing she was agreeing with her siren a lot more often of late.

Chapter Twelve

"Serah!" Draque and his brothers followed her through the maze of tunnels.

She'd taken too many wrong turns to count, but she refused to walk with them. When Draque latched onto her elbow, she angrily pulled away.

Stop fighting them, Thelix pleaded. *This is what you want.*

She made the mistake of looking into Draque's face. His cheeks were as red as the lava from Mt. Olion. "Serah," he groaned, dragging a hand through his thick beard. "We're walking in circles. You have no idea where you're going."

She crossed her arms, impatiently tapping her foot. "I'm not marrying you."

Teju caught up to them, panting rings of smoke. "Would you please just listen to reason?"

Ladon joined his brothers. The look in his eyes broke Serah's heart all over again. "Our marriage could prevent war between the witches and the shifters."

"Or start one."

Would it be so bad being married to three gorgeous dragon princes who shower you with affection and endless orgasms? Thelix asked.

"War is inevitable." Teju gave her a know-it-all look. "Your grandfather will be under pressure to back off if you are with us."

Yeah, right. Grandfather never backed down from anything. "You seriously think that?"

"At least he won't make another attempt on your life." Ladon grasped her shoulders. "You'll be safe with us."

Unable to withstand Ladon's pleading eyes a moment longer, she gazed at her feet, then grimaced when the smell of sulfur hit her again. "What makes you think I want to spend the rest of my life in The Grotto?"

She hated having hurt them by insulting their beloved realm. Other than the smell, the strange creatures with hair as thick as twine growing out of their ears, and of course her lovers' evil, jealous admirer, this place wasn't too bad.

"You won't *have* a life if you go back up there." Draque closed in on her, speaking in a soothing baritone as he cupped her chin. "You're nothing but a pawn to Nathaniel Goldenwand. He tried to murder you and frame us."

Great fucking goddess, not this again. She jerked away from him so fast, she nearly tripped over her own feet. "I'm not listening to you anymore. You're like a broken record. I get it—my grandfather's an asshole!" She marched down the tunnel, not caring if she was going in the wrong direction. Her need to get away from them was too great for her to care.

She stumbled and then stopped when a roar behind her shook the cave walls. She turned around in time to see Draque shift into the monstrous creature he'd been in the water—part human, part dragon, and scary as fuck with his glowing golden eyes focused on her.

"I give up!" he said with a deep growl and pointed a talon at her. "You're the most foolish, hardheaded girl I've ever known."

"Draque, calm down," Ladon said, reaching for him.

Draque shook off his brother with another rock-shattering roar. Serah could barely think over that and the din of her pounding heart.

After two giant wings sprouted from Draque's back, she ran. She'd only made it a few steps when the powerful beating of his wings above her nearly knocked her to the ground.

She screamed when his clawed fingers dug into her armpits and lifted her off the ground. "You asshole!" She thrashed, but he only tightened his grip. "You can't force me!"

He spun her around so fast, her head whirled. They flew through the tunnel at breakneck speed, then up into a drafty cavern, ascending so high she couldn't see the ground.

She screamed when he released her and then tossed her like a doll in the air. She landed in his arms, terror freezing her limbs as she looked into eyes that shone like twin suns.

"You're ours!" he boomed.

Powerless, and too frightened to use her siren's voice, she could do nothing to stop him. Even mouthy Thelix had gone silent.

There was a burst of fire over Draque's shoulder; his brothers had also transformed into dragon hybrids and were following them, eyes glowing unnaturally bright.

Well, holy fuck. So this is what happened when you pissed off dragons.

HECTOR FIRESBREATH paced the worn fur rug before the hearth of the secret cave he shared with his brothers, impatiently waiting for a message from the resistance. Tired of being stuck in a cramped cavern, he and his brothers had shifted into their human skins.

"How long must we wait?" brother Thaddeus asked, his long, dark hair hanging over his eyes while he shoveled pizza in his mouth. Yeah, he looked real worried.

"Until they send for us," Hector grumbled. Why had they agreed to kidnap the heiress? Supposedly she was the key to preventing war, but Hector worried this plan would have the opposite effect.

"We should've heard something by now," Bastian said, He leaned against the cave wall, crushing an empty beer can in his hand and blowing smoke rings out of his nose.

"Patience." Hector heaved himself from his chair and peered through a slit in the wall, shoulders slumping when he saw nothing but a stray bird. "They don't want our communication traced."

Bastian glanced at the dark tunnel leading to their prisoner's cell. "She's being so quiet."

"I know." Thaddeus flashed a triumphant grin. "She's not even putting up a fight."

Alarm bells went off in Hector's head. The little siren had been a mouthy banshee during the entire flight. "Did you offer her any supper?" he asked Thaddeus.

"No." Thaddeus frowned. "It wasn't my turn to check on her."

"What do you mean, it wasn't your turn?" Hector snapped.

He pointed at Bastian. "He was supposed to take care of supper for her."

Bastian pushed off from the wall, throwing his empty beer can on the ground. "No, you were!"

A sick feeling soured Hector's gut. "Both of you shut up!" He glared at them. "When was the last time anyone checked on her?"

They shared anxious looks. "A few hours ago."

"Imbeciles!" Hector raced down the tunnel, his brothers following close behind.

His heart lurched when he saw the door was open. He nearly lost his supper when he noticed the cot was empty, and their prisoner's bindings were lying on the floor.

He screeched, furious, flames shooting out of his mouth and setting the bed ablaze.

Bastian grabbed a fire extinguisher and put out the fire.

The cold, gray stone walls of the cell were a stark reminder that he'd completely fucked up. "Where the hell is she?"

Thaddeus threw up his hands. "How would I know?"

Bastian threw the fire extinguisher on the bed and punched Thaddeus in the arm. "This is your fault!"

Thaddeus punched him back. "Don't blame me!"

When Bastian let out a roar, his eyes and nose shifting, Hector jumped between them. "Stop it! We need to find her."

"Sorry, bro. You're right," Thaddeus said. "She can't have gone far."

"There's an ocean outside, genius," Bastian rumbled. "She's long gone."

Fuck, he was right. She was a mermaid, after all. When Demona found out they'd lost the prisoner, she'd string them up by the balls.

Hector jumped when he heard a loud bang outside.

Thaddeus's eyes widened to saucers. "What's that?"

"Sounds like it's coming from the kitchen," Bastian said, running out of the cell with Thaddeus at his heels.

Hector followed more slowly, spouting obscenities. "Keep your guard up," he warned, but his brothers were long gone.

When he reached what they referred to as "the kitchen"—a small alcove with an ice chest, barbeque pit, and a few folding chairs—Hector had to do a double take. What was his high school headmistress doing in their secret lair, and how the fuck did she find them?

"Dame Doublewart?" Thaddeus rasped, sharing looks of horror with his brothers.

"You look surprised to see me." She searched the open ice chest. "Have you no butter?"

"No." Bastian's dark brows were scrunched in confusion. "What are you doing here?"

She flung a piece of moldy cheese on the ground. "'No, ma'am.'"

Bastian's tanned cheeks colored. "No, ma'am. What are you doing here?"

Standing, she arched a pencil-thin brow. "You tell me, and by the way, you're terrible hosts."

Hector scratched his head, puzzlement fogging his brain. "We don't follow."

Her hook nose twitched. "You brought me here."

Thaddeus's jaw dropped. "No, we didn't."

"Are you sure?" She flashed a condescending smirk, the same look she'd given them after announcing they'd have to spend every weekend of their last semester in the dungeon.

A twine noose tightened around Hector's spine and he felt like he'd been caught in some strange magical déjà vu spell. He certainly hoped not. He couldn't imagine any scenario where he'd long to see the woman who'd haunted his teenage nightmares.

"Positive," he said, though even he could hear the doubt in his words. Dame Doublewart had a habit of making him question every decision.

She turned her back on him, digging through the ice chest once more. "How can you have enough beer to hydrate an army and not a stick of butter?"

Hector shared a look of annoyance with his brothers.

"We have cooking oil," Thaddeus said.

"Oh, you boys. Was the food at my school so horrible you'd kill your tastebuds?"

"What are you making?" Bastian asked.

"Macaroni and cheese, since you don't have much else to eat."

"We have leftover pizza." Hector fidgeted with the watch in his pocket. "Do you want some?"

"Please." Before Hector could send him for it, Bastian was already marching to their modest sitting room. Luckily, Thaddeus had gone for pizza earlier before joining them in their secret lair. Which apparently wasn't so secret after all. They were down to the last box, and a good thing, too, because they were going to have to abandon the cave soon anyway. As soon as they got rid of the headmistress from hell, of course.

When Bastian returned with box of half-eaten, cold pizza, Dame Double-wart snatched a slice from him, sat in a folding chair, and bit into it with a groan, acting as if she hadn't eaten in a week.

Again, Hector shared a puzzled look with his brothers.

"We're sorry, but we can't stay long," Hector said. "We're looking for some-one."

She looked at him as if he'd grown a second head. "Are you really that thick-headed?"

What the devil was she talking about?

"Beg your pardon?" Bastian said.

"Do you have any wine to wash down this cardboard?" She waved her half-eaten slice of pizza.

"Hang on." Thaddeus's hands shook as he dug through the cooler. He finally pulled out bottled water and handed it to her.

She glowered at the bottle as if it were poison. "No wine?"

"Sorry." Thaddeus colored. "We have beer."

"Yes, I know about the beer." She waved away the water. "Get me a mug then."

A mug? Thaddeus mouthed to Hector.

He shrugged. What did she expect? This wasn't a pub.

When Bastian offered her a disposable plastic cup out of a grocery bag, she clucked her tongue before accepting it. After Bastian handed her a longneck beer, she popped the top with her teeth and poured it into the cup.

Hector gave Bastian the side-eye. The longnecks were for special occasions, and the cans were for guests. Not that Doublewart was a guest. She hadn't even been invited. And why exactly was she here, anyway?

"Dame Doublewart." He nervously cleared his throat when she fixed him with that eagle-eyed stare. Damn, seven years out of school and she still un-nerved him. "Could you please tell us what's going on?" He tried not to sound annoyed that she'd crashed their party. He'd been raised to treat his elders with respect, even if they didn't deserve it.

She took a long swallow of beer before slamming it on the cave floor, the clanking sound ricocheting off the walls. "How did you dimwits get diplomas? I'm a djinn, remember? If memory serves me, your mother is a djinn, too."

"She is." Hector wondered how in fuck his mother had anything to do with this.

"And like me," she continued in that same condescending tone, "she can transform into any person."

The sharpness of her glare was so severe, he practically felt it piercing his chest.

"Yes, but—" He stopped mid-sentence when it hit him. Dame Doublewart had disguised herself as Seraphina Goldenwand, which meant they'd failed in their mission. What fools they'd been! He slapped his forehead, wishing instead he could bang it against a wall. "Aw, fuck!"

His brothers gave him blank stares, and he was annoyed with their stupidity. "She disguised herself as the fucking heiress," he snapped.

Flames lit in their dull eyes and they launched into a tirade of curses.

"Boys, boys!" The headmistress waved. "Enough with the language." She finished the beer and handed the empty bottle to Thaddeus. "It's okay. I understand the need to overthrow that tyrant. He's determined to war with the shifters. I can feel it in my bones."

Struck by a throbbing stress migraine, Hector slumped into a folding chair across from Doublewart, rubbing his aching temples. "We thought kidnapping Goldenwand's granddaughter would give us leverage."

Doublewart snorted. "Kidnapping his granddaughter is a surefire way to *start* a war. How do you think shifters will fare against an army of wizards armed with the latest wands?"

Hector couldn't find the right words to answer that question. They hadn't thought that far ahead.

A visible knot worked its way down Thaddeus's throat as he slumped into a chair beside Hector. "We were just following orders."

She gave them a pitying look. "You poor sorry idiots. Please don't tell me you're part of the resistance?"

"They are the only shifters willing to stand up to the witches," Hector said, but even he was doubting the sanity of the group's leaders. Why had they trusted him and his brothers with the task of kidnapping the heiress, and why hadn't they bothered to check in?

"They're reckless and dangerous, and the future kings of the shifter world should not be connected to a group of outlaws."

Great Goddess, she sounded like their parents. Hector hated to admit it, but maybe she was right.

Bastian hung his head. "We're sorry, ma'am."

Hector clenched his hands, claws extending and digging into his skin. He didn't know if he was angrier with himself for foolishly entangling his family with the resistance or at his brother for capitulating so easily.

"Really sorry," Thaddeus added earnestly.

Hector held his breath, afraid to release it lest he capitulate and apologize for wanting to save his species. Nathaniel Goldenwand was evil. Something had to be done about him. No good had come from his fathers continuously trying to make peace with the witches. Goldenwand had simply put more pressure on Parliament to restrict trade and commerce in The Grotto, reducing the shifters to beggars and thieves.

Dame Doublewart eyed Hector for a long, tense moment, her gaunt face making her look like a ghoul. She was obviously waiting for an apology.

Let her wait. She wasn't going to get one.

She caved first. "I'm only relieved you didn't take the true heiress. Can you imagine the consequences of such an action?"

"What do we do now?" Thaddeus begged, hanging on her every word like a pathetic puppy.

"Now you take me back to school. We will tell the authorities it was just a prank, and you will be punished accordingly."

"But we haven't received word from the resistance." Hector fought off panic.

She looked at him in astonishment. "Haven't you heard a word I've said?"

Hector wasn't quite sure he was prepared to take on Doublewart. "Yes, but—"

"Great Goddess!" she hollered, jumping to her feet and jabbing his chest. "If you three don't start acting like kings, shifters are all but doomed."

The dragon inside him sprang to life and demanded he bite off her head. Instead he hung his head, and some pathetic wimp said, "Sorry, ma'am."

OVERRIDDEN WITH GUILT, Draque couldn't even look his lover in the eye as he carried her through the maze of tunnels to the chamber he shared with his brothers. He flew close to the dark ceiling, so others wouldn't see them. Not that it mattered. Her screams echoed through the caverns, making her sound like a banshee. About halfway home he realized he hadn't handled the situation well. Actually, he'd fucked up big time, but between Katherine goading him, and Serah refusing to listen to reason, he'd lost his temper and let his dragon take over. He wasn't sure how he'd clean up the big pile of dragon dung that was his love life.

The flapping of his wings slowed to a dull thud as he neared their chamber. Serah had gone eerily silent. He chanced a look at her, hating himself when he saw her face streaked with tears. This wasn't how he'd imagined courting their bride would go.

Hovering above the door, he waited for Ladon to open it and then fell to the ground, cradling her close to his heart. He thought about setting her down after they went inside, but he couldn't let her run back to Laden's chamber when they had so much enmity between them. He had to find a way to make things right.

"I will despise you for eternity if you force me to marry you. Is that what you want?"

Stunned by her admission, he looked at her.

"Brother," Ladon said at his back. "Let's all discuss this."

Draque thought of shifters suffering for decades at the hands of Parliament's sanctions, introduced by Nathaniel Goldenwand. He hated himself for what he was about to say. "To prevent war, it's a sacrifice I'm willing to make."

Her eyes swirled with brilliant violet, blues, and greens, the colors matching the irridescent scales of her tail. "Release me at once," she said in a voice surprisingly dark and powerful.

An odd compulsion to do whatever she said washed over him. He blinked hard at her, loosening his grip, his knees weakening. When his dragon roared, he snapped out of the trance, holding her tightly once more.

"Don't try to use your siren voice on me." With brisk strides he marched across the room and kicked open the door to his chamber, grunting when she swore and kicked at him.

He kicked the door shut on his brothers. Pinning her wrists in one hand, he locked the door, ignoring the pounding on the other side.

He pushed back a curtain and dropped her on his bed, which was a feather mattress and a mound of furs tucked in an alcove carved into the cave wall. This luxuriously soft bed had been made for loving. It was a shame Serah's first experience on it wouldn't be pleasant. He snatched the rope off the heavy crimson drape and grabbed her ankle when she tried to scramble away.

"This is for your own good." He made quick work of tying her up, barely missing a kick to the groin. "Enough!" he bellowed. "Even if you don't want to prevent a war between shifters and witches, maybe you'll care about your safety."

When her eyes shifted to a brilliant violet and her cheeks turned a rosy hue, he thought maybe he'd gotten through to her, but then she reared up like a cobra and spit in his face.

"Let. Me. Go."

Her voice was even darker, and his fingers itched to remove her bindings. Instead he ripped off a section of drape and gagged her, hissing when she bit his finger. Shaking off the pain, he went back to the door.

He flung it open as his brothers were about to rip it to shreds with extended talons. He gestured to their reluctant mate curled up on his bed. "She is to remain here until the betrothal ceremony. Do not let her leave."

Ladon gaped at him as if he'd just eaten his puppy. "You should've let me handle it."

Resentment welled in Draque's chest at the censure in his brother's tone. "You?"

"Yeah. I could've convinced her."

Great. Now his brothers were angry with him, too. "Her little lamb?" A sardonic laugh escaped his throat. "You wouldn't persuade her. She has you by the bollocks."

"We have a special connection," Ladon insisted. "At least, we *had* one."

"Great goddess!" Smoke poured from Draque's nostrils. "Would you listen to yourself, you giant twat? You're hardly fit to be called a Firesbreath."

"You guys," Teju interrupted. "Cool down."

Ignoring him, Ladon puffed out his chest, stepping up to Draque in a bold move. Draque could reduce his brother to ash in seconds.

Ladon looked Draque over as if he was no more significant than the crusted dirt on his talons. "You think forcing women into submission makes me worthy of the name?"

Extending a claw, Draque jabbed his brother's shoulder. "Putting your people before your cowardice makes you fit to use our family name."

Ladon jerked back as if he'd been scalded. "So now I'm a coward?"

Teju groaned louder and tried to get between them. "Stop this."

Draque pushed Teju away. "Your actions speak for you."

Draque saw Ladon's fist coming too late. It connected with his jaw with a *crack*. Draque fell against a table, knocking it on its side and landing on one knee. Rubbing his sore jaw, he got to his feet.

Ladon held his ground. "What about *that* action? What does *that* say?"

Draque blinked, hardly believing Ladon had had the balls to hit him. His claws extended, and his dragon roared for vengeance. Throwing back his head, he released a stream of fire. "That you're a dead man." He plowed into Ladon, sending him flying across the room.

Draque didn't know why he'd expected Ladon to back down, but he bounced off the wall, smoke pouring from his lengthening snout as he readied to reengage.

"Stop it!" Teju shouted. "This isn't helping."

Ladon leaped into the air, his wings beating heavily. With a roar, Draque jumped up and slashed Ladon's wing.

With an ear-splitting howl, Ladon landed on Draque's shoulders. Draque spun, whipping his brother off him, but not before Ladon tore a hole through his wing. Pain shot through him, and he fell to one knee, panting. Ignoring the throbbing, he got to his feet again, preparing to charge Ladon.

Teju jumped between them, letting out a roar that shook the walls. "Both of you separate at once!" he hollered, horns sprouting from his head.

Draque pointed at him, inwardly cursing when pain shot through his injured shoulder. "You are not alpha brother."

"I'm not going to argue with you, Draque. For Serah's sake, you both need to cool down."

When he nodded to the open door behind them, Draque realized Serah had witnessed their fight. His back stiffened when he heard her loud sniffle. If she'd loathed him before, she probably hated him even more for fighting with her favorite brother.

He said to Teju, "I'll leave if Ladon leaves." The thought of Ladon running to Serah for sympathy filled him with such a jealous rage, his head spun.

"Fine." Ladon threw up his hands. "So long as you stay the hell away from her. She's suffered enough of your abuse."

Draque's chest ached as if his brother's words were barbed with venom. Unable to stand the censure in Ladon's eyes a moment longer, he turned to Teju. "Are you going to watch her?"

Teju smirked. "What do you think?"

"Don't take off her gag, do you understand? She will use her siren's voice to escape." He strode past his brothers, jarring Ladon's hurt shoulder. Ignoring Ladon's howl, he shifted, jumped into the air, and flew away without a backward glance. He didn't know where he was going, but he needed to be alone, somewhere he could cool down and escape his brothers' censure. As dark thoughts plagued him, he knew he'd never be able to escape his conscience. Ladon was right. He'd really fucked up this time.

SERAH COULD HARDLY believe Draque and Ladon had fought over her or how bravely Ladon had stood up to his brother. If only she could just marry one brother, or maybe Teju, too, who'd tried so hard to keep the peace. But Draque? How could she ever marry a brute who'd not only bullied her but his brother? Not to mention, he was impossible to control. She'd hoped her siren voice would be effective, but he'd broken her spell. Maybe that's why her mother and grandmother had tried to sacrifice her. She was a terrible siren if she couldn't even master a basic compulsion spell.

Draque had wrapped the gag too tightly around her mouth. Her hands were bound too tightly, too, which meant she'd have rope burn for sure. That fucking asshole. He clearly cared nothing for her. She was just another fuck, no doubt. She'd no idea how long he planned on keeping her tied up, but one thing she knew for certain—she wasn't marrying him, and not just because she was not fucking ready, but because no way in hell would she call that steaming pile of troll dung her husband. She could only imagine how he'd order her around after marriage. No thanks. She dealt with enough condescending demands from her grandfather. She didn't need to put up with it from a mate, too. Her thoughts turned to Grandfather, who'd also often made her life miserable. When she wasn't at school, he disapproved of her behavior and told her what to do. Honestly, it was tiring. The week she'd spent with him after she'd been expelled had been a nightmare, so much so that she'd welcomed the idea of attending an academy for misfit witches, even if she felt her punishment was too severe.

"Serah, are you okay?"

Teju was bent over her. Rolling onto her side, she looked away from him, unable to stand the pity in his eyes.

The bed dipped as he sat beside her. "Please don't cry," he said, smoothing a hand down her back.

If only he knew she wasn't crying because she was sad. No, she was pissed. Her eyes always leaked when she was furious, like the time her mother and grandmother had tried to sacrifice her. Her eyes had leaked for several weeks after that. It had nothing to do with being crushed by their betrayal and rejection.

No way was she hurt by Draque, a stupid, selfish dragon who frustrated her too much for her to care about his opinion.

"Serah, I'm so sorry. We never wanted this to happen. Won't you look at me?" She stiffened when he tugged on her shoulder. "Please don't turn away from me," he pleaded.

She winced when he reached around her, trying to hold her hand.

He touched the rope burn on her wrist. "Draque tied this too tight. I'll find something else to bind you."

As if that would make it all better. She stared at the dark wall opposite her. Hanging on it was a display of medieval weapons, or maybe they were kink toys. She wouldn't put it past Draque.

Teju tried to dig under her gag. "Damn. This is tight, too."

Rolling on her back, she blinked at him, then coughed to emphasize his point.

Indecision was written in the lines etched into his forehead. "If I take off the gag, do you promise not to use your siren voice to compel me to release you?"

She vehemently nodded. She'd still try to compel him, but only to get him to listen to reason. It probably wouldn't do any good anyway.

"Okay." He quickly strode to Draque's dresser and dug through the drawers until he found a bag of cotton balls. "Hang on," he said and shoved them in his ears.

So much for trusting her.

He returned with cotton sticking out of his ears. She should've been grateful that he'd offered to remove the gag, but she'd still be a prisoner. Their betrothal wasn't off to a good start.

As he leaned over her, a talon extended to cut through the gag, she caught movement from the corner of her eye. She tried to warn him, but it was too late. She screamed into the gag when someone smashed a bottle over Teju's head. Shards of glass sprayed her hair and face, and Teju slumped on top of her, a visible knot growing on top of his head.

Eyes glowing red, Katherine came into view and rolled Teju off her. He hit the ground with a thud.

Serah fought when Katherine dug sharp talons into her shoulders and blood pooled in the deep cuts.

"How convenient." Katherine laughed. "They've already tied you up for me. This makes killing you so much easier."

Chapter Thirteen

Doris Doublewart's heart sank as she took in the ruins of her school. Every wall had been reduced to charred rubble, every desk turned to cinders, and there were no signs of life other than crickets and hooting owls in the nearby forest. She smelled the scent of fresh rain. Tears cascaded down her cheeks as she peered up at dark clouds, which looked poised to unleash a torrent on them at any moment. How could this have happened to her beloved school, and had her students and teachers escaped in time?

She looked at Hector Firesbreath, who was still in full dragon form. "Did you do this?"

His large golden eyes widened. "We didn't do this, I swear. We only knocked down the wall to your office. Bastian did a reveal spell that showed us where the heiress was before he knocked it down."

"At least, we thought you were the heiress," Bastian mumbled. "I need to modify the spell next time."

Dame Doublewart threw out her hands. "There will not be a next time!"

"You had to have seen the school was still intact when we flew away," Bastian said, lower lip quavering.

Doris bent down and picked up a charred book, her heart shattering when it crumbled to dust in her hand. "I should've been here to protect them." Damn those stupid dragons and their fool's quest. If they hadn't taken her, she could have defended the place.

A tear slipped down Thaddeus's long snout. "We're so sorry."

She turned away, unable to look at him or his brothers. Whistling, she held out her hand, pleased when her trusty wand flew to her from the rubble. Turning it over in her palm, she noted it was smeared with soot but otherwise unharmed. Running her hand over it, she felt the magic and summoned the memory enchantment she'd placed on it after too many episodes of the mischievous Firesbreath brothers trying to steal it.

She closed her eyes, and the wand told a story. After she'd been kidnapped, an ominous brick-hued cloud approached the school. Six translucent dragon heads appeared in the storm. An illusion, to be sure, but who would do such a thing? Though her wand couldn't see what had happened to her lover or her children after the explosion, she prayed her teachers had been able to save the students in time.

"Halt in the name of the governance of the third realm!" Six third-realm witches—deputies, no doubt—were pointing their wands at her and the Firesbreath brothers.

When Hector Firesbreath foolishly stepped in front of her, puffing up his massive chest, she ducked around him, wildly waving her hands. "Stop!" she cried. "I'm Dame Doublewart. These dragons had nothing to do with the destruction of my school."

The witches refused to lower their wands. A tall, handsome blond man, who looked suspiciously familiar, stepped forward. He aimed his wand directly at her chest. "Then tell them to shift back to human form."

She didn't like the gleam in his eye. "Please lower your wand," she said tightly, doing her best to maintain her composure.

The gleam in his eye magnified, followed by a twitch above his lip. "I will do no such thing."

Doris recognized him then, the witch who'd delivered the check on Nathaniel Goldenwand's behalf and who'd also insisted Seraphina not serve detention. He was a deputy, too?

"Then you leave us no choice," Hector bellowed.

Before she could stop him, he pushed her behind him and released his flame, fighting the bolts that flew from their wands with fire.

She ducked, casting a protective bubble around herself, and watched helplessly as dragons fought witches. A flash of red flew by, and a dragon roared, then wailed, the keening, high-pitched sound of injury. She watched in horror as Thaddeus stumbled and fell.

The bolts from the witches' wands were too many, flying through the air like erratic balls of energy. Clutching her wand, Doris cast her protection bubble outward until it shrouded Bastian and Hector, with the exception of their jowls, which poured fire onto the witches. She couldn't reach Thaddeus and doubted it would do any good if she could. She suspected he'd already perished.

It was forbidden to use the unbreakable curse, but one had shot out of a witch's wand as a red bolt. Every wand manufactured had a special spell put on it, preventing the wand from releasing the hex. Parliament had even passed a law decreeing any witch using the curse would be sentenced to a slow and painful death.

Thaddeus didn't stir. Doris's chest seized with grief. *No, not him. He'd been such a sweet boy.*

These witches were playing dirty. She couldn't let any more Firesbreaths die. Controlling the movement of the protective bubble, she pulled it back, and the dragons came back with it.

"We can't hold them off forever," she called to Hector. "I'm afraid they've already summoned reinforcements."

Hector cast a glance at his supine brother. "I'm not leaving Thaddeus."

"We have no choice," she said sadly, the energy in her protective bubble wearing thin under the onslaught of attack.

When a red bolt bounced off the bubble, she fought a surge of panic. These "deputies" weren't the law. They were law*breakers*!

When Hector and Bastian shared knowing looks, Doris knew they were about to make yet another stupid decision.

Hector broke through the bubble, blowing a stream of scorching blue fire as he galloped toward his inert brother. He snatched up Thaddeus in his talons, stumbling and then flailing in the air, crying out when he was struck by a blue bolt. He crashed into the trees and then flew low, dragging his poor brother across the treetops as a red bolt flew over his head.

"Hold on!" Bastian snatched her up in his jowls and tossed her on his back. She tried to cast a protective bubble around them, but they were moving too fast.

Bastian burst through the flames, striking the witches from behind and causing them to go on defense until his brothers were out of striking distance.

Doris flung bolts at the witches, forcing them back as Bastian jumped into the air, chasing after his brothers.

It didn't take them long to catch up. Hector still struggled to keep his brother above the treetops.

"He's too heavy!" Hector cried.

Doris gasped when she saw what appeared to be a flock of birds, all in a line, heading toward them. She didn't need a magnifying spell to know they weren't birds but an army of witches on broomsticks, heading straight for them.

"Drop him!" she commanded. "Or we're all dead."

"No!" Hector roared.

With a heavy heart, she pointed her wand at Thaddeus's lifeless body. "Expediramos!"

Hector cried out as his brother fell from his talons and crashed to the ground.

Doris waved her wand and chanted, "Abscondo!" and Thaddeus was swallowed by a copse of leafy trees that concealed the dragon.

Hector dove for his brother, then pulled back mid-air, the branches below him swaying in the battering wind from his wings but not revealing Thaddeus's hiding place.

"We will return for him!" she hollered above the din of their wings.

With an earth-shattering howl, Hector flew away from the witches on broomsticks, Doris and Thaddeus following closely. The dragons flew faster than any broomstick, and with a sigh of relief, she saw the line of witches and the charred remains of her home fade in the distance.

She faced forward once more as they climbed above the heavens, flying just below the mystical frost-covered clouds of the elven fourth realm. Only then did she surrender to tears, crying over the destruction of her beloved home and the souls that may have perished. She also cried for Thaddeus Firesbreath. His brothers did as well, howling and honking like dying phoenixes descending into ash. How her heart broke for them. As she mourned, she wondered what could have led to this moment.

Something made her suspect Nathaniel Goldenwand was behind the attack, not just because of his connection to the murderous deputy. Who else could override restrictions on a wand? She remembered how oddly he'd behaved at their one and only meeting, and the many times he'd called his granddaughter a whore. He could've paid her way into any of private school in the third realm, or even hire a private tutor, but he'd insisted she attend Doris's school and that she not serve detention. It was as if he'd planned for his granddaughter to perish in the school attack. The thought made her stomach churn.

His strange behavior, coupled with his thirst for power, made her suspect he was far more evil than she'd ever imagined.

DRAQUE SPED AWAY, FLYING close to the ceiling of the cavern, shrouded by shadows. It was a maze, but he'd grown up here and knew the area like the back of his hand. He'd intentionally flown toward Master Eagleheart's quarters, since most shifters were too frightened to get close to the griffin. There he knew he could get some peace, as long as Katherine didn't discover his whereabouts.

He landed on a granite ledge and was so deep in remorseful thought about how he'd treated Serah, he almost didn't hear footsteps echoing down the tunnel, followed by the occasional scrape of wood against stone. Still concealed by darkness, he peered over the ledge, his sharp dragon senses recognizing the sound of Master Eagleheart's staff.

The hood of his cloak pulled low over his forehead, Master Eagleheart cast a surreptitious glance over his shoulder before tapping on a rock three times with his cane. A crack materialized in the wall, and he slipped through it.

How odd. The entrance to Master Eagleheart's chamber was at the far end of the tunnel, and it was a door, not a secret entryway.

Without a second thought, he swooped down and edged through the crack before it closed. Pressing up against a damp wall, he waited until he heard the scraping of Master Eagleheart's cane down the hall.

Keeping a good distance between them, he followed the sound of the cane down a winding staircase of damp stone, which was lit only by the occasional wall sconce. Draque had to rely on his dragon-touched eyes to see anything, for it seemed the farther they descended, the darker it became.

Eagleheart reached a landing, and Draque pulled back into an alcove as the mage wove his way through a maze of man-sized boulders that glowed an eerie red. He squinted, trying to count them and failing. There had to be at least a thousand—a veritable forest of stones bathing the underground cavern in a soft crimson glow. What were those things?

Master Eagleheart placed a palm on one of the stones. "How are my babies?"

Babies? They must be eggs. Great Goddess!

A creature that resembled a malformed griffin sidled up to Eagleheart, one side of his body drooping like it was made from melting wax. "They done growing, Master," the creature answered in a nasal voice. "They ready for war."

Uneasy and apprehensive, Draque's dragon stirred. *War? What war?*

"Good, good," Eagleheart touched another egg. "But you must not hatch them until I give the signal."

"Rem know." The creature bowed low. "Rem wait for Master's whistle."

Eagleheart patted the creature on the head. "Good boy." He turned to the eggs and raised his staff. "Hello, my precious darlings," he said aloud, his voice echoing across the cavern. "Don't fret. Daddy will release you soon, then all five realms will know the might of the griffin."

Draque's dragon let out a menacing, dark growl. What the ever-loving fuck? Draque suspected his fathers knew nothing of their mage's eggs.

"Will griffin fight dragons, Master?" Rem asked.

Eagleheart rubbed his pointed chin. "If the kings do not relent, yes, but they would be fools to cross me."

Relent? Holy flaming troll turds!

The creature looked at his master with the hungry eyes of a baby bird begging for food. "If they do cross Master?"

Eagleheart laughed. "Then my army will rip off their wings and shove them down their throats."

Well, fuck. He had to alert his fathers, but not until he'd incinerated every last egg.

AS KATHERINE FLEW THROUGH the tunnels with Serah in her talons, Serah fought against her captor to no avail. The griffin bitch was strong, too strong. If only she could tear off the gag that restricted her siren tongue. Her compulsion spells didn't always work, but her siren voice might stall Katherine long enough for her to escape.

They landed with a hard *thud,* and Serah tumbled out of Katherine's talons. She cracked her head on the ground, and a sharp pain shot through her skull. Nausea rose as her head spun.

Great Goddess, save me! She couldn't throw up with a gag in her mouth. She'd choke to death.

Rolling onto her side, her head whirled fiercely, like she was stuck on the merry-go-round from hell with no end in sight.

"I see the way you're looking at me. Don't judge me, you bitch," Katherine hissed. "I'm not just doing this for me, but for the entire shifter race."

With surprising strength, the griffin picked up Serah and tossed her over one shoulder, then took to the air, flying across the underground lakes. Serah couldn't check her earrings to see if they'd come loose. She thought she could still feel them in her ears and prayed they wouldn't fall out. It was an odd time to worry about jewelry, but the thought of losing them was almost as frightening as losing her life.

Her heart pounded double-time when they flew through a narrow opening and out into the open sky. She closed her eyes against the glare from the setting sun. She'd never survive the fall if the griffin dropped her, but she swooped down and deposited her beside a small boat tied up in a cove. Shifting back into human form, Katherine untied the boat, then dropped Serah in it. "Do not fear, little slut. I'm not killing you today. The last thing I need is your mates extracting your murder from my lips with a truth spell."

Serah flopped in the hull like a fish out of water.

Katherine raised the sail. "I'm going to place an enchantment on the sail, and it will take you to Siren's Cove. Your family can finish what they started."

Her mother and grandmother had intended to sacrifice her, and they were most likely very upset with Serah for escaping her fate. They might be successful if given another chance.

She shifted into siren form. Though she was bound and gagged, her powerful tail still made a good weapon. She thrashed, trying to slap Katherine's face.

Katherine lunged for her and wrapped a cord around her neck. "Immutatus!" she said, pointing her wand at Serah's tail.

The tail instantly shifted back into human legs.

"Now you can't shift," Katherine sing-songed.

She gaped at the obsidian tau stone pressed against her chest. That stone, combined with the spell, trapped her siren inside her skin. As Katherine grinned nastily, her nose lengthening to a bird beak, she squawked, and Serah thought of the sharp contrast to Ladon's sweet smile. She wept for him, for she doubted she'd ever see him or his brothers again.

Chapter Fourteen

Keeping the hoods drawn low, Kron and Vepar Firesbreath stood in the shadows of the Parliament Hall in their human forms, waiting for the assembly to call their emergency session to order. No witches knew of their presence, thanks to Vepar's concealment spell. Nathaniel Goldenwand would speak to the assembly first, and Kron couldn't wait to expose the deceitful mage.

The assembly hall was grand, a large round room built in the Guilded Age. No expense had been spared. Golden fae statues balanced the world in their slender hands and polished mahogany benches with padded cushions offered comfortable seating. The benches descended to a polished podium, where speakers could look at the assembly and easily measure their temperaments, and hear their jeers or applause.

Assembly members wore traditional powdered white wigs and long black robes, attire left over from the Renaissance. Preserving history was never foolish, though Kron did find grown witches parading in wigs with powdered rolls of bouffant hair to be comical.

Prime Minister and majority leader, Sir Gais Goblingout, a member of the Optimate party, who stood more for lining his pockets than helping his fellow witch, called the meeting to order, despite the fact that several members of the assembly hadn't taken their seats. Gais's family name suited him perfectly, for his goblin heritage, and his rumored affection for ale, had saddled him with a quadruple chin, a distended gut, and hands and feet that looked like stuffed sausages. His voice was far more unflattering than his figure—so phlegmy, he could hardly speak without coughing up a prodigious amount of snot.

Luckily Kron didn't have to listen to him for long, as he yielded the floor almost immediately to Nathaniel Goldenwand. Kron didn't like how the assembly had quickly returned to their seats, appearing ready to hang on Nathaniel's every word. Nathaniel unfolded himself from a chair behind the speaker's podium, like a vampire waking from his coffin. Tall and lanky, almost skeletal, with oily dark hair and a thin moustache, he looked so villainous, it bordered ridiculous.

Holding out his hands like a martyr on the cross, he addressed Parliament. "Dear honorable council and fellow mages, I have come to you today with an urgent plea—and I will not deny it—a thirst for revenge. The Firesbreath kings have sought to harm us all by murdering our innocent children and kidnapping my granddaughter. Goddess knows what they are doing to my sweet Serah at this very moment."

When Vepar let out a low growl, Kron settled a hand on his shoulder. *Remain calm, brother,* he said telepathically. *We shall give him enough rope to hang himself.*

The grumbles from the crowd were not reassuring. Kron even thought he heard a few mutter, "Eradicate the beasts."

He was briefly afraid, then steeled his resolve. He was the mightiest shifter in all five realms. He would not be discouraged by a few prejudiced politicians who were probably on Goldenwand's payroll.

"How can we be sure it was the dragon kings who did this?"

Kron scanned the attendees, searching for the one who'd spoken. It was Marcus Moonbeam, a somewhat eccentric member of the Demagogue Party, a noble one in principal but bumbling leaders had reduced them to a handful of instigators who were barely a threat to the ruling party and Goldenwand's interests. Of average stature, and with an unremarkable face and skin the color of polished mahogany, Moonbeam more or less faded into the crowd. What separated him from the rest was his temerity to defy the majority, even when his party remained suspiciously silent.

Goldenwand chuckled, leveling Moonbeam with a look that made the politician sink low in his chair. "Their four-toed prints were found in the cemetery beside the school."

"They could've been made by the princes, who were students at that school," Moonbeam squeaked.

Goldenwand gave the bumbling politician a long, dark look, one meant to silence him, no doubt. "No shifting is permitted at school," he said. "Witnesses say they saw dragons fly toward the school moments before it was incinerated. Who else but a dragon has the power to burn down an entire edifice? There was nothing left but cinder and ash." Goldenwand paused and wiped his dry eyes.

His show of grief was blatantly false, yet the assembly witches sniffled in commiseration. Just how stupid were they?

"A powerful mage could've done it," Vepar called, then slunk back into the shadows.

Goldenwand looked around for the dissenting voice, his hawkish eyes scanning the hall and his mouth twisted in a knot.

"Look outside your doors!" he yelled, whipping out his wand and banging the podium. "There are dozens of heartbroken parents demanding swift justice against those responsible for murdering their children."

Sir Gais Goblingout got to his feet, gazing at Goldenwand as if he controlled the very rotation of the sun. "What do you propose we do?"

"What we should've done years ago." Goldenwand banged the wand again, the sound of wood striking wood ricocheting through the hall. "Raze The Grotto and annihilate every shifter living there."

Vepar growled again, his yellow eyes lengthening to oblong slits.

Kron laid a steadying hand on his arm. *Patience, brother. We will expose him soon.*

We must act, Vepar snapped. *Before they put a war resolution to a vote.*

"Even while your granddaughter is their captive?" Moonbeam countered. "Don't you think it's best we speak to the dragon kings first?"

At least one person in Parliament made sense.

"How many years have we wasted with words?" Goldenwand threw up his hands, sparks flying from the wand when he waved it at a massive, low-hanging crystal chandelier. "What good has speaking to them done in the past?"

"I-I'm sorry, Master Goldenwand," Moonbeam stammered, wiping sweat off his brow when he was met with disapproving scowls from his fellow members, "but I don't think war is the answer, not until every avenue of diplomacy is explored."

"You would use diplomacy with murderers?" Goldenwand raged.

Thrusting a fist in the air, Vepar's hood fell back, exposing glowing dragon eyes. "We're not murderers!"

Swearing under his breath, Kron joined his brother, pushing back his hood. He ignored the gasps and mutters that raced through the hall.

Goldenwand pointed his wand at them. "You dare show your faces here?"

Kron's spine stiffened. "You dare lie to Parliament when you know full well it was your mages who burned down the school?"

"Lies!" Goldenwand shrieked. The sound reminded Kron of Master Eagleheart and his daughter.

"Our family is innocent," Kron said. "Your granddaughter will testify to the truth. She is not our prisoner. She is betrothed to our sons."

Murmurs and whispers rose from the Parliament floor.

"More lies!" Goldenwand cried, twitching as if he was about to have a seizure. "Serah would never defy me. She knows she'd be disinherited if she did such a thing."

Kron growled. Their sons were dragon princes. Any woman would be honored to mate with them.

"Your wealth and status mean nothing to us," Vepar boomed. "Serah will be safe with us, and she won't have to worry about her bewitched fairy godmother trying to murder her."

The onlookers fell silent. They turned to Kron and his brother in shock. The accusation of attempted murder was a serious charge, but when the third realm threatened war against The Grotto, they were left with little choice.

Moonbeam shot up from his bench. "Bewitched godmother?"

"He sent her to kill the heiress," Kron said, the words ringing through the hall. "If it wasn't for my sons, Serah Goldenwand would be dead."

"They lie!" Goldenwand wailed again, sounding like he was on the edge of panic.

Goldenwand wilted under the glares of Parliament. Kron could smell the wandmaker's guilt from across the hall.

"He's incensed that his granddaughter is betrothed rather than relieved she is well." He pointed at Goldenwand. "Is it not obvious he sent her godmother to murder her after she escaped the school massacre?"

Goldenwand stopped wilting. Fueled by some unseen force, he straightened, visibly regaining control of himself. "More lies, but I'd expect nothing less from shifters. I demand Parliament declare war on these low-life scoundrels."

Kron's breath hitched. If they sided with the wandmaker, he and his brother would have no choice but to unleash their might on Parliament. They couldn't let the threat of war spread beyond the hall.

A deputy carrying a missive raced toward the prime minister.

"Order, order!" Sir Gais Goblingout yelled, waving the scroll above his head. Nathaniel Goldenwand reluctantly stepped aside as Goblingout waddled to the podium.

"We've just received word from the Werewood Constable," Goblingout announced, clutching the podium with whitened knuckles, the rest of him turning as red as an overcooked beet. "The elder dragon princes attacked the school once more."

Kron's heart skipped a beat. "No! That can't be."

Goblingout's many chins shook as he spoke. "They took Dame Doublewart captive and badly burned three deputies."

Vepar held out his hands defensively. "This has to be a trick. Our sons wouldn't do that."

Moonbeam gave Kron and his brother an apologetic look. "Where are the dragons now?" he asked the prime minister.

Goblingout quickly scanned the parchment, his red face expanding like a balloon ready to pop. "Two escaped and one perished."

Kron's world ground to a halt, and his heart shattered into a million sharp shards. "What?"

Goldenwand's gaunt face split into a wide grin. "Bring me the deputy who felled the dragon, so that I may reward him."

They had to be wrong. One of his sons wasn't dead. He couldn't be. No way could mages fell a mighty dragon. Kron shifted into a behemoth beast in seconds. He released his fire in an irate stream. Members of Parliament summoned protective bubbles, but they neglected to protect their beloved hall. Kron intended to burn it to the ground. His brother joined him in destruction fueled by grief.

Crushing burning benches beneath his massive paws, Kron and Vepar stalked the assembly, transfixed on Goldenwand like cats cornering a mouse.

"This is all your doing!" Kron roared.

Nathaniel waved his wand like he was trying to catch a unicorn with a lasso. His eyes turned as black as tar. "Exsuscito!"

Every council member stood at attention, their protective bubbles popping as they raised their wands. "Master," they said in unison, their lifeless eyes fixed on Goldenwand, unfazed by the fires burning around them, "we are yours to command."

Ice flowed through Kron's veins. "What is this twisted magic?"

"Twisted magic?" Goldenwand's laughter reminded Kron of a serpent's hiss. "It's the new Goldenwand 2050, the latest in magical technology. Every member of Parliament was given one just last week. They come with a special hidden feature that allows the wand's creator to control the user." His black eyes turned deep crimson. "Genius, isn't it?"

Vepar kicked the crumbled remains of the hardwood floor, steam pouring from his nostrils. "You are the devil incarnate, and you will pay for killing our son."

"Will I?" Goldenwand's confident smile thinned into a dour line. "Assembly, kill the dragons."

When they turned their wands on them, Kron launched into the air. *Let's go, brother,* he said. *We'll take our vengeance later.*

I will kill that mage with my last dying breath, Vepar roared, flying after him.

Kron blew the top off the glass-domed ceiling with a mighty breath while Vepar shielded them from the sparks flying off the wizards' wands by hitting them with fire.

Magic pinged off their scales as they dove off the top of the building and took to the sky.

Kron's heart was heavy as they flew back to their homeland. One of their sons could very well be dead and war between shifters and witches was imminent. Goddess save them.

BY THE TIME MASTER Eagleheart left the creature named Rem alone to tend to the eggs, Draque's feet had gone numb, and his legs were stiff from squatting in the shadows of the alcove. He waited for several tense heartbeats, listening to the retreating sound of the mage's staff ricocheting off the stone floor. With his dragon-touched hearing, he heard the stone wall sliding open, then shut, before heaving a sigh of relief. When Rem's back was turned, Draque wove through the maze of eggs, his heart stuttering when he saw the labyrinth extended well beyond his line of vision.

He might not have enough firepower to destroy them all, but he sure as hell was going to try. He shifted and released his flame at once, burning Rem, who ran off, squealing like a stuck pig. Projecting the flame, he spread it across one cavern after another. The eggs began to bubble and pop, and malformed creatures escaped, crawling over each other like a nest of agitated spiders.

He spun at the sound of several cracks behind him, reeling when hundreds of spindly creatures raced toward him. They launched, pulling at his scales and digging their claws into his neck, and he knew he was out of time. Shaking them off with a roar, he flew to the top of the cavern and cut a swath through the hordes of hatchlings, vicious creatures with pointy beaks, bloodshot eyes, and gray wings with translucent membranes. Then he dove for the tunnel leading to the exit, shifting to human form and racing up the stairs, praying to the goddess he'd escape before they reached him.

LADON COULDN'T STAY away from his sweet Serah for long. She might never forgive him for forcing her into a bonding, but he had to see her. The thought of causing her anguish cut him up inside, and he hoped he could find a way to soothe her.

He followed her scent to Draque's chamber, but then her smell suddenly dissipated, and he heard no sounds coming within.

He paused at the door, which was partly ajar. Draque always kept his door closed. Fingering the wand in his pocket, he nudged it open and saw Teju on the floor.

"Teju!" he cried, running into the room with his wand drawn. Falling to his brother's side, he scanned the chamber for any sign of Serah, but she was gone.

"Wake up!" He shook Teju's shoulder, alarmed when blood trickled from his ear. Broken glass was scattered around his head.

Teju moaned, and his eyes opened. "Wh-What happened?"

"That's what I want to know." Whoever had injured Teju probably had Serah. His dragon grumbled to be set free. "Where's Serah?"

Teju sat up on his elbows, blinking. "I think I left her tied up on the bed."

Ladon scowled at the empty tangle of furs on Draque's bed.

"Ouch." Teju rubbed the back of his head, then pulled his hand back, gaping at the blood on his fingers. "Someone knocked me out."

"Did Serah break her bonds and hit you?" he asked.

"No." Teju still looked disoriented. "She wouldn't do that to me. I remember looking at her face and then I was hit." He shot to his feet, then half fell on the bed. "She's gone?"

"We need to find her."

Teju howled, and a stream of fire burned the drapes. "I failed to protect her!"

He had, but there was no time to lament that now. Snatching the drapes, Ladon stomped out the fire. "We need to go find her." Ladon's dark dragon voice spoke for him. "Let's go."

"Where?"

"Where else?" Ladon growled. "Wherever Katherine is hiding."

Chapter Fifteen

Ladon stalked past his fathers' three-headed guard dog, shoved open the doors, and flew toward the dais, leaving Teju behind. His brother had lagged most of the way, his wings giving out more than once, slowing them down. He needed medical attention, but finding Serah came first. Ladon was alarmed when he saw only Dagon and Mother were at court, with the mage advisor, Master Eagleheart, sitting in a much smaller chair beside them.

"Where is Katherine?" Ladon asked brusquely.

"I don't know." Eagleheart rose, clutching his staff. "Why do you ask?"

"You know why!" he roared. "She took Serah."

"Took her?" The mage's eyes widened. "Where?"

The mage's shock sounded forced, which automatically made him suspicious.

"We don't know," Ladon said, "but Serah's in danger."

The mage leaned on his staff. "Are you saying my daughter would harm your mate?"

"That's exactly what we're saying," Teju said as he landed beside Ladon.

Their father, Dagon, focused his one eye on the mage but surprisingly said nothing. Mother climbed on his shoulder and whispered in his ear.

Eagleheart blinked. "Do you have any evidence of this?"

Ladon had no time for games. He pounced on the mage. "Where is she?" He shook him by the collar. "You know where she is!"

"How dare you!" Eagleheart's nose and mouth morphed into a giant bird beak. "Your mate probably ran away from you."

When he snapped at Ladon's hand, Ladon let the mage go but not without a hard shove.

He smiled when Eagleheart tripped over his staff and fell to the ground. "She wouldn't run away from us."

Crossing one paw over the other, Dagon still said nothing.

The mage used his staff to pull himself up and brushed dirt off his robes. "How can you be sure?"

Rage threatened to split Ladon's skull in two. "Because she was tied up!"

The mage chuckled. "It sounds like she's much better off wherever she is."

"It was for her own safety. Whoever took her attacked Teju." Standing beside him, his brother swayed. Shame washed over Ladon. He shouldn't have let Draque bind and gag her.

"You didn't see this person, Teju?" Dagon asked.

Teju's hand flew to his blood-streaked head. "They attacked me from behind."

Mother sprang toward Teju and inspected the injury. "Sit down, son." Pulling out her wand, she waved it over Teju. Her magic wasn't strong enough to completely heal him, but the open wound closed enough that the blood stopped flowing.

Ladon didn't know whether to be relieved or worried by her support.

"You have no evidence for your preposterous claim." The mage struck the stone floor with his staff. "Yet you level these charges against me and Katherine."

"We know it was you!" Teju insisted. "You and your daughter have motive."

"Where is your daughter, Master Eagleheart?" Mother asked, giving him a long, cool look.

"I-I don't know." The mage stepped back as if to escape the weight of her stare.

"Find her," Dagon said, his ominous tone leaving no room for refusal.

Eagleheart bowed low. "Yes, Your Highness."

"Not you," Dagon grumbled and gestured to two feathered guards standing by the door. "Make haste," he added.

Squawking, the guards flew toward the exit as the doors were thrown open, and two massive dragons flew in, nearly running into the birds with their talons. After a lot of screeching and flying feathers, the guards left and Ladon's older brothers, Hector and Bastian, landed heavily beside him.

Ladon was surprised when Dame Doublewart slid off Bastian's back. "What are you doing here?" he asked, not meaning to sound rude.

She reprimanded him. "Mind your manners."

"Where are our other fathers?" Hector demanded shakily.

His obvious anguish made Ladon's knees weaken. Something was seriously wrong.

"They've gone to Parliament," Dagon answered, extending his neck so he towered above them. "It's about time you returned home. Where is Thaddeus?"

"We were attacked by third realm deputies." Bastian hung his head, and a tear slid down his snout. "He did not make it."

Mother cried out, and Teju grabbed her elbow to steady her.

Ladon shared a look of shock with Teju. He and Teju and Draque had often clashed with their older brothers, but they'd never wished them dead. Thaddeus being killed was like a knife in his chest.

Mother was starkly pale, her eyes like black holes in white paper. "What do you mean, he didn't make it?"

Hector looked sick. "I'm sorry, Mother. They killed him."

She slumped in Teju's arms.

Black smoke poured form Dagon's snout. "No, this can't be. Where is his body?"

"He was in dragon form." Hector hung his head, his wings and tail drooping like a wilting flower. "I carried him as long as I could."

"This can't be!" Dagon bellowed. "Witches can't take down a dragon."

Their mother threw herself on Hector with a wail. "Take me to him."

"We can't." Hector frowned as he nuzzled their mother's head. "It's too dangerous."

"You can't just leave him there!" she said shrilly, then narrowed her eyes on Dame Doublewart, who'd been standing stoically by Bastian's side. "Why is the academy headmistress here?"

"It's a long story, Mother." Bastian placed a protective arm in front of her.

"Queen Firesbreath." Dame Doublewart bowed low. "My condolences."

"Did you see them kill my son?" Mother demanded.

Dame Doublewart wiped watery eyes. "I did. I also saw red bolts come out of their wands."

Gasps filled the hall.

"This does not bode well for us," Hector said. "If the witches attack, we will fall like flies."

Dagon stood, shaking his wings, his chest and throat turning as red as molten lava. "I will send every murderous witch to hell!"

"That curse is illegal!" Teju growled. "Their wands should have spells to prevent it."

"Who modified their wands?" Mother asked.

"Nathaniel Goldenwand!"

Kron flew into the hall and landed on his throne. Vepar arrived moments later, the displaced air from his heavy wings beating down on Ladon's back.

Shielding her eyes, Mother raced to the dais. "Have you heard? Our son is dead, killed by the unbreakable curse."

Vepar and Kron appeared to be barely keeping themselves under control. "We have."

"I want vengeance!" She thrust a fist in the air. "I want Goldenwand to suffer as we do!"

"If I may be so bold, Your Highnesses." Master Eagleheart bowed low. "A tail for a tail would only be fair."

Ladon's blood ran cold, and his dragon issued a warning growl.

"What are you saying, Master?" Mother asked sharply.

The mage shrugged, avoiding eye contact with Ladon and Teju. "That we kill his heir."

"You want to kill Serah?" Ladon boomed. "Have you lost your mind?"

He flashed an oily smile that did nothing to hide the malice in his eyes. "It's only fair."

Teju was visibly angry. "You sick, twisted demon!"

"He knows where she is," Ladon said, suddenly very sure of that. "Why else would he suggest killing her?"

Kron lifted a scaly brow. "Has she gone missing?"

"Yes, Father," Ladon answered, glowering at the mage. "They attacked Teju and took her."

Eagleheart gazed at Ladon coolly. "They've no proof it was me or my child."

Ladon clenched his hands into fists, his dragon claws unsheathing and breaking skin. He was one heartbeat away from slitting Eagleheart's throat.

Kron turned to the mage. "Do you know where Serah Goldenwand is?"

He paled. "I do not."

"And yet how easily you speak of murdering her!" Ladon roared.

The guards returned in a whirl of feathers, dragging a shrieking Katherine. "We have brought the griffin girl, my kings," they said and deposited the griffin in front of the dais.

Ladon ran to her, hauling her to her feet and desperately searching her eyes. "Where is she?"

She shook him off. "Where is who?" she asked nonchalantly, her disinterest too practiced, her voice too hollow.

"Don't play dumb with me." Ladon jabbed her with a long talon. "Or I swear I'll burn you to a crisp."

"You will do no such thing!" Eagleheart said, whacking Ladon's leg with his staff.

Ladon blew out a stream of fire, but the mage threw up a shield in time to prevent being flamed. Too bad. Ladon needed revenge, and he needed it now.

"Tell us where she is, Katherine," Kron said sternly. "Tell us now, or we will use the truth spell."

Katherine let out a wistful sigh. Ladon longed to smack her smug face.

"I found her tied up and gagged by your sons," she said, "so I helped her escape."

"Liar!" Ladon yelled.

"That is enough, son," Kron cautioned before turning back to Katherine. "Where did she go?"

"She's on a boat to Siren's Cove. She'll be much safer there than here. Plus, she'll be with her own kind."

Ladon was so upset at that news, it was a wonder he didn't wring Katherine's neck. They were going to sacrifice Serah.

"Did she tell you that's where she wanted to go?" Teju asked.

She hesitated, then said, "Yes."

"Now I know you're lying!" Ladon advanced on her, his dragon barely in check. "The siren queens want to kill her."

"Oh!" Her hands flew to her face. "I didn't know that."

Latching onto her arm, he dug his claws into her skin, all too aware of her father hovering nearby with his wand. "But Serah knew, and she would've told you."

She smile was contemptuous. "I guess it slipped her mind."

Kron nodded to Lord Crowfoot and two other bird-beak guards. "Arrest her."

"My kings!" Eagleheart banged his staff to draw their attention. "I implore you to be reasonable."

Kron said evenly, "We are." After his guards had Katherine in their grasp, he said, "Arrest her father, too."

The mage backed away from the guards, brandishing the staff and his wand. "You don't want to do that."

Kron straightened to an imposing height. "Name one reason why we shouldn't."

Master Eagleheart's eyes gleamed. "Oh, I can name thousands of reasons." His face transformed to that of an eagle and he let out an ear-shattering screech.

Ladon's blood turned to ice. "What are you doing, Eagleheart?"

"Summoning my family," the mage said.

Vepar took their mother under his wing. "Your family?"

He let out a sinister chuckle. "You'll regret crossing me."

The guards knocked the staff and wand from his hands and bound him and his daughter by the wrists.

Ladon heard a rumble beneath him, followed by several ear-piercing screeches that sounded like rabid bats. Goddess save them.

"CLOSE THE DOORS! CLOSE the doors!" Draque flew into his fathers' hall, hell birds nipping at his tail.

When the guards saw them, they whistled to Cerberus, who helped them push the massive doors shut. Draque added his weight, then bolted the door as the first griffin hit. Hundreds of them slammed into the doors, their beaks and claws sounding like hail hitting a tin roof.

Vepar flew to Draque's side. "What in the devil's name are those?"

"Demons," Draque said and turned to those behind him: his birth brothers, two of his older brothers, his fathers, Mother, and Master Eagleheart and Katherine, who had been restrained by guards. About time his fathers arrested the Eaglehearts. Draque only hoped it wasn't too late.

"Over three thousand griffins, my spawns." Master Eagleheart smiled triumphantly. "Surrender the throne to me, and I'll call them off. If not, they will destroy your kingdom and everyone in it."

Kron towered over Eagleheart. "You've gone mad."

"I'm the same I've always been." The mage turned up his chin. "I have served your family faithfully for three generations, and I would've served you faithfully, too, but for your cowardice."

A hush fell, with the exception of the noise the griffins made on the other side of the door. Draque wondered why his fathers hadn't crisped Eagleheart yet.

"You've allowed the witches to strip your powers and your sovereignty," the mage continued. "You are a disgrace to the Firesbreath name."

For the first time in his life, Draque saw Kron flinch, his golden scales coloring to an almost crimson hue. "We did what had to be done to prevent war."

There was much Draque wanted to say to Eagleheart, but he held his tongue. It was true his grandparents had been far more confrontational, but they'd also suffered an untimely end because of it.

"Yet war is at our border even now." The mage banged his staff on the stone floor, and the demons outside squealed and pounded the door with more ferocity. "The witch army will be here soon, and you can't defeat them without my griffins."

"Fathers," Draque said, trying not to gloat, "I burned most of the griffins while they were in their cocoons."

He enjoyed the look of horror in Master Eagleheart's cold, black eyes.

"You what?" the mage rasped.

"How many are left?" Kron asked.

"Probably a third their original number," Draque answered.

"Excellent job, son." Kron grinned, his dragon teeth long and sharp. "We will not yield the throne. Call off your griffins."

Eagleheart's face twisted into a grotesque cross between man and bird. "A thousand griffins can still raze your kingdom."

Smoke rings blew from Vepar's flared nostrils. "And it only takes one dragon to fry you like an egg."

Master Eagleheart was unfazed despite the guards holding tightly to his bound arms. "I'm the only one who can control them."

"We are eight mighty dragons," Kron said. "They don't need to be controlled. Our cunning son has already destroyed most of them, and we will kill the rest."

Draque shared shocked looks with Teju and Ladon.

Cunning, huh? He never compliments you, Teju's thought echoed in Draque's head.

I know, Draque answered, a strong sense of pride surging through him. *I have never heard such sentimental words from him.*

Ladon hung his head. *He is probably sentimental because Thaddeus was killed.*

Draque heard the words, and then their meaning became clear. *What?*

Witches attacked him with the unbreakable curse, Teju said sorrowfully.

War is imminent, Ladon said. *We know Nathaniel Goldenwand was behind it.*

Draque was stricken by the news. He and his pack brothers had never gotten along well with their older siblings, but the loss was devastating. He couldn't imagine how he'd handle losing Teju or Ladon.

He jumped when the griffins renewed their attack on the door, and the wood splintered down the middle. Not much longer, and they'd breach the barrier. Draque prayed he'd burned enough of their cocoons to shift victory in their favor.

Ladon and Teju shifted into full dragon form, flanking Draque to form a line with their other two brothers and father.

You might have saved us, Ladon said. *Thank you.*

I did what had to be done. Draque felt like a pile of troll dung for the way he'd treated Serah. *You were right to chastise me earlier. I'm sorry we fought.*

Me, too, Ladon answered. *And now Serah is gone.*

A resounding *crack* ricocheted through the cavern as the splinter widened, the door buckling inward. The creatures would break through any moment. But right now Draque was more concerned about Serah. *Where is she?*

Katherine sent her on a boat to Siren's Cove, Teju said.

What the fuck are we doing here? Draque rose on his hind legs, as upset as he'd ever been. *We need to go save her now!*

The demons burst through the doors, and Draque had to shift gears from saving Serah to fighting for his life and his kingdom. He and the other dragons blew out blue fire, engulfing the hall in flame. Mother and the others huddled behind the throne, protected by a blue bubble of magic.

The winged creatures came toward him in what could only be described as suicide missions. He and his family incinerated them the moment they drew near, like electrocuting bugs in a zapper. The more demons that flew at him, the more he killed. It was so easy, fighting them became tedious. As he settled into complacence, one broke through the barriers and landed on Kron's neck with an ear-splitting howl. Kron swatted it away but not before it bit his neck, ripping out a chunk of flesh. Kron bit the demon in two. A wave of leathery, winged creatures washed over them, using their burned brethren as shields. Debris from overhead rained down on them when their dragon tails swept the walls. Draque howled when a big chunk of rock sliced open his arm.

"I thought I'd killed most of them," Draque said when he paused to stoke his fires. "There are more than I imagined."

"We can hold them off," Kron said and flung another demon off his back. "I'm more worried about the witches. They will be here soon."

"Father," Ladon said, slinging a demon off his tail, "Serah is in danger. The sirens have tried to sacrifice her before."

Kron didn't hesitate. "Then one of you must save her."

When Teju surged forward, Kron blocked him. "Not you. We need your magic when the witches arrive."

"I'll go," Draque said. He was probably the best dragon for the job, though she'd like seeing him the least. He needed to make amends with her. He hoped saving her would earn her forgiveness.

Ladon puffed up his chest. "I'll go with you."

Kron shook his head, then stomped on a crawling griffin that was missing a wing. "We need you here." He turned his dark gaze on Draque. "Go, son. May the goddess bless your journey."

Ladon gave him a dark look. "Do not fail her, brother."

A renewed sense of energy washed over Draque, fueled by determination. "I will save her or die trying." He released a ball of fire and charged through the wall of griffins, treading on their heads and beating them down with his heavy wings. He fought his way through the busted doors and out into the tunnel, shifting into a dragon-human hybrid after he passed the griffins. He flew through the tunnels until he reached the underground lakes. He couldn't summon strong protective bubbles like Teju, and he had no time to learn. Drawing in a deep breath, he dove into the water, letting the current sweep him into the lagoon. By the time he surfaced, his lungs were begging for air. He shifted into full dragon form, emerged from the lagoon, and shook water off his wings.

"I'm coming, Serah," he yelled. He only hoped he wasn't too late.

THE WIND BEAT DOWN on Serah, drying her skin and cracking her lips. Clouds passed in a blur overhead, blotting out the moon's light as her boat swiftly sailed her to her doom. She wondered how long it would take her to reach Siren's Cove. Her heart raced when she recognized the familiar scents of honeysuckle and lilac. She was nearing her homeland.

She'd tried several times to loosen her bonds, but it was no use.

Damn you, Draque, for tying them so tight.

If Katherine hadn't put that spell on her, she could've shifted into a siren and flopped out of the boat, but she couldn't even hear her siren's voice, much less transform.

She heard a splash, followed by another. When the boat slowed, she tensed, wondering what had caused those splashes. She tried to temper her breathing, but her chest heaved from fright. When long fingers grabbed the side of the boat, she nearly pissed herself.

A woman with moss-covered hair poked her head above the gunwale and looked at Serah with a mixture of curiosity and alarm. "Serah?" she hissed. "My daughter?"

Serah blinked at her mother, her eyes filling with tears. She'd never see her dragon princes again.

Chapter Sixteen

Teju and Ladon pushed through the wreckage with their fathers and older brothers, sweeping away dead griffins with their tails. Luckily only the great hall was damaged; the rest of the kingdom had been spared. Their fathers' spies had reported no signs of the witches yet. Teju wondered why they were waiting. Even though he was exhausted after fighting the griffins, the agony of not knowing their fate was worse than war. He wanted to get this over with, so he could fly to Siren's Cove and help Draque save Serah. He only prayed he survived and that Draque and Serah weren't already dead.

Dame Doublewart chased Kron's tail, a determined glint in her eyes. "I could pretend to be her and ask them to call off the battle."

"Dame Doublewart." Kron heaved a sigh, blowing out a weary ring of smoke. "I appreciate your offer, but I doubt it will matter if we show them Serah is alive. These witches are possessed, like zombies. We saw it with our own eyes."

"And they are also armed with the unbreakable curse," Hector added, his eyes red and swollen from crying over Thaddeus.

"To say they're fighting dirty is an understatement," Bastian added emotionally, wiping tear stains from his face.

Teju ached for them. Though he, Draque, and Ladon had never been close to their older brothers—heck, at times the rivalry between them was so fierce, he'd considered them more enemies than family—now was not a time for enmity. Losing a member of a pack was more than just losing a family member. It caused a deep rift in their tightly bonded group. Other packs that'd lost family had compared it to losing a limb. It affected their number of offspring as well. When they did find a mate, she would most likely only produce two eggs at a time. Dragon kings had always ruled in threes, which meant Teju and his brothers would probably inherit the throne, a burden he did not wish to bear. He also suspected this would make Hector and Bastian resent Teju's pack more.

He wanted to go to his older brothers and offer them comfort, but he worried they'd resent his pity, so he felt sorry for them from a distance while praying to the goddess that their fate didn't befall his pack, too.

"I don't care. I want to help." Doris waved her wand wildly. "They killed Thaddeus! They destroyed my school!"

Kron gazed at her as if she was a wayward child, his upper lip pulled back in a snarl. "We appreciate the gesture, but please—"

"It's no gesture," she interrupted, jabbing his snout with the slender piece of wood. "You won't find anyone more skilled with a wand than me, other than perhaps Teju."

Teju's scales warmed when his headmistress and Kron turned their eyes on him. He gave Dame Doublewart a subtle nod. "Thanks, ma'am."

She eyed Teju as if she was sizing up his worth. "As a matter of fact, Teju would serve you best fighting with his wand, not his fire."

Ordinarily, Teju would've felt pride at his headmistress's faith in him, maybe even rub it in Ladon's face, but he just felt numb.

Kron studied Dame Doublewart for a long moment, and Teju didn't know if his father planned to eat the pushy headmistress or thank her. "You're right. Thank you for your counsel, Dame Doublewart." Surprisingly, he bowed low to her.

Her expression was as dour as ever. "Anything to stop that madman."

"Why aren't they here yet?" Teju asked.

Kron scanned the cavern ceiling as if expecting witches to crash through the granite any moment. "My spy reports they're waiting until dawn to attack."

"Why?" he asked.

Kron frowned, his long whiskers nearly dragging the ground. "I don't know."

A chill went through Teju as he scanned the ceiling, worrying they were planning a surprise attack.

SERAH FOUGHT HER CAPTORS, but it was no use. They pulled her from the boat and dragged her into the warm water. Doing her best to keep her head above water, she nearly fainted from fright when her mother bared her fangs, but the woman only cut through her bonds. When she was free, she lurched for the boat, trying to scramble back inside.

"Seraphina!" her mother cried, pulling on her shirt. "My precious child, do not fear me."

Heart racing, she kicked and flailed, desperately trying to pull herself into the boat. "Stay away from me!"

"Seraphina, darling." Her mother pulled her back into the water, spinning her around with a surprisingly strong grip. "Don't you recognize us?"

Several other sirens had joined her mother, their gleaming teeth shining in the moonlight that reflected off the water.

"I know who you are," she said venomously.

An older siren with a long silver braid draped over her shoulder frowned at Serah. "Nathaniel has poisoned her against us."

Serah recognized her grandmother and trembled. "Grandfather saved me when you tried to kill me!" Biting down on her knuckles, she spun around, unable to look at them a moment longer.

Resting her forehead against the hull, she clung to the side of the boat, flinching when someone placed a hand on her shoulder.

"We'd never try to harm you," her mother said at her back. "Please turn around, child, and see that my words are true."

Emotion tightened her chest as she refused to look at her mother. "You tried to sacrifice me to Maiadra."

"Is that what he told you?"

She bravely turned around. "Have you so easily forgotten dragging me to the altar and lighting a fire at my feet? If Grandfather hadn't stopped you, I'd have burned to death."

Her mother arched back, clasping a hand to her heart as if she'd been wounded. "Seraphina, we don't do sacrifices. We haven't in over two thousand years."

Grandmother frowned. "Nathaniel has placed a memory spell on her." She spoke about Serah as if she wasn't right in front of her.

A memory spell? Messing with a witch's memory was forbidden. Any witch caught using it was sent to prison for life. Grandfather wouldn't have done that to her.

"He's not here to enforce it." Mother gazed at the vast sea, an endless blackness that reminded Serah of her personal hell.

"Something is anchoring the false memory to her," Grandmother hissed. "Remove her earrings."

"No," she screamed, but the other sirens pinned her arms. "He gave me these," she cried as they were slipped from her ears. She let out a wail when her mother tossed them in the water. She heard the *plop* of each earring as it landed and then sank.

"I must get them!"

"Hold her!" Grandmother said. "She'll calm down when the spell wears off, and she remembers."

"Seraphina, my darling girl." Mother cupped her face in her hands. "Wake up from your spell. Please come back to me."

Panting like a wounded animal, she stared into her mother's eyes as tears cascaded down her face. Why was Mother crying? She loathed Serah, didn't she? But memories started to come back, like pieces of a distant dream. Grandfather had invited her for a swim and then trapped her in a net. She'd been dragged into a boat by mean faces. Miss Pratt had been one of her captors, calling Serah a hideous whore with a tail. A man had helped Miss Pratt haul her in. She thought hard, trying to remember out who it was.

But, no, how could that be? Prometheus Periwinkle? His hands had roved over her breasts when he tied her up, then he'd pinned her to the ground with his wand, immobilizing her while she tried to scream in terror. Grandfather had returned, dripping salt water on the deck and sneering at her, casting a shadow over her while she squinted against the glaring sun. She'd pleaded with him for help, but he'd forced those earrings into her ears, making holes where there were none. The memory of the pain shocked her back to reality.

"Oh, Mother!" she cried, throwing her arms around her neck. "He kidnapped me!"

Mother held her tight, kissing her forehead. "He asked to take you from us, but when we refused, he stole you."

She felt her earlobes, the memory of the pain from the forced piercing making bile rise at the back of her throat. "He said I was never to take them off, that they were worth one million merlins and the rarest jewels in the world."

But that had been a ruse to make sure she kept them on and remained under his spell. The thought of how badly she'd been used made her sick to her stomach.

"You are far more rare a jewel than those earrings." Grandmother, stroked her hair. "We've mourned every day since he took you from us."

The pain in Grandmother's eyes made her ache with guilt.

She pressed her forehead against Grandmother's. "I'm so sorry."

"Don't be sorry." She brushed her lips across Serah's forehead. "It is I who should be sorry. I knew that wizard wasn't to be trusted. I would regret taking him as a lover, except then I wouldn't have your mother and you."

"All of that is behind us now." Mother pulled them both into a hug. "Our Seraphina has returned to us, and that's all that matters."

"Who sent you here?" Grandmother asked, the fine lines running across her brow deepening with concern. "Why were you bound?" She frowned at Serah's blood-crusted shoulders. "And why are you injured?"

Serah repressed a curse when she remembered Katherine's twisted features. She'd thought she was sending Serah to her doom. Ha! She only hoped her mates didn't think she'd deliberately run off. "A jealous bitch who's trying to separate me from my mates."

Mother was surprised. "You have mates?"

"I did." Her shoulders fell. "Three dragon shifters. They saved me after someone burned down our school, and my fairy godmother tried to kill me." She decided to leave out the forced marriage. "It's a very long story," she said, wishing their last encounter hadn't been so unpleasant. They probably did think she'd escaped and she was positive that's exactly what Katherine was telling them. What would happen if Grandfather showed up, demanding her release? As much as Serah would have liked to enjoy a reunion with her family, she couldn't stay.

Her mom hooked an arm through hers. "Let's go home, and you can tell us everything, my darling."

Serah remembered the way home was through a maze of underwater tunnels that took them to their private lagoon.

She closed her eyes and embraced the change, but she couldn't summon Thelix. "I can't shift. That bitch put me under a spell."

Grandmother shook her head. "You've been bewitched again?" She ran her webbed fingers over Serah's body. Grandmother laughed softly. "This one is easy." She pulled the tau stone off her neck and pocketed it.

It's about fucking time! Thelix bellowed.

"Well?" Grandmother asked with a smirk. "Did it work?"

"Yes, unfortunately," Serah chuckled. "Thank you, Grandmother."

She changed with fluid grace, so pleased that she didn't have to look like a fool in front of her family. She'd missed them, yet she'd no idea until a few moments ago how much. She had to return to her dragons soon. There was no telling the desperate lengths Grandfather would go to in order to wage war, and Serah had to make sure she was there to stop him.

SITTING AT THE BASE of Grandmother's watery throne, Serah drank the sweet juice from a palma pod and laughed with her and Mother. Her injuries felt much better after Grandmother had rubbed ointment on her. They were in their private cove, accessible only by swimming under the island through a maze of tunnels or by flying over the jagged rocks that protected them from winter's rough waves. It wasn't accessible from the beach, for the foliage was too thick to traverse. Tall palma and many other fruit trees and flowers flourished here, making it look like the images of paradise in the elven fourth realm. Grandmother's throne was placed between two waterfalls. It was a carefully constructed succession of stone slabs half submerged in the water. Below the throne was a large slab, where Serah and her close friends and family sat, languidly splashing the blue-green water with their tails.

She enjoyed the soothing sounds of Acacia's harp while relaxing in Mother's arms. Warmth flooded her cheeks when Acacia kept giving her sly looks as she plucked the harp strings with dexterity.

A little tryst won't hurt, Thelix begged.

Be quiet, she scolded. *I'm not cheating on my mates.*

Serah's loyalty to the dragon princes surprised her, especially after Draque had tried to force her to submit to their betrothal, but she was smitten over them and couldn't help it.

But Acacia has such delectable breasts, Thelix pointed out. *Creamy and heavy, like two ripe palma pods.*

Serah admired Acacia's perfectly round breasts but wasn't tempted.

Redheaded Acacia had been one of Serah's two lovers and the primary reason she'd refused Grandfather when he'd asked her to return with him to the third realm. He'd promised her riches and jewels, but she'd found heaven in Acacia's arms. Funny how when she closed her eyes, it wasn't Acacia's sweet smile she pictured, but Ladon's. The dragon prince had stolen her heart, and she'd forever pine for him if she remained in Siren's Cove. Loathe though she was to admit it, she'd long for Teju and even Draque, too. Her gut twisted at the thought of not being able to stay long with her family; she didn't want to break their hearts all over again.

Mother stroked her cheek. "Tell us about the world of witches."

She rested her head against her mother's shoulder, feeling more at home than she'd ever felt with her deceptive grandfather. "It was far different," she said, looking around at her friends and family. Some were laughing and splashing each other, others were brushing each other's hair with coral shell combs. A trio had transformed into humans and were making love on the shore. "They place great value in material things, especially their wands," she said, feeling a blush creep into her cheeks as she looked away from the lovers. She remembered making love on that very spot with Acacia and Violante.

"Your grandfather thought his wealth would impress me," Grandmother said. "But we sirens don't care much for material things."

No, they didn't. And to think her grandfather had brainwashed her into believing that expensive shoes and jewelry mattered. Holding tightly to Mother's hand, she knew what mattered.

"Tell us about your mates," her mother said.

She smiled when she thought of Ladon holding her and stroking her back. "They are dragon princes."

Grandmother arched a brow. "Sons of the Kings Firesbreath?"

She swallowed back a knot of apprehension at the concerned look in her grandmother's eyes. "Yes."

But Grandmother nodded. "A wise and noble family."

She heaved a sigh of relief. Her approval meant so much, especially as it wasn't typically the siren's way to mate with males—unless a siren wanted to conceive, and even then the bond was temporary. "Grandfather wishes to wage war on them."

Her mother gasped. "Whatever for?"

"He's hated them since their grandmother spurned him for the late dragon kings."

"Ah, yes, I remember," Grandmother said wryly. "He sought solace in my arms. It obviously wasn't enough."

"Obviously," Mother answered with an eyeroll.

"The dragon queen was a powerful witch," Grandmother added. "There's a rumor that she not only broke his heart but cursed him, too."

I hope she shrunk his balls, Thelix hissed. *Periwinkle-style.*

Serah sat up, jaw dropping. This was the first she'd heard of her mates' grandmother cursing Grandfather. Had she put a curse on his heart? Was that why he was so cruel? Serah hoped it was so. It made the heartbreak of him abducting and trying to murder her more bearable. "Did she?"

"I believe so." Grandmother grimaced. "He'd only allow me to see him during the day. He sought solace in his guest quarters each night."

Serah remembered Grandfather's sour moods the few times she'd dined with him at supper. He'd retire after eating only a small portion of his meal and didn't reappear until breakfast. "He was the same way with me." She worried her bottom lip. "What kind of curse would keep him hidden away each night?"

"There's no telling." Grandmother tossed her long silver braid over her shoulder. "Perhaps he shifts into a hideous creature. All I know is that he can fly, for he appeared on our island one morning, no ship in sight and no broom."

That didn't make sense. "But he hates shifters." *Because he's got small-ball-itis,* Thelix teased.

"Ironic, isn't it?" Grandmother laughed. "He's an enigma. I could never figure him out during the short time he stayed with us." She paused, tapping her chin. "He showed no interest when I sent him word of your mother's birth. He didn't bother calling until he'd learned of *your* birth." She shot Serah a pointed look.

"Why me, Grandmother?"

Her tail changed into legs, and she stood, holding a hand down to Serah. "Come, child. We'll discuss this privately." She flashed a smile that appeared forced as she waved to the other sirens in the cove.

Taking Serah's hand, she led her to her private chamber accompanied by Mother. As she studied her mother's toned legs and smooth back, she thought it strange that her siren family refused to wear clothes, yet witches covered themselves as if they were ashamed of their flesh.

They reached an underground cavern with a deep pool illuminated by flickering sconces. Mother and Grandmother waded into the pool, shifting into sirens once more, reminding Serah that most sirens couldn't stay out of water long or their human skin became scaly and brittle. She joined them, treading water in the deep part while they sat on a narrow shelf, their shimmering tails curled up beside them.

"You're special," Grandmother said. "Able to survive out of water for long periods of time and walk among the witches as if you are one of them."

"But I *am* one of them. Grandfather and father are witches, right?" Mother had told her that she'd been conceived during a witch orgy, and she'd no idea who her father was. For the most part, it hadn't bothered her, as most of her friends didn't have relationships with their fathers.

"You are part witch from your grandfather's blood," her mother answered solemnly, "but your father was fae."

Fae, huh? Thelix's laughter rang in her ears. *That explains why you're so uptight.*

"Fae?" A shiver stole up her spine. She shot her mother an accusatory glare. "You told me he was a witch."

"I know." Her mother frowned. "I'm sorry. We kept that secret from you for your own protection."

She didn't understand why she wouldn't be safe. She swam over and sat between them on the shelf. After shifting, she pulled her human legs to her chest. "Why?"

"It's complicated," Grandmother answered, "but our siren goddess Maiadra was part fae, as you know."

Mother cupped her chin, a wistfulness in her eyes. "And her mates were dragon princes."

Pulling away, she tried to make sense of what they were telling her. "But the fae haven't left their realm in centuries."

"They haven't." Her mother bit her lower lip, twirling a long lock of auburn hair around her finger. "But your father was no ordinary fae."

Serah was momentarily shocked into silence when she realized her mother still had tender feelings for her father. It made her sad that their relationship hadn't lasted longer. "So I'm fae, siren, and witch?"

"You are." Grandmother's face hardened. "We believe you are the second coming of Maiadra."

Her throat tightened. "What?"

Thelix sighed. *I'm not calling you goddess.*

Her grandmother stood on human legs and held down a hand. "Let us show you."

They took her down a narrow hall, at the back of Grandmother's chamber, to the prayer room. Serah remembered praying there many times with her family to a shrine of the goddess, a beautiful mermaid carved in bronze. She studied the goddess's face and for the first time realized they had the same facial features. Behind the statue was a tapestry of a blue-green mermaid tail entwined with three golden barbed dragon tails.

Grandmother moved the tapestry aside, revealing a small wooden chest tucked in a niche in the wall. She set the chest on a table beside the tapestry and opened it, hinges squeaking. A faded scroll was revealed.

"What is this?" she asked as she unrolled it and flattened it on the table.

"Maiadra and her mates." Grandmother pointed to the faded image on the scroll. "This was painted over two thousand years ago."

Though the colors had faded, she recognized the people in the painting. The woman nestled in her three mates' arms looked just like Serah, and the men had to have been triplets of her dragon lovers. One of the young men, who looked at Maiadra as if she had stars in her eyes, had Ladon's smile. Another had Draque's dark eyes and flaring nostrils as he clutched her shoulder in a protective gesture. The third man had a wise look about him and held what appeared to be a primitive wand. It was as if Serah and her mates had traveled back through time to pose for this painting.

"She looks like you, doesn't she?" Grandmother asked.

"Exactly." Serah traced the smile of the one who reminded her of Ladon, wishing he was holding her. "They look like my mates."

"The very first dragon shifters," Mother said.

Her heart stilled. "So we are them reincarnated?"

Grandmother's smile thinned. "We believe so."

You've seen images of the goddess before. I'm surprised you didn't notice the similarities, Thelix scolded.

I was young then. Maybe I noticed similarities, but not as strong as now.

"Maiadra was a wise and noble queen, and her mates were strong, fair kings," Mother said wistfully. "During their reign we needed only one realm."

"What happened?" Serah asked.

Grandmother frowned. "A war hundreds of years ago, so violent and bloody that the unbreakable curse was banned, and our world was forced to separate into realms to keep the peace."

"The humans were sent to one realm," her mother said, "their minds erased of all memories of magic. The remaining realms were enchanted to prevent humans from seeing us. The sea folk dominated the second realm. The witches and shifters took the third realm, and the fae took the fourth."

Serah hugged herself tight as a chill snaked up her spine. "But most shifters broke from the witches and created a fifth realm."

Grandmother's eyes darkened. "Though the witches refuse to acknowledge it."

"How do we get them to do so?" Serah asked, for she now understood the need for the fifth realm. Shifters and witches were too mistrusting of each other. Separating seemed the only way to keep the peace.

Grandmother slumped on a bench carved into the wall. "I'm not sure more realms is the answer. What we need is a powerful witch to bring back peace."

Serah's heart stuttered, and she eyed them. "And you think I'm that witch?"

Mother beamed. "I know you are. Maiadra stopped a great war with her siren tongue. She brought peace to our world for centuries."

Serah's heart sank. How could they think her the second coming of Maiadra? She barely knew any spells, and she couldn't even command her mates to untie her bonds. "My siren tongue is weak."

"What are you talking about?" Mother looked at her in disbelief. "Your siren tongue is more powerful than any I've ever heard."

Memories washed over her, like the time she'd lured a ship of sailors to their shore all by herself. They'd eagerly jumped in the water, mating with sirens on the rocks and along the white, sandy beach. She hadn't been interested in men then, as she had only recently begun exploring her body with two siren lovers, but still her voice was powerful enough to draw a ship to shore. It usually took several sirens to accomplish such a feat.

"It was strong once, wasn't it?" She clutched her throat, thinking of how it didn't always work and how she couldn't convince Draque to release her. "I don't know what happened."

"Those earrings" Grandmother said. "They muted your memories *and* your powers."

Instinctively, her hand flew to the scars on her ears where her earrings had once been. Those cursed earrings. They'd not only robbed her of memories, they'd stolen her life. "Do you think so?"

"I know so." Mother's grin was confident. "Your voice should return to you now."

They were interrupted by a loud roar that reverberated through the hall, rattling the walls.

"What was that?" Mother asked.

Serah's heartbeat quickened. "Sounds like my mates are here."

"Time to test your siren voice," her grandmother said with a wink.

Chapter Seventeen

Serah's heart plummeted when she saw that only Draque had come for her. What had happened to Ladon and Teju? He had flown into their secret lagoon, cornering several frightened sirens on Grandmother's throne, moonlight illuminating his golden scales. Though they tried to duck behind the waterfalls' curtains of water, he drove them out with his tail.

"Where is she?" he demanded.

"With our queen," they said, their voices dark and powerful. "Now leave us be!"

Draque swayed, momentarily disoriented. "You can't use your siren voices on me!"

She hurriedly stepped forward. "Draque! Leave them be!"

When he turned toward her, steam pouring from his snout, her heart nearly broke from the pained look in his eyes.

"Serah? You okay?"

She waded across the shallow end of the pool, water splashing her ankles. "I'm fine, Draque. Now shift before you give my sisters heart attacks."

His eyes narrowed. "How do I know you're not under a spell? They tried to sacrifice you."

She heaved a weary sigh. "No, they didn't."

He arched a leathery brow. "Either you lied to Ladon then, or he lied to me."

"Neither." She held out her hands in a defensive gesture.

More smoke poured from his snout. "Then climb on my back and let us leave this place."

Crossing her arms, she eyed him through slits. "I'm not leaving yet. I've only just reunited with my family."

Grandmother and Mother came up behind her. The former put a hand on Serah's shoulder and addressed Draque in a low, melodic voice. "I demand you stand down at once and shift into your human skin."

Draque swayed again, eyes half closed, and then seemed to come back to himself. "I will not fall for your siren tricks. Release her!"

"Stand down, Draque!" Serah commanded, her siren speaking through her with a power so strong and raw, her throat ached.

Much to her surprise, Draque went down on all fours, whimpering like a kitten.

"And shift into your human skin," she added.

He shifted, huddling shirtless on the stone slab, revealing meaty biceps and rippling tanned muscles along his back.

One bold siren stepped forward, licking her lips.

Serah held out a staying hand. "Mine!"

She marched through the shallow water to Draque. Crossing her arms, she gazed at him. "You will calm down," she commanded.

Much to her chagrin, his eyes rolled back, and he slumped in the water. Well damn. Her siren voice *was* powerful—maybe too powerful.

Letting out a shrill laugh, Grandmother clapped her hands. "I told you so."

SERAH SAT ON THE EDGE of her bed, staring at her sleeping lover and wondering why he came by himself. She hoped his brothers were okay.

She refused to leave Draque's side as she waited for him to wake. Her mother had placed a tau stone around his neck and recited the spell that prevented him from shifting, and Grandmother had ordered her sirens to bind his wrists and ankles. They'd brought him to Serah's old bedchamber, a cavern much like her grandmother's, with a private pool. Only this cavern had a four-poster bed. Serah hadn't slept in the water with her siren sisters. She'd usually rested in her feather bed, which was piled high with cushions.

It all made sense now. Such luxury was uncommon for sirens, but not for fae. Yet her family had never made her feel like an outsider for her differences.

"Hello, Serah."

Acacia and Violante stood in the doorway, looking as lovely as ever. Acacia had generous curves, large breasts, and fair skin, and Violante, had dark skin and eyes, small, perky breasts with dusky nipples, and long black hair that hung down her back in thick braids. They had been best friends growing up and then lovers in their teens, learning their own body's needs while exploring each other. Serah had never wanted to leave them and wondered if their hearts broke after Grandfather took her away.

She smiled weakly, for their relationship would never be the same again. "Hello."

Acacia stepped forward, twisting her fingers together while sharing wary looks with Violante. "We've missed you."

Her heart seized at the longing in their eyes. "And I you."

"We are going for a moonlight swim." Violante said coyly. "Won't you come with us?"

She glanced at Draque. No way was she leaving him. "I can't."

"He's quite handsome." Acacia's otherwise smooth brow was drawn into a deep frown as she walked up to her bed and peered down at Draque. "I'd like to ride him if you're interested in sharing."

Serah tensed, her possessive siren issuing a warning growl. "I don't share my mates."

Expecting a rebuke, Serah was shocked when Violante knelt beside Serah and placed a hand on her womb. "I feel a quickening."

Serah's breath caught in her throat. "A what?" But she already knew. She'd forgotten to take maiden wart after having sex with her mates. She'd had a lot on her mind, starting with trying not to get murdered.

"You carry their eggs." Violante pressed her ear to Serah's belly. "There are three, maybe four."

Her mouth went dry, and she suddenly felt like an animal caught in a trap. "You must be mistaken."

Violente blinked at Serah with luminous almond eyes. "I've never been wrong before."

It was true. She had a sixth sense, no doubt inherited from her father, who'd been a seer. She'd accurately predicted every siren birth for the past ten years.

Serah moved away from her, clutching her belly, mind reeling. "I can't have babies. I'm not ready."

She shrugged. "Dragon eggs take a long time to hatch."

"Dragon eggs? But sirens only give birth to sirens." That's how it had always been. They gave birth to sirens, all females.

"Our goddess gave birth to boy dragons," Violente said. "Read the scrolls."

"Really?" Serah straightened. "You said they take a long time to hatch. How long?"

"Three to five years."

The tension that had felt like a noose around her neck slowly unraveled. Plenty of time to get used to the idea. At least she'd have more time than the standard nine months, but she still didn't think she'd be ready. Violente rubbed Serah's belly. "The hatchlings will wake when their mother is ready."

"Thank the goddess." They'd be waiting a while.

Acacia knelt beside Violente with a smile that looked forced. "I suppose this means you're committed to them now."

She didn't want to hurt her former lovers' feelings, but she couldn't imagine spending her days without her dragons. "I think I am."

"If you change your mind...." Acacia stood and brushed her lips across Serah's knuckles. "Just remember all the exciting things we can do to you with our tongues."

"I remember." She pulled back her hand as images of Teju's face, planted between her legs, flashed through her mind. She wanted all her dragon lovers, the fathers of her hatchlings. She wondered how they'd take the news. Would they be as confused and terrified as her?

SERAH HAD A DIFFICULT time processing what Violante had told her. Placing a hand on her womb, she closed her eyes, trying to envision dragon eggs growing inside her. She had so many questions, like how big would they get and when would she birth them?

Leaning over her lover, she stroked his bearded face, alternating between feeling bad that he was bound and smug that his bonds were tight, just as hers had been. Now that she'd found her voice, never again would he bind her. Well, at least not against her will.

Her hands roved across his muscular, tanned chest and then down the fine trail of hair leading to his groin. A thick erection pressed against the sheet, so long and perfect, she couldn't help thinking of mounting him.

His eyes opened. "Serah?" he asked, then realized he was tied up and strug-gled.

"Shh." She brushed her lips across his. "Where are your brothers?" she asked urgently, her siren once again speaking through her.

"I left them at The Grotto," he responded in a monotone as his shoulders relaxed.

"Are they well?"

"They were when I left them."

She heaved a sigh of relief. "Grandmother says you must stay bound until we know you won't hurt us."

The fog lifted from his eyes, indicating he was free of her voice. He fought the restraints, rattling the bed. "I came to save you."

Her heart did a little backflip. Draque flew across an ocean to save her! Was it because he cared about her or was he bringing her back to prevent the witch-es from declaring war?

"Thank you, but as you can see, I'm fine." She smiled, hoping he'd calm down. "I was wrong. They never tried to sacrifice me. My grandfather be-witched me with a memory spell."

"I wouldn't put it past him. So you believe us now when we say he's evil?"

"Yes." She hung her head. She wished she could erase the memory of Grandfather forcing those earrings through her unpierced lobes.

"Serah." His voice softened. "I didn't mean to upset you."

Her gaze snapped up to his. "Well you did," she huffed. "Many times."

"I know, and I'm sorry. I've only ever wanted to keep you safe." He held out his hands. "Will you loosen my bonds? They're too tight."

She showed him her wrists, which were still rubbed raw from the ropes he'd tied around her. "Like this?"

"I was a brute," he said. "I can't tell you how sorry I am."

She eyed him coolly, a smile tugging at her lips. "I cannot untie your bonds without my grandmother's permission, and she has gone to sleep for the night."

His eyes widened, making him look like a child who'd been caught with a forbidden book of spells. "So I'm to remain like this until morning?"

She shrugged, absently drawing a lazy circle around his navel. "Sucks, doesn't it?"

If it was at all possible, that stiff protrusion under the sheet pulsed and lengthened.

Pulling down the sheet, she admired his thick erection. The mere sight of his beautiful body sent her lust into overdrive.

Mount him, Thelix urged.

"Serah," he said. "We mustn't fool around. I need to return to my brothers." But his actions belied his words when he thrust his hips forward, aiming his erection at her lips.

"I can't untie you," she said, bending over and taking him in her mouth. She didn't want to untie him. She intended to torture him, as he'd tortured her. But though she hadn't forgiven him, her siren's lust needed to be sated. Besides, he'd traveled across an ocean to save her. She might have been pissed at him, but he deserved a reward for his bravery. And she deserved a few orgasms for putting up with him.

He let out a groan, flexing his hips and pushing his length deeper into her mouth. "What are you doing to me, woman?"

She sucked him in until his balls were pressed against her lips and his cock-head tickled the back of her throat.

He inhaled sharply when she moved up the shaft, then swore when she slurped him all the way down. She sucked him again and again, lathering his balls with her spit, tenderly cupping and stroking them until they firmed beneath her touch. Knowing he was on the verge of exploding, she pulled off again.

He thrust his hips at her. "Stop torturing me," he pleaded.

Straddling him, she smiled, breasts heaving as she sat on his erection. His eyes rolled back as she rode him, slowly picking up tempo, crying out when he lifted his hips, smacking into that tight bundle of nerves. After grinding hard against him, she came undone, her inner walls clenching him like a vice as he shot into her with a groan. Pleasure zinged through her and she fell onto his chest, panting. He kissed her forehead, whispering sweet words in her ear.

"Serah, my darling, I thought my heart would shatter when I lost you." His tender words set her heart aflutter. Lying against his chest, listening to the steady beating of his heart, was a balm to her soul. But even as her breathing slowed, her lust wasn't sated. She rode him harder this time, until their cries of passion echoed through the chamber.

Drunk on orgasms, Serah's lust was sated—for now. Rolling off of him, she wiped up their juices with a cloth and then climbed back into bed.

"Serah, as much as I enjoy being in this bed with you"—he rattled the headboard—"I must return to my family. Please untie me."

She sat up. "Why should I? You fucked me and then tied me up." She wanted to forgive him but not yet, not until she was convinced he was sorry and would never restrain her again without her permission.

He looked panicked. "Serah, please be reasonable."

Her breasts heaved when she wagged a finger in his face. "Oh, now you want to reason with me?"

"I'm sorry. I shouldn't have lost my temper."

Good. Now they were making progress, but she still hadn't forgotten he'd intended to force her into marriage. "And?"

"And I won't force you to marry us," he said. "War is coming to The Grotto, and now that I know you're safe, I need to return and fight with my family."

Bile rose at the back of her throat. "Are you sure war is coming?" she asked, hoping he was mistaken. Grandfather was obviously cruel and delusional, but would he persuade Parliament to declare war on the shifters?

"They murdered my brother with the unbreakable curse."

She cried out in shock, wondering which one was dead. Draque had told her they were alive.

"Not Teju or Ladon," Draque quickly assured her. "My older brother, Thaddeus."

Not Teju or Ladon. Thank the goddess. She threw her arms around his neck, stifling a sob. "I'm so sorry."

"Your grandfather activated a spell like the one he used on your godmother. He's controlling Parliament. They could've descended on my home already."

She jerked upright and grabbed his wrists. Extending her siren fangs, she tore through the bindings. "Let's go then, before we're too late."

He ripped the tau stone off and tore through the bindings on his ankles with a claw. "You're staying here."

Her siren voice took over. "You're taking me, and that's final."

His face went blank. "As you command."

Chapter Eighteen

Teju's stomach roiled as he watched the horizon for the witches. Ladon faced the opposite direction, watching the sea for signs of Draque and Serah.

His fathers, mother, two remaining older brothers, and several other shifters had surfaced, preferring to engage in battle above their beloved grotto, rather than risk the lives of thousands of innocents below. Master Eagleheart, his daughter, and their minions had managed to flee last night during the fight. Teju wondered if they'd met up with the witches during their escape and reduced each other's numbers. That might explain why the witches hadn't shown up yet.

At least, Teju prayed that was why.

An ominous cloud in the distance rolled in their direction, swathing the desert landscape in gloomy shadow.

"Fathers," he asked the dragon kings. "Were we expecting rain?"

Kron's long moustache hung over heavy jowls. "No." He released a deep, dark howl.

Clutching his wand, Teju climbed on Ladon's back. *Ready, brother?*

Ladon answered with a growl. *No, but let's get this over with.*

Hector released fire into the sky. "Today I shall avenge my brother's death!"

"This battle will be won for Thaddeus!" Bastian bellowed. He stood beside Hector.

Dame Doublewart was on his back, clinging to the horns on his head and aiming her wand at the sky. "Shields at the ready!" The dragons lined up, the kings standing protectively by their sons. Vepar stood next to Ladon and Teju, their mother on the Vepar's back.

"Be brave, sons," she said, her eyes as hard as stone. Teju admired her strength; she'd cried all night for Thaddeus.

The cloud rolled closer, billowy and black with swirls of red and violet. This was definitely no ordinary storm.

The witches were coming.

"WE'VE ONLY JUST GOTTEN you back." Mother hugged Serah close once more, her tears falling down her back. "Now we're losing you again."

She didn't want to leave Mother, but she had to reach The Grotto before Grandfather brought war to her mates. Knowing the witches were using the unbreakable curse only made the situation more urgent.

"I will return to you, I promise." She clutched her mother desperately, guilt weighing heavy on her. She turned to Grandmother, who was fighting back tears.

"Go, child," her grandmother said, her voice cracking like shattered glass, "and fulfill your destiny."

Turning up her chin, Serah felt a renewed sense of purpose surge through her. "I will." If she truly was a reincarnation of their beloved goddess, it was up to her to prevent war—a daunting task she hoped she could realize.

"Keep my granddaughter safe," Grandmother said to Draque.

He had transformed into a giant, hulking dragon. Serah was overcome with love for him when he bowed to her grandmother. "I will, my queen, with my last dying breath."

With one last forlorn look at her family, she climbed on Draque's back. Her heart dropped into her stomach when he lurched into the air. She held tight to a spiked spine, wincing when a hard rain stung her. This storm was much like the hurricanes that battered Siren's Cove, and she wondered if Draque would be able to navigate through it.

"Fly above the storm!" she yelled.

"I'm trying."

The higher he climbed, the slower his wings flapped. The air became thicker, pressing down on Serah's chest and constricting her lungs. She huddled close to his scales, praying to the goddess to see them through the torrent.

He pushed himself harder, trembling under the onslaught as the wind whirled around them.

When they finally ascended above the clouds, his wings were covered with scratches and tears, and the air was as thick as soup.

"I can't see where I'm going!" He said in a panic.

She squinted into the rising sun. "Fly toward the light," she called. "The fifth realm is east of Siren's Cove."

He slowed, soaring above the clouds, catching pockets of air beneath his wings. "So you acknowledge our realm now." His deep voice was touched with mirth.

Squeezing his neck tight, she pressed her lips against a thick scale. "Of course I do. It's my mates' homeland, after all."

He howled his approval and cut through a double rainbow. Looking over her shoulder, she watched them fade in the distance, hoping the beautiful phenomenon was a message from the goddess that they were headed toward The Grotto and her other mates. Then she remembered she was supposedly the reincarnated goddess, her mates, the gods, and feared there were no deities to answer her prayers. She had to stop the witch army before they killed any more dragons. If Teju and Ladon perished, she didn't know if she could go on living.

WHEN THE GIANT CLOUD enveloped them in a swirling vortex, Teju and the others raised their wands, spreading their shields across the line, protecting themselves from the red bursts of magic. The witches, many clad in black robes and white, powdered wigs, fell from the cloud like human raindrops. Some broke their legs when they landed. The rest gave the shifters no opportunity for negotiation. Spells were screamed and deadly magic was released. Those with broken legs showed no signs of pain as they crawled across the desert floor, clutching their wands, a singular determination to kill shifters in their fixed expressions.

Teju was on defense, unable to fight back as he protected his family from the barrage of forbidden curses. The witches were relentless, fighting with unnatural fervor, their eyes void of emotion as if they were puppets on a string. That's when he knew he'd have to destroy the puppet-master.

He scanned the sky for Nathaniel Goldenwand, focusing on the gray vortex swirling above their heads. The evil wizard had to be there.

"We should break away and go after that funnel," he said to his brother. "I think Goldenwand is in it."

Ladon blew fire, burning a hapless witch to a crisp. The poor soul didn't even cry out. Teju hated killing them. They might have been allies to the shifter race before they were possessed.

"Can you keep a shield around us and fight him at the same time?" Ladon asked.

Teju tossed a ball of energy at a witch who tried to sneak up behind them. "No. You'll need to hit him with fire."

"Then let's get it over with," Ladon huffed and leaped upward.

Teju focused on ensuring their protective bubble didn't pop as they climbed toward the vortex. He didn't notice the tall, blond mage until it was too late. He walked across the clouds as if he was a god. The mage threw a thunderbolt at them, shifting Ladon off his trajectory. The jolt made Teju's shield blink in and out. The mage threw more bolts at them, followed by a spark of red. Teju screamed when Ladon lit up as if he'd been electrocuted. He tumbled and spun, head over tail, before landing on his stomach with a *thud*.

Rolling off his brother, Teju tried to quell the swirling bubbles in his skull. "Get up, Ladon!" Blood pooled around Ladon's mouth, and he only grunted.

Teju's blood ran cold. He lifted Ladon's eyelid and shined his wand in his eye. "Are you okay?" he asked, not reassured when Ladon didn't answer.

Teju couldn't maintain his shield. When it fell, a trio of witches descended. He shifted into full dragon form and knocked them back with his tail before burning them. Enraged and distraught, he charged through a crowd of witches, crushing and burning them until the desert sand was painted red and black.

He stumbled and fell on his belly when he was struck by a blue ball of flame. Jumping on all fours and arching his back, he hissed. He snatched up a screaming witch in his jowls, crushing her and flinging her into other witches. When several of them climbed on Ladon's inert body, he swatted them off with his tail and fried them.

A heavy wind beat down on his back, and he ducked. The vortex above him was expanding, dipping and spinning through the battlefield like a tornado, tearing up a line of tree shifters, breaking off limbs and sending logs flying.

His fathers' trusted aid, Lord Crowfoot, squawked and flew straight at the tornado, slamming into a red bolt of magic like a bug striking a window. He landed on the ground in a motionless heap of feathers.

Teju guarded his brother while rebuffing attacking witches. His brothers and fathers were also playing defense as more witches descended on them. It wouldn't be long before the zombie witches wore them down.

A familiar shadow swooped down and landed. Teju was filled with a mixture of relief and dread at the sight of Draque, with Serah on his back.

"Ladon!" she shrieked and ran to him. Flinging herself on his long snout, she let out a heart-wrenching wail. "Please don't die, Ladon. Please!"

Draque nudged her. "Pay attention, Serah. We need to stop them." He turned to Teju, his luminous golden eyes watering. "Can you project her voice?" Serah clung to Ladon, sobbing against him.

A blue protective light fell over them like a translucent drape. Teju smiled at Dame Doublewart and Bastian, who hovered over them.

Teju shifted into human form and recited a spell. "Sonora."

Draque nudged Serah toward Teju. Her eyes glowing a dazzling violet, she took the wand. Teju shivered as the temperature rapidly dropped and his feet felt weighted in concrete, as if her strengthening magic had sucked all gravity into a vortex.

"Witches," she said, and the wand amplified her voice so it reverberated across the desert and was heard by all. "Drop your wands."

The zombie witches turned, mouths agape, and dropped their wands.

Whoa. Teju had no idea Serah had such a strong siren voice. He'd had no idea any sirens possessed such power. He, too, felt compelled to drop something, and since he didn't have his wand, he obediently followed her like a loyal puppy.

"Wake from the spell Lord Goldenwand has cast over you," she continued.

Gasps and groans raced through the witch army like wildfire. They looked around as if they were seeing for the first time.

"What the devil are we doing here?" one witch asked, and others echoed her question.

Several wands fell from the swirling vortex and then an unholy shriek resounded from the funnel,which turned bright violet, then crimson. It receded, rapidly retreating across the sky. Kron took to the sky, chasing after it, his brothers following closely at his heels.

"Flaming troll turds," Ladon groaned, rolling onto his side and shifting into human form. "What the hell happened?"

Serah raced to his side and fell to her knees, plastering his face with kisses.

Teju's shattered heart slowly fused together as he and Draque dropped beside them, alternating between crying happy tears and hugging each other. Teju had never been so relieved in his life, but relief turned to shock, and shock turned to disbelief. Had his beautiful, amazing mate just stopped a war? And how had Ladon survived the forbidden curse?

Still in dragon form, Bastian and Hector crawled over to Ladon and sniffed him in confusion.

"You were struck by the forbidden curse," Bastian said. "You should be dead."

Dame Doublewart climbed off Bastian and approached Ladon. "How do you feel?" she asked, pressing her fingers to the pulse on his forearm.

"Like a bucket of beat-up sea slogs."

"Hmm. The forbidden curse is meant to kill witches, but perhaps it's not strong enough to slay a dragon. I will have to consult the history books."

Bastian and Hector shared hopeful looks. "Thaddeus!" they cried in unison.

"I'm coming with you." Dame Doublewart climbed onto Bastian's back before he could argue.

When Bastian and Hector flew off, Teju sent a silent prayer that Thaddeus would be found alive. When all eyes turned to Teju and his remaining brothers, he realized they were the only dragons left on the battlefield. He and Draque quickly shifted, barking orders to the remaining shifters. After all Goldenwands had been collected, he and his brother burned them, then they burned their dead friends while the witches watched with sorrow and regret.

Their fathers returned, angry that Nathaniel and his cronies had escaped. After they negotiated a truce with the witches, Kron offered them food and water, and instructed the flying shifters to take them and their dead friends home. Sir Gais Goblingout apologized profusely to everyone, especially the dragon kings, his round cheeks reddening when it took three hawk shifters to lift him off the ground.

It was nightfall before Teju and his brothers finally returned to the shelter of The Grotto. They collapsed on the sofa in their living quarters. Teju was so exhausted, he wanted nothing more than to sleep for the next century. When Serah crawled into his lap and hugged him, his hard cock pressing into her round bottom had an entirely different idea.

Chapter Nineteen

Weary from battling witches all night, Hector looked for any signs of Thaddeus among the crushed trees and bushes. Though it was dark, his dragon eyes saw well enough under the light of the moon. "Are you sure you left him here?" he asked Dame Doublewart.

She gave him her signature condescending scowl. "Positive. I even set a tracking spell on my wand." She pointed it at the mossy forest floor. "This was the exact spot."

"Who could've moved him?" Bastian asked.

"He must have flown off." Hector sat on his haunches, scenting the air. "He's alive. I feel it in the marrow of my bones." Thaddeus was alive. He had to be. What else could've happened to him?

"The trees are only flattened in this area." Bastian stomped around, sniffing for clues. "He had to have flown off."

Dame Doublewart's thin lips twisted. "Or something carried him away."

Hector's breath hitched at the thought. "Who could carry a dragon?"

"Another dragon?" she suggested.

Bastian shook his head. "The only dragons nearby are our brothers and fathers." There were others, but most of them lived up north or with the elves in the fourth realm.

Bastian slapped the ground with his heavy tail, rattling the thin tree branches and causing a flurry of leaves to fall. "Then where is he?"

Hector frowned. "We would've seen him if he'd flown home." A dragon was hard to miss.

"Give him time." Dame Doublewart said. "I'm sure he'll turn up. If you boys don't mind, I'd like to return to my school."

"But there's nothing left," Hector said.

Dame Doublewart tapped her chin with the tip of her wand. "Don't be so sure."

AFTER DORIS DOUBLEWART unlocked the door to the emergency shelter, Bastian held her hand and helped her descend. Her breath caught when, instead of finding students huddled in the shelter, she saw a giant bubble suspended in the air above the benches.

Bastian laughed. "This looks like Teju's work."

He jumped into the bubble, then poked his head back through. "You're going to want to see this." He gave a lopsided grin.

Doris let him pull her through, and she nearly collapsed with joy when she saw her students were all safe and happy. Some were playing at a ping-pong table, others were huddled on a round velvet sofa, watching a flat-screen TV. Most were studying or at least pretending to be.

As soon they saw her, they cried her name, rushing her. She embraced each one, silently doing a head count, so happy they were all alive.

When she spied Athena sitting at the bar with Bodicea Bubblebosom, their knees and heads pressed together, she knew something was amiss.

Athena slowly rose, pulling Bodicea up with her, their faces masks of remorse. That's when Doris knew her relationship with Athena was over. She contemplated all sorts of reactions, from hexing them to throwing a tantrum and setting the entire bubble on fire. In the end, she settled for a warm handshake with each of them.

"Thank you for keeping our students safe," she said.

Athena frowned. "It was due to Bodicea's quick thinking."

A rosy hue tinted Bodicea's porcelain cheeks. "I only did what you taught us, Dame Doublewart."

She nodded, then glanced curiously at their joined hands before giving Athena an expectant look.

"I'm sorry, Doris." Athena sighed, her eyes misting.

"As am I," Bodicea echoed.

"Don't be." She waved them away indifferently, pretending she wasn't dying inside. "I put my students before you," she said to Athena. "I always will, and you need more than that."

Athena's jaw dropped, her thick brows drawing together. "You're not angry with me?"

"Of course not," she said stiffly, putting on a good show. "I'm just happy the children are safe... and you, as well."

Athena cheeks swelled as if her face was a balloon on the verge of popping. "Bodicea got a job offer at Sawran next year. I'm going with her. I'd appreciate a letter of recommendation."

"Of course." Doris's throat constricted, making it harder for her to speak. She waved to the children as they enjoyed their last few moments of respite. "I don't see how they could deny you after what you've done here."

Doris jerked at the sound of a high-pitched wail sounding like a wounded gnome in heat. "What was that?" she asked Athena.

The troll pointed to a woman strapped to a chair on the other side of the ping-pong table. Doris had no idea why she hadn't noticed her before. Her thick makeup was so badly smeared, she resembled a tragic clown. A pink wig clung to her scalp, flopped over her ears like a dead beaver. The poor creature's mouth had been sealed shut with thick tape.

Doris went over to her, wrinkling her nose when she caught the woman's scent: a mixture of old piss, shit, and stale alcohol. The woman's eyes bulged as she tried to speak through her gag.

Doris ripped the tape off her mouth in one quick snap, taking off pink lipstick, a few chin hairs, and maybe some skin.

"Ouch!" she yelled, bucking against her restraints. "Untie me, you cursed witch, and pour me a damn whiskey!"

Athena walked up behind her. "See why we had to use the gag?"

Doris scowled at the creature. "Yes."

She pulled out her wand and sealed the tape back over the woman's mouth.

Clucking her tongue, she turned to Athena. "Do I want to know who she is and what she's doing here?"

Athena said, "Probably not."

Doris joined Bastian and Hector. She could tell by the looks in their bloodshot eyes that they were impatient to leave.

Once they'd left the dungeon, Bastian and Hector shifted into hulking dragons and bowed.

"We have to search for Thaddeus," Bastian said. "We're sorry for all the trouble we caused."

Doris watched Athena and Bodicea hugging out of the corner of her eye. "Don't be. Your actions might have saved my life."

Hector frowned. "We're sorry to leave you so soon."

Doris waved away his concern. "Go find your brother. I will pray to the goddess he is safe and well."

"Thank you, headmistress," they answered and flew off, leaving Doris alone with several dozen confused and tired teens, a school in ruins, and a heart in tatters.

SERAH SMOOTHED LADON'S brow. She'd been fretting over him all evening. She'd almost lost him today. Just thinking about finding him with blood pouring from his mouth made her heart ache.

"How do you feel?" she asked for at least the hundredth time.

He sighed and pulled her into his arms. "I'll be okay."

She pressed an ear to his chest, listening to the thrumming of his heart. It was steady, but she'd expected it to be louder.

"Are you sure?" Teju sat across from them, holding his head in his hands. "Teju, is there anything you can do for him?"

He looked up. "The healer already examined him," he said wearily. Poor Teju looked like he'd been dragged through hell and back. His clothes were shredded, and his arms and face were covered in lacerations.

"I'll be fine, Serah." Ladon wrapped an arm around her, kissing her cheek. "I never apologized to you."

"For what?"

He frowned, his brows pinching. "For letting Draque tie you up and for not telling you about our fathers' crazy marriage scheme."

"That's okay, and it wasn't such a crazy idea," she said tenderly.

Yesss, Thelix hissed. *Make them ours!*

Teju brightened, suddenly hopeful. "You don't think it's crazy?"

A blush crept into her cheeks. "Not really."

Her heart skipped a beat when he and Ladon shared goofy grins. Dear goddess, what had she done?

The heavy door to their living quarters swung open, and Draque entered looking exhausted, his mouth drawn and dark circles framing his eyes.

"Well, what news?" Teju asked.

Draque strode to the bar and popped the top on a beer. "They can't find Thaddeus." He took a long drink.

Ladon struggled to sit up. "Where could he be?"

"How do you lose a dragon?" Serah asked.

Draque dragged a hand through his disheveled hair. "A search party has been sent after him."

Serah said apprehensively, "What about my grandfather?"

"He was last seen flying over Sawran with about a dozen witches." Draque grimaced, then gave her a pointed look. "Witnesses identified two of them as professors at your old school. One was named Prometheus Periwinkle."

She froze, feeling as if her heart was imploding. Ladon squeezed her hand, and she told herself she wasn't upset by the professor's betrayal. She'd traded up with three sexy dragon shifters. Besides, she'd already known Periwinkle was in on it after the memory of her abduction returned to her. It burned knowing the lengths Grandfather had gone to: orchestrating her abduction, downfall, and murder in order to enact revenge. She wondered if he'd felt any love for her at all during the three years he'd been her guardian.

"They've frozen your grandfather's bank accounts," Draque continued. "He'll turn up as soon as he runs out of money." He took another swig of beer and pulled out a few more longnecks. "Anyone else want one?"

She remembered what Violente had told her about the quickening in her womb, even though it had only been a few days since she'd first had sex with her dragons.

"No, thanks." She pushed away the beer when Draque tried to hand it to her.

He arched a brow. "We have wine if that's what you prefer."

"Or I can make you a sangria," Ladon said, waggling his brows.

She gave him a stern look. "You stay right there. You're supposed to be resting."

He cupped her chin. "I'm a dragon, not a mouse."

"I know." She shrugged, nervously biting her lip as she struggled for the right words. "But I don't want any alcohol."

Draque tried to shove the beer into her hands again. "It will help you relax."

She flinched. "No."

He knelt beside her. "What's wrong?"

"I'm pregnant," she blurted, wishing she could sink into the sofa cushions when they all stared at her.

Teju shot to his feet. "W-What?"

"A seer told me last night." She looked away, unable to withstand the looks of horror in their eyes. "She says I'm carrying three or four dragon eggs." She rocked forward. "I forgot to take Maiden Wart."

"Maiden Wart doesn't work for preventing hatchlings," Draque rumbled.

"Then what does?"

"Nothing. When it's time, it's time." One corner of his mouth hitched up in an impish grin.

Did he think this was a joke? "I'm not kidding, Draque. I'm pregnant."

He leaned forward, clutching her knees. A slow, languid smile spread across his face. "Dragon seed always finds a way, but only with a dragon pack's destined mate."

Destined mate? Heat raced through her like wildfire as her world tilted, then spun. "Oh." She slumped into Ladon's arms.

"You okay?" Ladon whispered.

"I'm not sure," she said, feeling as if someone else was speaking as a surreal sense of detachment washed over her. "Are *you* all right?" she asked her mates, cringing as she waited for their answer.

"Of course." Ladon pressed his lips to her ear.

"Serah, we're going to get through this." Draque looked at her with big, sweet dragon eyes.

Teju knelt on her other side, rubbing her knee. "We have at least three years. They won't come until you're ready."

Relief washed through her. "Are you ready?"

Draque squeezed her other knee. "We will be."

"I'm ready," Ladon said and tightened his hold around her shoulders. "I've wanted you to be our mate from the moment I met you."

She was humbled by the sincerity in his eyes. "How am I supposed to raise three or four baby dragons?"

"We'll help you," he said. "It's a group effort."

Sirens took care of their young without any help from the fathers. In fact, the fathers were usually more like sperm donors. But Serah wasn't a typical siren, and her mates weren't typical sperm donors.

"You're not going to go through this alone." Teju took her hand in his, brushing his lips across her knuckles. "We'll be with you every step of the way."

Her heart did backflips as she looked into Teju's golden eyes. "Thanks," she said, too choked up to say more.

"Come here, my love." Ladon pulled her into his lap, peppering kisses on her forehead and neck. "You make me so happy. I'm glad I'm going to live to see our children."

She clung to him, a shiver wracking her as she remembered she'd almost lost him today. "Me, too."

His loving gaze searched hers. "I love you, Serah."

She sucked in a sharp breath. "I love you, Ladon," she blurted, hardly believing she'd uttered the words so soon but knowing them to be true. How could she not love him or his brothers after what they'd been through? She surrendered when he claimed her mouth in a passionate kiss. He tasted of barley and sulfur, the perfect blend for the perfect mate. By the time they separated, she was panting heavily and her panties were soaked.

Someone's getting pounded tonight, Thelix teased.

"What about me?" Teju asked, nibbling her ear. "Do you love me?"

She leaned into him, giggling when he dragged his teeth down her neck. "Of course I love you. Do you love me?"

"With every breath in my body," he avowed, snaking a hand around her and toying with her nipple.

She groaned as more moisture flooded her panties.

Her breath hitched when Draque bent over in front of her and unzipped her jeans.

A hard pounding, Thelix promised.

"I'm going to show you how much I love you." He slipped off her pants first, then licked her through the flimsy cotton panties.

"Oh, yes, Draque," she cried. Impatient for the feel of his forked tongue on her clit, she tried to take off her panties, but Teju held her back, leaning over and suckling her breast.

"Submit to us, Serah." Draque gently scraped his teeth across her mound. "And we'll submit to you."

She surrendered, sinking into the soft furs while Draque and Teju feasted on her. She looked up at Ladon, who had her head in his lap. She felt bad he wasn't participating more but knew he needed rest.

Draque eventually removed the panties and licked her labia like she was a melting ice cream cone, dipping his tongue inside her before smoothing her wet desire across her slick ribbon.

Teju sucked her tits, swirling his tongue around pebbled nipples until she ached with unfulfilled lust. She jerked with pleasure when Draque stuck a thick finger into her.

"Tell me you love me," he said, sucking on her nub as if he was trying to draw a thick shake through a straw.

"I love you, I love you!" She bucked against his mouth. "Please."

Chuckling, he slid up the length of her body and drove into her with one swift thrust. When he was fully seated, he kissed her demandingly. He tasted of sulfur and beer and her sweet essence.

She let him dominate her as they began a slow dance of love, his thrusts timed to the steady rhythm of her heart. With each slippery stroke, they climbed higher and higher until she fell apart in his arms, whispering words of love, digging her fingers into his back and thanking the goddess for her brave dragon princes.

After he rolled off her, they tenderly kissed and toyed with each other until she was hungry for more. He handed her over to Teju, who carried her to Ladon's bedchamber.

Teju deposited her on the bed, and she crawled across the furs when Ladon sat on the bed, propped against the pillow with a goofy grin. He stroked her face, and she kissed his palm. "I hope you don't mind," he said. "I'm too tired to do much."

She stroked his lip, which still had a trace of dried blood. "Don't worry, sweetheart. I'll take care of you."

She took him in her mouth and slurped up and down his shaft, emboldened by his cries of pleasure. Thick fingers dug into the globes of her ass, and she paused, giving Teju time to anchor himself to her. He played with her labia, dragging moisture from her slick cunt to her puckered anus. Oh, great goddess!

When Ladon nudged her, she returned to sucking his cock, trying not to be distracted by the pressure of Teju's finger entering her puckered hole. She sucked Ladon deeper, lathering his balls, jamming him against her tonsils and groaning around his foreskin when Teju's cockhead pressed into her slippery anus.

Ladon exploded with a roar, bathing her throat with his seed. She swallowed, groaning as Teju slid deeper, stretching her and taking her anal virginity. The pain was so intense, she nearly bucked him off, but then he hit a spot that sent a zing of pleasure ricocheting through her. She slipped off Ladon's cock when Teju went deeper. By the time he was fully sheathed, her last band of sanity snapped, and she ground against him with abandon, blocking out the pain as every nerve ending sent thrumming pulses through her. The orgasm was hard and fast, making his cock feel twice the size as she tightened around him with each throb. Holy heck, it hurt like hell, and holy fuck she'd do it again. He pounded her with shallow thrusts, loosening her once more and priming her for another powerful orgasm.

Ladon pulled and twisted her nipples, heightening her pleasure and intensifying her pain. The orgasm hit her like a bullet, gripping her so hard, she thought she might faint. Teju came, and by the time he withdrew, she was so sore and spent, she could hardly move. Falling on top of Ladon, she let him wrap her in a warm embrace while Teju cleaned her up.

Draque and Teju crawled into bed beside her.

Teju stroked her back and nibbled her ear. "Did you mean it when you said marrying us wasn't such a crazy idea?"

She rolled onto her back, blinking up at them. They stared at her like she was a bone, and they were salivating werewolves.

"Yes, I meant it." She smiled when their gazes roved over her puckered nipples. "But maybe not right away."

Ladon sat up on his knees. "What about a betrothal?"

"I would love to be betrothed to you." She pulled him close. "Lie down. You need rest."

"How can I rest now?" He stroked her cheek. "The most beautiful girl in the world wants to be my mate."

She laughed and kissed the tip of his nose. "Keep calling me beautiful, and we'll be making love all night."

Teju toyed with her nipple, his wet finger making it peak and ache for his mouth. "We don't have a ring yet."

"You'd better hurry up and get one," she said while Draque massaged her inner thigh, her legs spreading like melting butter. "My siren is impatient to make you ours."

"We're yours, Serah." Draque chuckled. "We've always been yours. And we will get you that ring."

Draque climbed up her body and kissed her passionately, stoking her desire until she was left with no choice but to surrender to her dragons. That's when she knew she'd found the perfect mates, for she doubted ordinary witches would ever match a siren's lust.

Chapter Twenty

Ladon held tightly to Serah's hand as they stood in the center of what used to be their school, a virtual wasteland now. Where there were once walls, there was now blackened shells, making the place look abandoned next to the decrepit cemetery and overgrown forest.

This was supposedly neutral territory, where shifters and witches were meeting for a truce. Nervously scanning the skies for any sign of the witches, she twisted the betrothal ring on her finger. It was a beautiful work of art, three golden dragon tails entwined with a silver and green mermaid tail, twisted into the shape of a flower with an Elysian silver pearl in the center.

Her heart dropped when she heard a faint buzzing in the distance. Squeezing Ladon's hand tighter, she glanced at her other mates, standing beside their fathers, all of them in dragon form.

Their older two brothers were still searching for Thaddeus. With each passing day, Serah feared the dragon prince would never be found.

As the witches came into view, she recognized the prime minster, Sir Gais Goblingout, at the helm of an industrial-sized broom that sagged like a wet noodle under his weight.

Sir Gais landed hard, flipping over the broom and nearly falling face-first into the ground. A much younger witch caught him with a flick of his wand, setting Sir Gais down gently.

About a dozen other witches flanked him, clutching their wands and nervously darting looks at the dragon kings and princes.

Sir Gais coughed a good amount of phlegm into a handkerchief before giving them a forced smile. "Thank you for meeting us here, dragon kings."

Kron and his brothers eyed the prime minster, their low growls shaking the ground under Serah's feet.

"Your Highnesses, if you please, Prime Minister," Kron requested.

Sir Gais blanched, then mopped his brow. "Very well, Your Highnesses. I suppose we should get down to business."

Kron straightened, his long neck bowing over Sir Gais like a cobra about to strike. "I suppose we should. Have you heard anything of the whereabouts of our son?"

Sir Gais looked momentarily puzzled, then recognition dawned in his beady eyes. "No, I'm sorry. My investigators still haven't found anything, but they are already stretched thin, searching for Goldenwand."

Vepar's low rumble sounded like an approaching freight train. "Have you read our terms?"

"We have." Sir Gais furiously nodded. "Have you read ours?"

"We do not speak for the resistance." Dagon narrowed his one eye on Sir Gais. "We can't guarantee peace with them, but we can promise our sons will no longer do their bidding."

"We will lift the sanctions." Sir Gais coughed and sputtered, wiping more sweat off his brow. "But recognizing your realm takes an amendment to our constitution."

His answer elicited growls from every dragon, including Ladon, who tensed like a granite statue. Serah leaned closer to him, hoping her presence would calm him.

Kron moved so close to the prime minister, he dampened the witch's hair with steam from his nostrils. "Then I suggest you get to amending."

Sir Gais squeaked and a distinct bubbling sound erupted from somewhere behind him. His round face turned an alarming shade of purple.

Serah sniffed the air. The witch had sharted his pants! When Kron drew back, glowering, Serah hid a smile behind her hand.

Draque cleared his throat. "What about Serah's money?"

The prime minister crossed one leg over the other, no doubt in an attempt to ward off any more sharts. "Several families have filed suit against the Goldenwand estate for the deaths of their loved ones. We can't release all of her inheritance until after the lawsuit has been settled, but we can free up fifty million merlins."

Draque turned to Serah. "Is that acceptable?"

"I just need enough for my godmother's rehab and to rebuild the school." Her mates' fathers had refused her offer of financial assistance, saying The Grotto would thrive again once the sanctions were lifted. She suspected their stubborn pride had a lot to do with their decision. What did she need with that much money, anyway? She smiled at her dragon mates. She already had everything she desired.

"That will do... for now," Kron said, giving the prime minster a dark look.

"Good, good." The prime minister not-so-subtlety picked at a wedgie. "Does that mean you'll sign the peace treaty?"

Kron nodded. "On the condition that you declare The Grotto a realm within six months.

"Six months?" He gasped, then coughed into his fist. "I'm not sure that will be enough—"

"That's plenty of time. See that it gets done."

The prime minister bowed. "Yes, Kro—Your Highness."

Serah breathed a sigh of relief. The shifters and witches would finally have peace between them. She hoped it lasted this time.

SERAH LOUNGED ON THE shore, playfully slapping the waves with her long tail. She was leaning against Ladon as he ran a pearl comb through her hair. After the stress of the past five months, they'd needed this escape to Siren's Cove.

Thaddeus still hadn't been found, which was odd and frightening. How does one lose a dragon?

Her studies were brutal. She'd memorized so many spells this semester, she thought her head would explode. Sneaking off with her mates during the week had been nearly impossible, which meant Thelix could only be sated on weekend visits to The Grotto. Her siren was less than pleased, and she made it known on a daily basis.

Hiding the eggs growing in her womb had been challenging as well. Teju's concealment spells didn't prevent her from having a difficult time squeezing into her desk. There were no pregnant students at their school, and Serah didn't want to be transferred to Auntie Agatha's Academy for Expectant Witches. She was only carrying eggs after all, which she hoped wouldn't hatch for another five years.

Serah's godmother had escaped from rehab and gone on drinking binges at least half a dozen times. One time she'd *poofed* into the middle of Serah's potions class, demanding she brew her witch's whiskey while spewing demon daiquiri vomit and sparkles all over the floor.

Even though finals were this week, Serah needed time to unwind. If only Teju would leave her alone. He sat across from them, nudging her tail and trying to get her to recite spells.

"Focus." He waved a wand in her face. "We need to study for exams. Tell me, what is the spell for concealment?"

She slumped against Ladon with a dramatic sigh. "I'm tired of studying."

"Do you want to fail your finals?" Teju chided.

She thought her mates had taken her to Siren's Cove for some much needed R&R before finals, not to ruin her time in paradise with more studying. She sneered at the Pegasus-feather wand she'd tossed on shore. Since Parliament had banned all Goldenwands, sending witches back to the stone ages, her crappy school-issued PF wand was no longer uncool, but it sure was unwanted.

Teju snapped his fingers under her nose. "What is the spell to compel someone to do what you want?"

Serah bit her lip. Everything made her horny lately, from her mates' spicy, sulfuric scent to their broad chests and tanned, rippling muscles. All they had to do was look at her, and her libido sprang to life. The condescending smirk Teju was giving her made her nipples tighten and her inner goddess awaken.

She slapped sand off her tail. "I don't need a spell. I stopped a war and donated five million merlins to the school."

"Serah, Dame Doublewart can't be bought. You know this."

Ha! Who did he think he was fooling? Everyone could be bought.

"Serah's right," Draque said as he trudged through the sand toward them, a cooler of beer in one hand and a tall lemonade in the other. He kissed her forehead and handed her the lemonade. "Do you seriously think Doublewart will want to put up with us another year?"

Teju's shoulders slumped. "No, but that doesn't mean she'll pass us."

"I'm exhausted." Shifting into human form, she got up on her knees and rubbed her slightly swollen belly. "We've been studying all day."

"Considering all the breaks you've been taking," he said wryly, "we've only been studying a few hours."

She grinned and let Thelix take over her. "Pleasure me," she said to Teju, pleased when he threw down his wand and fell to his knees. She eagerly shifted back into human form.

Draque chuckled and stripped out of his clothes. "I'm next."

Ladon threw off his shorts. "This is way more fun than studying."

"You didn't have to use your siren voice." Teju said. "I'd have licked your pussy anyway." He dragged his tongue across her slick folds, and she sank into the sand, her eyes rolling back. Hot damn, she loved being their mate.

SERAH DIDN'T KNOW WHY she was nervous when Dame Doublewart called them into her portable office. It's not like the headmistress would deliver bad news to the school's biggest, and only, benefactor.

Holding Ladon's hand, she followed her mates up the wobbly ramp and into the trailer. The entire school was currently made up of portables until workers finished construction on the main building.

To her delight, Dame Doublewart had laid out tea and cakes. She shouldn't have worried. Clearly the headmistress had brought them here to thank them. She helped herself to a teacake covered in white chocolate topped with raspberries and cream. She ate it way too fast, not even caring if she looked like an insatiable troll in front of her mates. She'd been hungry all day, no doubt from expending all that brain energy on her tests. They were a lot harder than she'd expected, making her wonder if she should've listened to Teju and studied more.

Too late now. Besides, Doublewart couldn't fail her most generous benefactor. She thanked Ladon when he handed her a cup of tea. It was delicious, with just the right amount of sugar. She smiled into her cup. Though she wouldn't miss the strict teachers and the interminably dull homework, at least school was ending on a positive note.

As soon as everyone was seated around Doublewart's desk, the headmistress cleared her throat and addressed Teju. "Our potions teacher is leaving at the end of the school year. Dr. Clawfoot is taking her place, which means I'll need a sorcery and spells teacher to take her place. I prefer to fill my job vacancies with former students. Are you interested?"

Serah's jaw dropped. She hadn't been expecting that. She beamed at Teju, proud of her wickedly smart mate.

Teju was surprised. "Me?"

His brothers hooted and hollered, slapping his back and congratulating him.

Dame Doublewart remained impassive except for a slight twitch above one eyebrow. "You'd have to take the teacher certification exam, but I'm sure you can pass it in your sleep. If you have other things to do, I understand, but it would be a shame for you not to share your brilliance with our students."

His brilliance! She sat on the edge of her seat and reached for Teju's hand. When he entwined his fingers through hers, she kissed his knuckles, happy for her mate.

"I'm flattered," he said. "I'll have to talk to my family, especially Serah, before making a decision."

Dame Doublewart looked at Serah, thoughtfully rubbing her chin. "There is also a secretarial position open."

Serah's eyebrows rose. "Lady Hoofenmouth is leaving?"

Dame Doublewart folded her hands on the desk. "She's going to live in Sawran with Miss Bubblebosom."

"Oh?" She'd heard rumors that Lady Hoofenmouth had once been Dame Doublewart's lover. She wondered how the headmistress was taking the news. She squirmed under the weight of Dame Doublewart's heavy glare. She was not cut out for secretarial work. After graduation she wanted to spend more time with her family at Siren's Cove, not answer phones and deal with bratty teens.

"Thanks for asking," she said, "but I don't think I'm secretary material."

"I wasn't asking you." Dame Doublewart snorted. "I was asking Ladon."

She jerked. "Oh."

"You failed the sorcery and spells final exam." Dame Doublewart's mouth twisted as if she'd sucked on a sour lemon. "Looks like you'll be here one more year."

What the ever-loving fuck?

She sneered at Draque when he laughed. "Thanks a lot, asshole."

"You failed, too, Draque." Dame Doublewart sipped her tea. "Three classes."

He shot from his chair, steam pouring from his nose. "What?"

"Perhaps with your brothers on staff, you'll be motivated to study harder," she said wryly.

Serah and Draque shared horrified looks, then she threw up her hands in exasperation. "B-But I donated all that money to rebuild the school."

"And I can't thank you enough." Dame Doublewart's smile was so tight, it appeared to be etched in stone. "Certainly you didn't intend that money to be a bribe?"

"N-No." She struggled for the right words to say. "But I thought—"

"You thought what?" The headmistress stood, peering down at Serah over her hook nose. "That I would do you the disservice of letting you graduate without getting a proper education?"

Draque mumbled a curse. "I can't be a twenty-one-year-old senior."

"And you can't be an uneducated father either." The headmistress inclined her head to Serah.

Her hand flew to her abdomen. She'd worn loose shirts and pants, and she only had a slight poof. How did her headmistress know? "Who told you?"

"Nobody." She chuckled. "You have the glow, which puts me in a predicament. Never before have I allowed my staff to sleep with the students." She gave Ladon and Teju pointed looks and then heaved a sigh that sounded staged. "I suppose I will have to allow one exception, as long as you keep it on the down-low."

Draque paced. "Holy troll turds!"

Dame Doublewart banged her wand on the desk, making Draque jump. "My sentiments exactly." She turned to Teju and Ladon again. "Well? Are you going to accept my offer, or do I need to look elsewhere?"

Teju looked at Serah, who gaped at him. She'd flunked her senior year, and her mate was going to be her teacher? How fucked up was that? Last time she'd had sex with a teacher, she'd been expelled from school.

Teju stood and held out his hand. "I'll accept."

Ladon did the same. "Me, too."

Burying her face in her hands, Serah slumped in her seat.

"Excellent. I'll see you this fall. Have a wonderful summer."

Peering through the cracks in her fingers, Serah saw Dame Doublewart standing by the door, impatiently waving them toward the exit.

Ladon helped her up and escorted her to the door, at which point, she finally found her voice. "Wait!"

Dame Doublewart smiled. "Don't try to use your siren voice on me."

Blowing out a breath of frustration, she marched back and snatched a teacake off the table, stuffing it in her pocket. Then she grabbed another one for good measure. "I paid for the damn things," she snapped, raising her chin as she stalked out.

By the time her mates caught up to her, she'd traversed the length of the cemetery and was almost to Werewood Forest.

"Serah, wait!" Teju pulled her to a halt and looked into her eyes.

"What?" She regretted her tone when she saw the hurt in his eyes. "Sorry." She slumped onto a tree stump. "I can't believe we're stuck here another year."

Teju sat beside her and pulled her hands into his lap. "It won't be so bad."

She fought the urge to roll her eyes. "Not for you."

"I'll tutor you." His enthusiasm sounded forced. "Every night. And if you study hard...." His eyes gleamed mischievously. "I'll reward you."

Electricity raced up her spine. "With your tongue, I hope."

He nibbled her ear. "Lots of tongue."

Clutching his collar, she moaned. Nobody licked pussy like Teju. Maybe having him as her professor wouldn't be so bad.

"Hey, guys, come look at this."

Ladon and Draque were at the edge of the forest, squinting at something on the ground. Teju and Serah joined them.

"Fresh dragon tracks," Teju said. Jaw dropping, he looked at his brothers. "How can this be?"

Serah's hand flew to her throat when she saw a massive four-toed print followed by another and another, the trail leading into the forest.

Draque rubbed his bearded chin. "Were any of you out last night?"

"You know we weren't," Teju answered.

"Who is it?" Ladon rasped.

Draque stepped to one side, eyeing the print from another angle. "Whoever it is has a limp."

Teju followed the tracks until they vanished in the underbrush. Sinking onto his knees, he looked at them as if he'd seen a ghost. "We must alert our fathers. Thaddeus is alive!"

The End.

Dear readers, I hope you enjoyed my new series. Be looking for *School of Stolen Secrets, Academy for Misfit Witches, Book Two*, January 2020.

Books by Tara West

Eternally Yours
Divine and Dateless
Damned and Desirable
Damned and Desperate
Demonic and Deserted
Dead and Delicious
Something More Series
Say When
Say Yes
Say Forever
Say Please
Say You Want Me
Say You Love Me
Say You Need Me
Dawn of the Dragon Queen Saga
Dragon Song
Dragon Storm
Whispers Series
Sophie's Secret
Don't Tell Mother
Krysta's Curse
Visions of the Witch
Sophie's Secret Crush
Witch Blood
Witch Hunt
Keepers of the Stones
Witch Flame, Prelude
Curse of the Ice Dragon, Book One
Spirit of the Sea Witch, Book Two

Scorn of the Sky Goddess, Book Three
Hungry for Her Wolves Series
Hungry for Her Wolves, Book One
Longing for Her Wolves, Book Two
Desperate for Her Wolves, Book Three
Tempted by Her Wolves, Book Four
Fighting for Her Wolves, Book Five
Academy for Misfit Witches
Academy for Misfit Witches, Book One
School for Stolen Secrets, Book Two (January 2020)
Academy for Courting Curses, Book Three (April 2020)

About Tara West

Tara West writes books about dragons, witches, and handsome heroes while eating chocolate, lots and lots of chocolate. She's willing to share her dragons, witches, and heroes. Keep your hands off her chocolate. A former high school English teacher, Tara is now a full-time writer and graphic artist. She enjoys spending time with her family, interacting with her fans, and fishing the Texas coast.

Awards include: Dragon Song, Grave Ellis 2015 Readers Choice Award, Favorite Fantasy Romance

Divine and Dateless, 2015 eFestival of Words, Best Romance

Damned and Desirable, 2014 Coffee Time Romance Book of the Year

Sophie's Secret, selected by The Duff and Paranormal V Activity movies and Wattpad recommended reading lists

Curse of the Ice Dragon, Best Action/Adventure 2013 eFestival of Words

Hang out with her on her Facebook fan page at: https://www.facebook.com/tarawestauthor

Or check out her website: www.tarawest.com

She loves to hear from her readers at: tarawestwriter@gmail.com